A Palette of Magpies

SOULLA CHRISTODOULOU

KINGSLEY
PUBLISHERS

First published in South Africa by Kingsley Publishers, 2023
Copyright © Soulla Christodoulou, 2023

The right of Soulla Christodoulou to be identified as author
of this work has been asserted.

Kingsley Publishers
Pretoria, South Africa
www.kingsleypublishers.com

A catalogue copy of this book will be available from the
National Library of South Africa
Paperback ISBN: 978-1-7764317-9-3
eBook ISBN: 978-1-7764317-8-6

Also by Soulla Christodoulou

Alexander & Maria
The Village House
The Summer Will Come
Broken Pieces of Tomorrow

To my dear friends Carmen and Chris for taking the time to show me around and experience some of the most beautiful Cotswolds villages... and for introducing my tastebuds to the most delicious cruffins.

Chapter 1

Another handmade postcard. She ran her fingers lightly over the waxed paper taking in the tiny bumps and ridges, breathing in the soft vanilla, experiencing the weight of it. She turned it over, hesitating for a split second. But she had already guessed what it was going to say. She'd already worked it out.

She peered through the porch windows, the white light of morning dazzling her, bouncing off the leaded lozenges of glass. *Was someone watching her?*

Judith sat at her kitchen table and read, "Two for Joy". Along the bottom of the card, holding it landscape, two magpies faced each other, their feathers ruffled as they played in a watery blue puddle, tiny water droplets falling off their shaking wings, petrol bright, as they shook them: the crystal beads sparkling in the light of the yellow sun overhead. The delicate paint strokes were precise yet created movement, a fluidity on the page; the birds so life-like, moved in front of her. The watercolours had created joyful birds; alive and vibrant. Black, purple, turquoise and a smidgen of leaf green added gloss to the rough pleating of their tail feathers.

'Certainly jubilant. Just beautiful. And that purplish-blue iridescent sheen… whoever you are, you certainly know how to use a brush,' Judith sighed, flicking her long red hair over her shoulder. *Have you used a Winsor & Newton mini sable? Or are you a skilled artist?* She stared at the card, hoping it might reveal its secret.

Having taught art for over thirty years Judith was familiar with every style of painting and recognised the strokes created by different brushes as well as the names of almost every colour palette which existed across water, oils, and acrylics.

She recalled her first ever paint tray in 1960, a birthday gift from "someone we used to know" her mother had said before strict instructions of when and where she was allowed to paint. She had always had a knack for spoiling her highs, squashing her joy. Judith remembered colour names to this day and as the years whooshed by her memory had always amazed her more artistic students. She reeled them off in her head: Dorchester Pink, Hick's Blue, Julie's Dream, Pale Lime, Verzino Violet, Naples Yellow, Tawny Red, Croft Green.

The two-bedroom cottage resembled a treasure trove of every piece of art material imaginable; filled to the brim with paints, brushes, palettes, and easels. Against every blank vertical space canvasses, of all shapes and sizes, lined up haphazardly against the walls like a stack of tarot cards waiting to be shuffled.

Over the years, Judith, as Head of Art, had created a reputation for herself as an art collector and had been contacted by many art historians sourcing vintage items. Judith's paraphernalia had been included in local art displays in events celebrating the world of art and as props for filmsets and TV.

She placed the card on the stone mantle above the Aga, next to the first one. She didn't feel unnerved. She felt a tiny flicker of excitement which sent a shot of colour across her cheeks; as if she had lightly painted blusher in scarlet with a fan brush of camel hair. She felt her face, the heat coming off her. It had been a long time since she had put on any make-up. Perhaps today she would add a little rouge. Brighten up her day.

She untied her robe, all at once claustrophobic. The morning's first hint of light snaked its way past the shuttered windows of the kitchen, highlighting the bumps and dimpled crevices on the flagstone floor and a ball of dust collecting round the base of the bin; she needed to sweep and mop. Later, she told herself.

She thought back to Monday and the arrival of the first postcard. She had heard the clank of the letter box as it pinged shut before going for her morning shower. 'That's too early for the mail,' she'd thought. 'And I haven't heard the postman's usual whistling as he trundles down the lane on his bike, or his swearing as he jolts over those pesky potholes.'

The card had landed on the door mat in the porch, the door mat's word "WELCOME", faded over time, inviting it in. As she bent down to retrieve it a tiny shudder ran through her; someone was watching. A strange sensation seized her. Her hair dripped wet, and she shuddered against the coolness held by the cottage's thick stone walls.

'No post mark or stamp,' she said to herself. She tightened her gaping bathrobe around her and swiping the pale blue card from the horsehair mat disappeared into the warmth of the kitchen at Chrysanthemum Cottage.

"One for Sorrow" it simply said. And a tiny hand-painted magpie adorned the bottom left-hand corner of the note. A grey cloud poured down onto the magpie as he perched all alone, on a tree stump, its head bowed in sadness as if disappointment tugged at his jawline. Nothing else. No signature. No message. No hint as to who it might be from, yet despite her initial irritability a warm, calming tingle shot through her. Nothing sinister, nothing to be alarmed about.

She wondered whether her best friend, Louise, across the lane, always twitching behind the frilly curtains of Wisteria Cottage, may have seen anyone, seen anything. She would drop the question into the conversation, casually, as they took their customary morning walk around the village after breakfast, though Louise was prone to getting excited.

The brass kettle, old and tarnished, whistled on the stove; one of the few items she had kept when she inherited the cottage after her parents died.

The whistle brought back a faint memory of her father drinking his daily cup of tea, after work, while Judith fussed around him with her schoolbooks open on the floor, pens and pencils rolling under his seat as she chatted about her school day. Her mother was rarely interested in hearing about her lessons, but her father was always ready with a keen ear.

'Forgot the kettle,' she said and, with her hand to her chest, ran to lift it off the burner. 'One for me and one for the pot,' she said out loud, throwing two teabags into the teapot.

Her morning ritual had not changed much over the past few years despite having lived in many different places; it was the one constant she held onto, her anchor to normality, to staying sane, to remaining buoyant. She took the saucepan off the range, her one egg bobbing furiously in the boiling water. She spooned it into her chicken-shaped egg cup – another childhood item she had rescued – and with her one slice of toast on a floral-edged plate she sat at the table.

She scraped butter onto the toasted bread and cut it into five soldiers. 'You can't beat a good hearty breakfast,' she said to Jasper, her elderly cat, who, following the trajectory of the sun, had moved from his favourite warm spot in the kitchen to another outside the open back door.

So fat was he now he rarely wandered much further than the first couple of yards into the garden, often lying in the suntrap of the south-facing plot for hours at a time. Jasper didn't even jump up at the birds anymore: blackbirds, finches, robins, and tits tentatively edged towards him, and he would lie like a bronze statue, unmoved.

It was as if he had taken Judith's lead and, much like his owner, had resigned himself to a slower pace of life. At least that had been Judith's unimaginably boring retirement until the cards began to arrive. And though at first discombobulating, thank goodness they had.

Chapter 2

Life in the village had begun with a frenetic kind of energy; cleaning out the cottage, moving back in and reconnecting with old friends and neighbours. But it had quickly slumped to a slow and unexciting existence, which plagued Judith's mental health and well-being.

Three nights in a row she had woken seeped in sweat from a nightmare; drowning in the hushed gossipy whispers of faceless people. Nearly everyone in the village had something to say about someone and though she avoided being drawn into judgmental and critical conversations she heard the sting of sharp tones and condemnation wherever she went.

Perhaps moving back to the village had been a mistake. Perhaps she should have sold her inheritance, in the form of Chrysanthemum Cottage, and left the past exactly where it merited to remain, in the past.

A short walk from her home to the village shops crowded around the green created an anxiety in her which she found increasingly difficult to keep to herself.

One morning, as she stood in the queue at the pokey post office, with its trendy greeting cards and an eclectic selection of books, poking out from the squeaky metal display stand, her ears pricked up at the mention of the vicar. She thumbed through the assortment of sci-fi and horror, memoir, and thriller, and then romance and travel, until she found "Discover Cyprus". She picked it up and willfully moved her head back and forth over the inside front cover, pretending to read.

'He's on his own. Most odd if you ask me.'

'Maybe he has no family.'

'Of course, he does. He wears a wedding ring.'

'True. How can he not have brought his family with him?'

'He's sure to be hiding something,' said the woman in the pink headscarf.

'What is life coming to when we can't trust our local vicar?' said another, her grey hair pulled up into a tight bun.

'Whatever it is, the longer he hides it the more likely he'll be cast aside.'

It looks like he has been cast aside already, thought Judith. She fingered the weekly magazine promising to make you a car mechanic in as short a time as twelve weeks and let out a little sigh.

'And what about that Polish woman on the other side of the village?'

'And her daughter, always so glum-faced.'

'There's more to them than meets the eye,' the woman said, pulling off her headscarf and shaking her wiry silver hair from around her face. Judith watched only for the straw-like strand to flick back again, her efforts to smooth it down failing.

Judith wondered about Maja, the young Polish girl who lived alone with her mother, but suspected Maja's problem arose not so much from what she chose to hide but what she was afraid to stand up against.

Judith's sharp instinct came from her great-great grandmother on her father's side who had been accused many times of being a witch. In those days anyone who didn't quite fit in quickly became tagged a spellcaster. Of her thirteen babies and all of them died within days of being born apart from the last. A child, according to her father, who had the reddest head of hair in all the county and who from the age of four read all the obituary notices in the local newspaper fluently.

'And that poor Kerry. Not sure if she'll ever be the same again.'

'She's not been behind the bar at all for weeks now apparently.'

'Well, I wouldn't know. I'm not one for sitting in the pub.'

'No, no, of course not. I'm only saying…' and in a blink of an eye they strayed onto their next victim with such ease not stopping to take a breath, a seamless stream of discontent and criticism. Judith wondered whether they had a certificate in smooth-spouting gossip and trivial chatter.

'I saw Lou. Asked about her daughter. Very evasive.'

'Everyone's hiding something.'

'Well not everyone. I mean what do we have to hide from the world?' They both chuckled oblivious to Judith's eavesdropping.

Judith curled her until now limp hand into a fist and tutted under her breath. Lou was her friend. Her only real friend in the village. But Judith always took time out of her day to talk and say hello to anyone she passed while getting on with her daily business of making a new life in the village.

Judith paid for her first-class stamps; she liked to have a supply at home for any birthday or celebration emergencies. Her cousin in Liverpool, two of her former work colleagues, an old neighbour she still kept in touch with, a spinster aunt in Brighton, now in her nineties, a widowed uncle in Watford, somewhere north of London. And of course, there were the cryptic crossword competitions she entered with Lou. Lou was obsessed with them, and Judith liked doing them because it meant spending time with her; a joint effort and Judith laughed at her friend's own quirky ways of deciphering the answers. She smiled at the one they worked out together last:

'*She might have a part in current Hair production. Seven letters,*' *read out Lou. Judith had looked on, perplexed.* 'Ooh, I've got it,' Lou whooped, picking up the pen. 'Current Hair, current as in electricity is AC as in current of electricity and hair is TRESS.'

'And?'

'And the answer's ACTRESS.'

Judith thought back to the time she played an Oompa

Loompa in the school's production of The Wizard of Oz and smiled.

They always sent in their answers by post, Lou insisting on cutting out their answer grid and popping it into an envelope. They once won fifty pounds in Argos vouchers and they each bought a camping chair; orange with blue polka dots and the other striped candy pink and white. How they laughed at their frivolous purchases.

Outside, Judith shaded her eyes against the rising sun. She straightened up her mother's Dawes Duchess bicycle, stuffed her belongings into the basket and wheeled it off the verge before mounting it. The path back home, on a slight decline, allowed her to freewheel most of the way, giving her the opportunity to rest her legs. Harry and Charlie's cycle bells warned her they were approaching a few seconds before she felt the whoosh of them racing past. She waved hello and then quickly held onto the handlebars for fear of losing her balance.

At home, Judith put the book of stamps into the front compartment of her bureau drawer. She picked up the silver frame of the now faded wedding day photograph of her parents and wiped the dust off the glass with her sleeve.

She swung open the back door, Jasper slinked inside sniffing round his bowl for something to eat. Judith perched on the kitchen doorstep and slurped at her tea, smiling at her gaucheness. Her father habitually drank his tea like that, and it always made her laugh much to the annoyance of her mother.

'Teaching her bad manners,' she complained every time, but her father would give Judith a cheeky wink, tapping the side of his nose with his finger.

'Our little joke,' he would whisper and then tickle Judith until she cried out, 'I give up!'

Chapter 3

'What's wrong with you today? You're all…
melancholic.' Lou placed the two Gin and Tonics down
on the beer mats. 'They're out of Pork Scratchings,' she
said, passing Judith a bag of peanuts instead.

'I feel as if my life is a never-ending cycle of waking
up, having breakfast, walking, making dinner and going
to bed. Where's my purpose? What's my reason for being
here?' She split the bag of peanuts open and popped one
in her mouth. 'Oh gosh, what flavour are these?'

'I don't know. Some posh up-market one that cost me
£2.50 for that poxy tiny bag.'

'Wasabi flavoured peanuts…' she read off the packet.
'No wonder they're green.'

'Judith, enough about the peanuts. You're a little out
of sorts, that's all. The winter was harsh, the spring slow
coming and now that summer is here, you're itching to
do something. The best part of being retired is that you

don't have to rush anymore. You don't have to be up at a certain time or be somewhere you don't want to be. Be you, indulge yourself and enjoy each little moment. Be mindful.'

'Easy for you to say,' Judith said, popping another nut into her mouth and crunching down on it with an expression of trepidation.

'This isn't easy for me to say. I'm not one for dwelling on the past but it took me a long time to find myself after Brian left me, I was only thirty, and though life isn't what I imagined it to be it is a good life. I'm content with what I've done, managed to overcome the humiliation and embarrassment and I like the person I've become now more than ever. I have Ashleigh. I have found a new me.'

'Sorry Lou. I didn't mean to be flippant. I know how hard it's been for you. I feel so useless… so out of the loop of life. I thought being retired would bring some happiness, a freedom I craved, especially these last couple of years. But…'

'I know, I know. You'll find something to reignite the fire in your belly. And you have your art… I can't imagine that will ever leave you.'

'My art, yes. I suppose I'm free to paint and draw but I've no inspiration. All the hours stretch on like that endless fog in winter. It's nothing like I imagined. With no curriculum, no students bearing down on me, no student data, no exams, no parents complaining, I feel lost.' She shook a few nuts into her hand and passed the bag to Lou. As she crunched on them the little cards popped into her head. Should she mention them to Lou?

Perhaps now was not the time.

'Then fill your canvas with all your feelings, set yourself free through your… creativity. There's no hurry. This is your new timetable of life. You can spend your hours and energy doing whatever makes your soul happy. Be selfish, Judith. Do whatever you want.'

'New timetable of life. I like that. You're right. There's no rush and whatever I decide to do it's up to me to make it happen. I can only rely on myself now and I should certainly be used to that by now.'

'And me, Judith. I'm here for you too. Every step of the way,' said Lou and she squeezed Judith's hand as Judith tried to hold back the tears.

Chapter 4

Judith sat alone in the garden, a glass of red wine that smelt tired, in one hand, The Little Prince in the other, as she watched the day's final golden haze of sun fade into a dusky evening wash of pinks and oranges. The light fragrance of the clematis danced, softly present in the summer air. She fingered the dog-eared book, its pages sepia-brown, harkening her back to the warmth of her father's embrace and his unconditional love. She'd read it as a child, sitting in his lap. They read alternate pages in turn. She smiled and continued to read until it became too dim to read any longer; the sting of her straining eyes, forcing her to put the book down. She sat, sat in contemplation of life.

'Oh Jasper,' she said, 'it's all so complicated yet so simple too. How can I ever truly be happy? Nostalgia's like a strange sickness, making me painfully melancholic and yet extraordinarily content. There's no escaping our past. It's in our bones whether we like it or not. It sits there, a silent companion, holding our hand, squeezing our hearts.'

Jasper opened one eye. He surveyed Judith from his position, still undoubtedly warm, coddled under the trailing tendrils of the clematis, the plant barely visible in the night. A spider climbed a silken thread, weaving a fine web, fragile but perfect.

'Would I change things if I could? Would I turn back the clock? I guess despite what I missed through absent parents in my young adult life I gained through the privilege of moulding the lives of so many teenagers. So many of them... the naturally artistic, the ones who excelled at their friendships, the ones who battled daily with alcoholic or drug-dependent parents, those who defied their parents and then came running back, those who realised their dreams, and there were quite a few let me tell you,' she rambled on.

'But now... sitting here I ask myself was the sacrifice worth it? I'm lost. I can't find my happy. The balance has been tipped too far one way, the wrong way, I fear. School and the students anchored me to a life which I loved, relished, and set my heart on. And now? What do I have to look forward to?'

She sipped desperately at her wine and the shadows grew longer, like fingers reaching out to her but she made no attempt to move. She needed to be anchored yet felt herself slipping away.

Chapter 5

'So where do you want to stroll this fine morning?' asked Louise, her feathered bob, though rather modern for her in Judith's mind, suited her childish, dare-devil personality.

'I don't much mind,' said Judith. 'It all feels so pointless. This retirement malarkey is not all it's made up to be, is it? How do you do it, Lou?'

'I find things to remember. I resurrect them in the present moment, and it makes me happy. It gives me purpose and reminds me of what has gone and that without it I wouldn't be here now, the person I am.'

Judith nodded absent-mindedly, her friend's philosophising washing over her, remembering the colours on the second card. The golden honey amber took her back to the summer of 1972. Her mother had entered the village's 57th Beautiful Bloom Competition and Judith had never seen her so excited about anything. She lived and breathed her golden yellow chrysanthemums for days leading up to the competition. She even slept under a make-shift tent made of fishing tarpaulin and garden canes the last three nights before the show "just to keep an eye".

Judith, though she thought it rather odd at the time, relished the time he had alone with her father. They baked fairy cakes together; she remembered the gooey pink icing and the hundreds of multi-coloured sprinkles. They watched a silly programme on the television, snuggled on the sofa, their bodies pushed up close even though there was plenty of room to spread out, and ate all the fairy cakes which Judith had piled up like a pyramid on one of her mother's "special" blue and white plates.

Her mother's chrysanthemums were voted second place and though Judith saw a little dull hint of disappointment in her mother's eyes she also knew how wonderful she had felt, a week later, when her photograph appeared in the local paper and on St Barnabas' noticeboard for all to see.

The priest's wife had come third so that in itself had been an achievement and had given her a reason to smile and celebrate for what seemed like weeks. Judith remembered their celebratory meal of penne pasta with a rich, cream sauce and lardons of bacon and mushrooms in it. 'It's Italian,' her mother had proudly announced.

'And what are you thinking? Because you're certainly not listening to me.'

'Did you see anyone push something through my door a little before seven this morning?'

'Why would I notice?' Lou prickled with irritation.

'Come on Lou, you're always peeking out from behind your curtains.'

'I slept in and didn't have my morning cuppa until after eight. What was it?'

'A card.'

'Is it your birthday?' asked Lou.

'You know full well it's not my birthday until November.'

'Who was it from? What did it say?'

'Two for Joy,' stated Judith matter-of-factly.

'Is that all? At least it's a cheery message.'

'The card which arrived three days ago said, "One for Sorrow".'

'Now that's not so very cheery, is it?'

'No.'

'Who's sending them? What does the postmark say?'

'There's no postmark and each one has been hand-painted, so beautifully, with such detail and care. The most magnificent magpies with the gentlest of brush strokes.'

'One of your students?' asked Lou.

'I doubt it. The pigment of the paint, the style. I think it's someone older, more mature. But who?'

'I have no idea but it's disconcerting all the same. What do they mean?'

They walked towards the green. Judith kept cocking her head left and right, the wispy ends of her ponytail tickling her neck as she moved, but nothing around her looked out of place or different. The Post Office had its doors propped open with an iron sandwich board which declared "WE ARE OPEN" in bright red letters above the

Post Office emblem. Either side the Cotswold Perfumery and the candle shop, Wick's Wax Works, their "Open" signs clearly displayed.

The silhouette of a woman in Wick's Wax Works sent a little shiver up Judith's spine. Something about her felt familiar, even though she didn't have a clear view of her.

'What are you dawdling for?'

'Nothing. I…' Judith's voice trailed off and they continued their stroll.

A little way down, the pretty tea shop, Cup of Happiness, with its candy floss pink shutters and blooming flower boxes was buzzing with an early coach load of visitors. Through the lattice windows Judith could see the boisterous interior filled with Japanese tourists tucking into their breakfast while outside the tables buzzed with laughing faces and outstretched arms taking selfies, heads thrown back, eyes blinking against the sun.

Cup of Happiness was one of those sought-after pit-stops for so many of the visitors to this part of the country. Enjoying a special Cotswold breakfast with its artisan bread, locally produced jams, chunks of soft-textured Stinking Bishop cheese, thick-cut Gloucester Old Spot back bacon and tea, lots of it, was a big part of the tea shop's marketing and branding. The owner had embraced and harnessed the Cotswold experience to her advantage with her social media posts garnering thousands of likes and hundreds of comments.

The off license and the local convenience store, next door to each other, flanked the opposite side of the green with their curved bay windows, moss-covered tiled roofs, and mildewed shingles. The outside of the mini supermarket was stacked with wooden crates arranged with bright fresh produce. A dispatch van, parked a few yards from it, had its back doors open and a man carried two plastic trays full of fruit and vegetables to the back of the store. Judith saw Ian, the owner, in his customary white apron and striped T-shirt chatting with a woman as she filled her basket with green apples and under-ripened bananas.

Further along and set back behind a freshly painted railing adorned with baskets of overflowing pansies and peonies, trailing ivy and wispy grasses, the idyllic English country pub rose above the spray of colour in a monochrome of black and white. The landlord, Paul, was looking down at his watch, waiting for the day's brewery delivery.

In one of the upstairs windows, the silhouette of his wife, Kerry, who had lost her baby at twenty-one weeks last autumn, nearly eight months ago, shimmered behind the glass. No one had seen her out for months and Judith had noticed how the locals had stopped asking after her; people soon forgot and carried on with their own lives, yet Judith continued to send her best wishes to Kerry every time she saw Paul.

'Who do you think sent them? Do you think they mean something?'

'I don't know. At first, I thought the card had been posted to the wrong address. I half expected someone to come knocking to ask if I'd received it but so far there's been no enquiry made, no further clues or indication as to the identity of the sender. And now there's a second one.'

'It's all very cloak and dagger. We need to put our thinking caps on. They might send a third. Three for…'

'Three for a Girl.'

'No, that's not right, my nan always said, "Three for a Funeral".'

'Ever the positive one,' said Judith with disdain as she pulled out the gold elasticated band around her hair, leaving her orange locks to hang loosely around her shoulders. 'In China, it is believed a singing magpie will bring good fortune and symbolises happiness.'

'I'm only repeating what she used to say.'

'In Korea, Magpies are thought to deliver good news and invite good people into your life.'

'You've got me!' laughed Lou.

'When the card arrives, if it arrives, we'll see what rhyme the sender is following. Might give us a clue as to their age.'

'This is exciting. Like something from that TV series, Rosemary and Thyme. Do you think we'll have to work something out?'

Judith nodded and smiled at Lou's "we" and they strolled around the outside of the green, their daily morning exercise energising them. It was quite unremarkable until Ian's twins, Harry, and Charlie, whizzed past on their bikes, racing against each other, at break-neck speed. If it hadn't been for their bicycle bells ringing out Judith and Louise may both have been badly hurt.

'You little swines,' yelled Lou, her hand clasping her chest, her brown eyes wide in shock.

'Aww, we were young once, leave them,' said Judith.

'Ian's got his hands full being a single dad and running the store.'

'Yes, you're right, but we had manners. They should behave themselves.'

'I remember racing along the river's edge and the slope catching me by surprise. If I hadn't pressed my feet to the ground to slow myself, I would've flown over the handlebars and in the water. Instead, I scuffed my toes red raw; I hadn't been wearing any shoes and the blood stained my feet red. I had to walk around barefoot for days after that they were that sore and bruised. Mum went mad at me, but it was either that or ending up in the river.'

On the way back to their cottages, Judith looked up to glimpse Kerry still at the window of her bedroom.

'You go on ahead,' she said to Lou. 'I'm going to pop into Kerry. Today might be the day she wants company. I have a feeling she needs something from me.'

Judith walked towards the pub. Paul looked up, shielding the morning's sun from his eyes and Judith gave him a tiny wave.

'Good morning, Paul. How are you?'

'As well as can be, my dear Judith. You know.'

'I do. I thought Kerry might welcome a bit of company, a chat. I saw her by the window, up and dressed today.'

'You can try though heaven knows I can't get through to her.'

Judith took the back stairs, following Paul's directions to the top landing. She rapped on the door. After a few minutes she went back down to the pub.

The following morning, after her walk with Lou, she

went upstairs again, with Paul's permission. Again, she knocked on the bedroom door, which was shut tight. 'Kerry. It's Judith,' she called out gently and waited.

'I appreciate you checking on me,' Kerry eventually said, her voice muffled by the closed door. 'I don't want to talk to anyone, though.'

Judith left quietly, not wanting to push Kerry, make her feel uncomfortable or bullied into doing something she wasn't ready to do but she vowed to persevere. She had to persuade Kerry, no, show her, that everything happens for a reason and Judith felt this was the right time to approach her, talk to her.

'There is a time for everything, and everything has its time,' she said out loud to herself. But she had to bide her time, this was something that had to unfold slowly, like the snowdrops in winter and the crocuses in spring.

She visited the following day again, after seeing Kerry at the window. Something about her stance told Judith to try one more time. And after knocking on the door, she said, 'Give me five minutes, Kerry. I'll be back. I have an idea.'

'She won't be going anywhere, and you'll be wasting your time,' said Paul, when Judith told her she would be coming back. 'She refuses to see or talk to anyone but thanks Judith. You're very kind.'

Fifteen minutes later, and out of breath, Judith approached the pub pulling a lime-green shopping trolley behind her.

'What's all this?' asked Paul, surveying her bundle.

'It's my box of tricks. It worked every time while I was teaching. Curiosity brings people out of themselves.

They can't help it. Trust me.'

'I miss her, Judith.'

'I know you do. Your patience will be rewarded.'

'Whatever you have planned, I hope it works for all our sakes.'

'You'll have Kerry back before you know it,' said Judith.

Chapter 6

'Kerry, it's me, Judith. Can I come in?'

Silence. Judith pushed her ear up to the door. Perhaps she wasn't there now. Then she heard a shuffle, heavy footsteps. She's carrying the world and all its problems, thought Judith.

'Kerry?'

The doorknob turned slowly, and Kerry cracked open the door. Her pale face, sunken blue eyes and dried cracked lips stared back at Judith, in stark contrast with the sunburnt orange sundress she wore. 'Judith,' she said, sweeping her overgrown fringe from her face.

'I have an idea and I'm hoping you'll let me explain.'

Kerry leaned into the door, hesitating. Judith reached out and stroked her hand, which felt cold to the touch. Perhaps she was ill. Perhaps it's a doctor she needed.

Judith gently pulled away and made to leave but changed her mind. She had to give it one last shot.

'Please, Kerry, can I come in?' Judith asked, holding her breath, expecting to be rejected again.

Kerry stepped back and swung the door wider, ushering Judith in as if afraid to be seen, her eyes darting back towards the staircase. Judith bustled in, dragging in her pull-along, her neck scarf an abundant array of pinks, blues, and yellows, bringing a kaleidoscope of colour into the otherwise drab room.

'I'm not going to ask how you are. No point making silly small talk.'

Kerry cocked her head and half-smiled, but the smile didn't reach her eyes and she retreated into the room as if to distance herself from the conversation, but Judith carried on regardless of Kerry's agitation. 'I'm here to help. Here to show you that even when life seems impossible there is always something we can do to make it bearable once more and, in time, worth living too.'

Judith took a step further into the room. She held out her arms and Kerry fell into them, sobbing as if her heart would break. Judith recognised the shaking in Kerry's body, the release of its burden of pain and guilt and loss. Judith held Kerry, rubbed her back, stroked the top of her head, absorbed the weight of her. Eventually, Kerry's sobbing subsided, she finally pulled back from Kerry's frail body.

'Sorry. I'm so embarrassed.'

'There's nothing to be embarrassed about. Goodness, after what you've been through.'

'I feel empty, Judith. Empty of everything,' said Kerry as her words seemed to unspool. 'I don't feel love or hope. I have no energy, no will to carry on. I've lost interest in life, in Paul.'

'Grief does that, Kerry. It's all-consuming. It swallows you up until you can't think straight. This is grief. It's nothing to be ashamed of.'

'Not what all the wagging tongues will be saying. Have been saying.'

'People are kinder than you give them credit for.'

'Sorry, I know. I feel so alone. Like there's nothing to get up for anymore,' said Kerry and her face crumpled as the tears came again.

'Look, this is real. You're going through something enormously difficult, painful.'

Kerry continued to cry, and Judith let her have the time she needed to unburden herself, though she also recognised how grief stayed with you, under your skin, behind your eyes, in your heart and in your thoughts forever. It never went away. It changed energy. It altered the way it felt as you allowed more good days to come to you. She knew those feelings of hopelessness, of wondering what the point was.

'Paul mentioned, a while back, you wanted to paint your bedroom and then, well, you lost your vava-voom. Totally understandable and I'm so sorry for what you're still going through.'

'My vava-voom,' said Kerry.

'I'm sorry maybe that's not the right phrase... the students used to say it all the time. You lost your baby. Your adorable little girl and you're hurting. You're hurting so much you feel as though you'll never be able to ever recover happiness or joy. But let me tell you. You will. I know.'

'How can you possibly know?'

'Let me help you. Let me show you. I know you'll start to feel better Kerry. I promise you. Dry your eyes. This is the first day of your new beginning,' Judith said.

Judith bent over her shopping trolley and unzipped the bag all the way around to reveal its contents. Kerry looked on, her blue eyes wet with tears, rimmed red from crying. But Judith noticed something else too; a sparkle in her eyes beyond her tears, which hadn't been there earlier; sorrow was replaced, even if for a moment, by something else.

Hope?

Resilience?

Acceptance?

Chapter 7

That same evening Judith sat on her cobbled patio enjoying her meal of a shop-bought chicken and mushroom pie. She had cooked it to perfection in the oven and ate it with a portion of frozen vegetables she had not been so mindful of but still she gobbled them down. The local radio station played in the background and though she was tired, her bones ached and creaked in a way she hadn't felt before, she eagerly lifted her food to her mouth and still managed a smile. Today was a good day. The start of many good ones for Kerry and she hoped for her too.

'I've found my new purpose,' she mused to herself as she took another bite of pie and savoured the thick creamy sauce and crisp buttery pastry. 'I know all will be well,' she said, prodding at the soggy, mushy vegetables. 'At least the pie is edible.'

For the next three days, Judith woke early. She ate

leisurely, propped up in bed with a breakfast tray on her lap: instant oats, chia seeds and milled flax seeds, soaked overnight, sprinkled with blueberries and a drizzle of honey. She dressed casually in wide-legged trousers and plain but bright T-shirts and walked across the village to meet Kerry. Each day, Kerry waved to Judith from her open bedroom window with a child-like enthusiasm.

'I don't know what's happening up there Judith but thank you,' said Paul, running a scrim over the pub's windowpanes. 'I've not dared to think I'd ever have my Kerry back and yet last night she was humming one of our favourite tunes in the shower. Singing and showering. I never thought I'd be this happy about anything so simple. Her singing voice these past few days has been the sweetest... thank you,' he said, choking up and squeezing Judith's elbow before wiping away a tear.

'You're welcome. She's done this all on her own. And I know that she'll let you in when she's ready, Paul. Everything takes time. I won't hurry back. I think my work here is done.'

Another week passed and Judith received a text message from Kerry asking her to drop by. Kerry, still hiding from the punters and the hubbub of the pub's busy lunchtime trade, greeted Judith with a hug at the bottom of the back stairs. 'Come,' she simply said, and Judith trailed up the narrow staircase behind her.

'It's amazing what magic a few paint pots and letting go can bring to our souls,' said Judith and she followed Kerry back upstairs with a pot of ochre yellow paint and a long brush, each scuff-marked step bowing under her tread. 'I hope this is the colour you wanted,' she said, passing the pot to Kerry.

'I've never done anything like this. I didn't think it would make me feel so hopeful. So, dare I say it, happy.'

'My art has brought me a lot of happiness over the years. It's incredibly cathartic, starting with a blank sheet and watching the paint build up, connecting to our experiences, our thoughts. Some of the best art has come from discomfort, from tension.'

'It's like my therapy,' said Kerry.

'It is. Art is a great form of therapy for all sorts of ailments and worries. I can't pretend to be an expert on the subject of art therapy, but I read how it can help alleviate anxiety, depression, and stress, inducing a sense of calm and self-awareness.'

'Did art help you?'

'In many ways it did, yes. It has boosted my confidence over the years, I made a career out of it.'

'Paul's mum mentioned you left the village a long time ago. Why did you leave?'

'Stubborn teenage passion. Narrow-minded parents. A community which didn't accept anyone who blurred the boundaries.'

'I'm glad you're back,' said Kerry, squeezing Judith's arm.

'It was an incredibly difficult time. I was stubborn, of course, only young. A teenager who thought she had it all worked out until my parents let me go. That's what has hurt the most I suppose. They didn't seem to care enough to put their own embarrassment to one side.'

'That must have been awful for you.'

'It made me resilient and taught me to rely on no one

but myself. But yes, it was hard.'

As they talked, Judith watched as the sun, bouncing off the walls, cast one side of Kerry's face in shadow, no longer a tired shade of magnolia. Kerry was becoming alive again. She had a long journey ahead of her, but Judith hoped she would find her way out of the abyss of grief for her lost child, find a permanent hope and love and a happier, tangible reason to keep going. And in the short time they spent together they shared some of their most intimate thoughts.

'I lost a baby too,' said Judith, revealing her own despair. 'Long before I was married but, in the end, the pain of it, though years later, coupled with Brian leaving me, pushed me over the edge.'

'I'm so sorry, Judith. And here I am, self-obsessed, not considering how this might be inflicting pain on you.'

'Not at all, you didn't know. And you're not. It's just that you don't forget. You just wander, sometimes a little lost, in life until you find something worth holding onto, something which keeps pulling you forward.'

'The circle of life.'

'It's what keeps us nourished. Gives us life.'

Both women sat very still, two figures on the edge of the bed, holding hands, breathing in harmony.

Chapter 8

A week later, Judith woke and didn't have to head off to Kerry's; her work was done, and though she felt a sense of peace sitting on her shoulders, cooing softly like a dove, she also missed the routine her visits to Kerry had created, missed their conversations, their shared confidences.

With time falling away in front of her like a sheet to the wind, she wondered whether any more cards would fall through her letter box. She still had no idea who had sent them but no longer worried about it.

'One for Sorrow,' she said out loud as a robin flew from the branch of the crab apple tree to the lower boughs of the twisting sweet cherry wound around the arbour. Another bird joined him, and they sang in harmony. 'Two for Joy,' she said and remembered the second postcard sitting on the mantle. *What underlying message did it carry?* Her mind wandered and she began to form an idea. *Were the cards prompting her to seek out those needing her attention? Who needed her help next?* Life was full of both good times and bad times, and she wondered why anyone would need support at a time of joy.

Judith was beginning to think no more mysterious postcards would find their way to her letter box. She had been delayed at the off license where she bought a bottle of medicinal brandy.

One of the local busy bodies was digging for details of Judith's visit to Kerry, but Judith simply commented, 'You wouldn't want me breaking a young woman's confidence would you. After all, we all deserve some privacy.' The woman fled the store, her hot cheeks clashing with her overtly bright pink rinse.

Judith, pushing open the porch door, arrived home to a third postcard on the mat. It was facing downwards. She turned it over, excitement banging in her chest.

'Three for a Girl,' she read. 'What a beautiful picture,' she exclaimed. Three bowing magpies surrounded a young boy with golden curls poking from beneath his bonnet. Each bird played a musical instrument; a French horn, a trumpet and a tiny pair of symbols as musical notes floated in the air around them.

Each feathered friend seemed to smile at her; its beady black eyes gleaming off the white card. The tiniest brush strokes had shaped thickly plumed wings and a long lustrous tail on each image. 'You've outdone yourself this time,' Judith clapped as she studied the detail carefully, in awe of the beautiful artwork. 'Three for a Girl. Lou's speculation was wrong.'

She poured herself a generous measure of brandy and sitting at the kitchen table she held onto the card, turning it in her hand. *What did it mean? How would she know what to do?* She took a sip and then another. The burning liquid warmed her, firing her senses.

She looked up and Maja, who lived with her mother in one of the modern-builds on the outskirts of the village, walked by; her head bowed, she moved as if in a trance, the wires of her ear pods trailing down into the pocket of her huge, oversized lime-green hoodie.

She had heard how she had only been eleven when she and her mother moved into the village and though friendly, they had kept to themselves. Judith surmised that must have been a few years before; she was easily fifteen or sixteen now, gangly, lanky looking. Her experience of Polish people was that they were kind and she certainly had one Polish individual to be thankful to… she remembered him fondly.

Maja, like her mother, shied away from others too. The walk to the school bus pick-up point in the village coincidentally pushed Maja into the path of Harry and Charlie, and some of her peers, who always seemed to be messing around and laughing, yet she appeared too reluctant to join the rest of the crowd; the banter, the joking around, the usual pushing and shoving which came with the bravado of raging hormones and the presence of boys. The other schoolgirls joined in the fun, the teasing. Judith had seen the interactions around Maja when she had once persuaded the school bus driver to let her have a ride part of the way last winter when the ground was too frosty for her to walk any distance safely.

A likeable young lady, Judith imagined she would be popular at school though she had more than once caught the tail-end of chatter between parents of how *she kept herself to herself* and *didn't socialise with any school friends outside of class.*

Sullen.

Moody.

Unfriendly.

The comments were unkind, and Judith didn't dwell on those, recognising them for what they were; empty, hurtful mindless gibberish about the girl's weight and her accent which didn't warrant a second of Maja's attention. Though, once, she caught the last few words of a not-so-nice trail of banter from two students and had tutted extra loudly to alert them to stop. They did instantly, but Judith had wondered how long for.

The brandy warmed the back of her throat, and she closed her eyes, the fire of the cognac igniting passion within her. Her thoughts changed focus; the sender of the postcards giving her something to think about and something to do. Though she had been feeling discombobulated not knowing who they were from, a new sense of direction, a new path, seemed to be emerging and she wanted to trust their guidance. She needed something to drive her.

Retirement had not been what she had imagined... afternoons painting with layers of paint under her fingernails, cross-country rambling with mud caked on her boots, mushroom foraging and endless days reading —her to-be-read piles precariously growing and looming in all corners of the cottage, rising in tall towers like the intensive housing developments which were springing up on unused brown land. She refused to throw away any books, even the ones she would likely never read, but she still rarely let anyone borrow them either.

The magpie cards had become like angel visits, giving her a sense of orientation and purpose. A sense of being able to trust herself again, to be in tune with her instinct. The magpies felt strangely familiar, comforting almost as if they were being sent to her for her own guidance and protection and maybe even her sanity. *Someone was prompting her to do something new with her life.*

'After all, isn't that what I have spent the last thirty years doing? Bringing joy to all those kids through my art, my lessons, my wisdom,' she said, suddenly snapping open her eyes. Jasper, who was having a snooze, shrieked; Judith's outburst left him shaking, his fur standing on edge. 'Sorry, Jasp,' she cooed but he slunk away, meowing his protest, his whipping tail erect.

Chapter 9

Through the window, she could make out a hazy evening sun; it boiled over into vapourous streaks of oranges and pinks and lilacs; the colours of a Baroque canvas. She continued to sit at her table, though she fidgeted, the seat uncomfortable, thinking, thinking.

She refilled her glass and took another swig, and its convex glass reflected her unruly long waves shimmering like a waterfall of fire. She reached up and touched her face; the sun had brought out her freckles, a spatter across the bridge of her nose, a bursting cosmos of stars across her cheeks. She remembered the words of her mother, *my orange sorceress* she said once, pulling her close and hugging her tight in a rare moment of affection. Just as quickly she had pushed Judith away telling her to stop being soppy. 'Emotions tear you down,' she had said.

Somewhere in the distance a thought began to take shape, Judith knew the person in the village she wanted to help next: Maja.

How would she do this? She had no relationship with the teenager, had never taught her or had contact with anyone who did. She recalled how, hitching a sneaky ride into town one time, she had sat next to her on the school bus; Maja had been the only one to shove over and make room for her to sit, moving her backpack onto her lap to make space. She did not speak, not to Judith or to anyone else. A solitary, quiet girl, she seemed to curl into herself, as if wanting to disappear, be somewhere else.

Occasionally Judith glimpsed her mooching about the village; a typical teenager with her lairy-coloured hoodie pulled up over her head, kicking at stones and fallen pinecones as she aimlessly wandered to the village shop and presumably back home. The route took her past Chrysanthemum Cottage. There was only one way into and out of the village from Maja's home and with only an unused water mill beyond her house there had to be a good reason for Judith, or anyone, to pass that way.

Maja's mother, Zuzanna, was a seamstress and though she didn't advertise her services Judith had heard how she prided herself in her nimble stitching and attention to detail. People from the village and surrounding areas had grown to like and rely on her for their hems to be shortened, sleeves to be restyled, buttons to be sewn, lace to be added, trims to be affixed.

She was a quiet woman, who rarely spoke, though always smiled hello on the rare occasion she was in the village. Judith wondered what her story was. *She had to have one, everybody did.* To be so far away from home, no husband or partner as far as she knew. It couldn't be easy raising a teenager alone, in a village where people were friendly but equally judgemental and critical.

The next morning, with the sun's rays falling through the curtains and warming the bed, Judith woke and spritzed a little rose water on her face; it left her skin tingling and it was a ritual she had kept for many years; a little old lady in Cyprus, clad in the colour of mourning from head to toe, had given Judith a bottle when Judith had been island hopping in the early eighties. She had continued to buy it and it was what kept her skin shiny and glowing, and her age a secret from those who wondered how old Judith really was. Openly mentioning her early retirement was something she did not do.

With a bubbling excitement and lightness in her step, she arranged her cardigan over her shoulders and walked down the front garden path. The cobbled paving meandered to the gate, flanked with drooping tulips, their open heads too heavy for their stalks, amongst a carpet of forget-me-nots, creeping thyme with its tiny white flowers and the last of the purple spotted deadnettle.

She swung open the gate and stepped into the street. It was a quiet morning and in the distance the mist swirled on the horizon creating a translucent scape and the dew glistened on the village green like a carpet of emeralds. Two jays flitted from tree to tree, calling to each other, their characteristic screeching filling the air with a tangible joy, incongruent with her own anticipation. A dog walker had stopped by the old pump, talking on his mobile, his hound pulling impatiently on the tight lead.

She knew Maja walked to the supermarket at the

weekend for a loaf of bread and milk. Village life, like clockwork, rarely changed or missed a beat. People relied on their routine and their knowledge of each other to create a safety net and a community which Judith had grown to accept, and maybe even, now loved.

Shading her eyes with her hand, she cursed for forgetting her horn-rimmed sunglasses on the kitchen table. As she approached the bend in the road, outside the church, Judith slowed her pace, realising she had been walking too quickly, something she did when anxious, and fanned herself with one end of her shawl.

The exertion of walking warmed her and, after stopping in front of the post box to mail a birthday card to her uncle, she dropped onto the nearest bench for a breather. The bench's plaque, tarnished by the weather, was inscribed with the words "In loving memory of Dotty and Arthur Jacobs, who loved this village and everyone in it, August 2020". Covid had taken too many of the village's older folk and a stab of melancholy momentarily forced her to close her eyes, to remember those lost during that terrible year.

The audible calls of a group of boys playing cricket on the green forced her to look up. She surveyed the batsman as he fumbled his shot and the ball looped easily into the hands of the fielder. The batsman shrugged. The game continued.

A warm prickle of gratitude filled her as she took in the village houses' neat hedges and picket fences, pale blue painted shutters and peeling arbours framing front doors. She thanked her parents in quiet prayer for Chrysanthemum Cottage. Though Judith never dreamed of coming back to live in the village, she felt a quiet belonging filling her and an overwhelming emotion threatened her with a public display of tears and the view began to soften and then blur.

Chapter 10

She knew she didn't deserve the cottage; she'd walked out on her parents, on her life there, on her sixteenth birthday after a massive row; it seemed her mother didn't approve of her posing nude for the evening art classes in the village hall and her boyfriend's mother, though they were hardly boyfriend and girlfriend, too young to understand the complexities of a relationship, had stopped him from seeing her, after the "dreadful incident".

'I knew you'd be trouble,' yelled her mother. 'Your father and all his wickedness with that woman has made me unkind, unable to forget what happened.' Her words often came back to Judith when she felt at her lowest, when she missed home, but never thought to ask what they meant. *What did her mother mean?*

Judith returned, in her mid-forties, to celebrate her parents' diamond wedding anniversary. She struggled seeing them so old after all those years, especially with the stress of her own failed marriage still haunting her and couldn't wait to get away. She faked an emergency on Sunday morning, so she could return to the city; escape her guilty torment, regret, and frustration at how little they had changed. Paying extortionate rent for a pokey one-bedroom flat with a sloping floor and rattling windows and which let in more cold than kept in heat, made Judith stubborn and stoically independent.

She had left home a young girl, having known nothing of life outside of the village or how the world worked and had returned a woman with knowledge and experience which far outweighed that of her parents. At least, that's what she believed.

She involuntarily shivered despite the warmth and peered back up the road. She just made out its shaggy, brown thatched roof, spindly chimney, and the pretty leaded windows flanked with the yellow shutters, now blistering under the sun, but which suited the chocolate box style of her home. Not much of a gardener, unlike her mother, she had lived most of her early life drawing.

She had only grown to love gardening with the help of Bill, a retired gardener in the village since moving back. She relished the easy attention needed by the self-sufficient cottage garden he designed for her. It gave her something pleasingly wild yet pleasant to look at; most of her rented flats had faced brick walls or overlooked unsightly concrete car parks. She had hoped the all-year-round colours would make her feel closer to her mum, even after all these years, though she knew she was kidding herself.

But she was grateful to Bill; one of the few people who didn't spur her on when she finally returned after her parents' deaths within two weeks of each other three years before. Their passing, desperately sad, yet romantic, had made her wish she had someone who, so heartbroken without her, would give up on life too.

She sat in contemplation. She let her mind wander to her own marriage. Mainly one of convenience, it had been respectful, quiet, until, one afternoon, searching for mythical books and books with illustrations of goblins in them for a college art project, she found her husband in the clutches of one of the librarians in the section marked "Fantasy" and too lost in their own fantasy to notice her.

Chapter 11

Maja's rounded, hunched figure appeared about the bend in the distance. Her head was bowed, her eyes welded to her mobile phone screen, one fist shoved deep into the pocket of her hoodie: bright yellow with a silver lightning strike across the front. Her jeans had rips in them, the rage apparently, and her black trainers padded almost as silent as a predator, as she ambled towards the village green and Judith's little sitting spot.

'Hello,' she called out.

Maja slowed down and peered at her from under long blond lashes. 'Hello,' she said, her voice heavy, her regard for Judith suspicious.

'How are you? How's your mother?' Judith asked, but she had already bundled past her, her steps having quickened with Judith's attempt at further conversation with her.

Not easily put off, Judith decided to try and speak

to her the following day. But again, after greeting each other with a *hello* Maja quickly disappeared, seemingly not hearing her efforts to engage her in conversation.

The following afternoon, at around the time the school bus returned to the village, Judith inconspicuously waited near the post box. 'Hello again,' she said as Maja brushed past her, her mouth full of crisps. She nodded and swallowed. Took another handful of the chips from the bag and then made a funnel, tipping the crumbs into her mouth. 'How are you?' asked Judith.

'Alright,' she answered, bolshie, but Judith caught the shiver in her voice, noticed her brightly painted, but bitten-down fingernails.

'I used to bite my nails. Nerves mostly. My mum hated it. Said it was disgusting.'

'My mum doesn't much like it either,' she said, scrunching the empty crisp bag as she got ready to launch it onto the green. Noticing Judith staring at it, she changed her mind and pushed it into the front pocket of her pink holdall.

'I wondered if you might come by the house on your way home.' Maja gave her a quizzical look and Judith almost lost her nerve. 'I have a small sewing project,' she continued. 'Perhaps you can pass it onto your mum for me, save me from the long walk in this heat.'

'I've got homework and Mum will be waiting for me. She worries if I'm late.'

'Maybe tomorrow? My feet are not able to carry me as well or as far these days,' she said with a little half smile playing on her lips.

'I don't know how busy she is,' she replied, with an

expression of tolerant detachment.

'That's not a problem. I'm in no hurry. Pass by. I'll be waiting tomorrow. Chrysanthemum Cottage…'

'Yes, I know where you live.' She dashed off, slowing down after only a few steps, in the direction of her home, clearly not in as much of a hurry as she had implied initially. Judith knew she wouldn't look back to wave, but she continued to peer after Maja even so.

'See you soon,' she called after her.

Why is the girl always on her own? She had a feeling about her and as she spent more time grappling with it the more she became convinced her hunch was right, though perhaps a little predictable. She wanted to help, her pastoral role and safeguarding training from all her former years in education coming to the fore.

Back at the cottage Judith half-heartedly tidied the small front room. With a renewed vigour and urgency, she cleared the kitchen of her breakfast dishes. It was not so much for wanting to create a good impression as it was to give her something to do with the nervous energy now fizzing in her. Like one of those indigestion tablets, you drop into water, she found herself bubbling with an almost unrecognisable excitement. She was sure she would come by the following day.

At four o'clock the next day, she filled the kettle and placed it on the Aga; she hoped Maja would stop by, maybe even for a natter. She wished she had coke or lemonade, or one of those energy drinks all the youngsters guzzled these days, but it was too late to worry about that now.

Within minutes of throwing away the rubbish into the

already overflowing bin and wiping down the kitchen worktops with a quick flick of her dish cloth, a light tapping at the front door alerted Judith to her visitor. A flush coloured her cheeks.

'You came,' Judith said, stopping herself from uncharacteristically clutching her in a tight hug.

Maja nodded, standing awkwardly in the porch, her overfilled school bag dangling from her arm. Judith waved her in, stepping aside to let Maja, tall and broad, into the cottage.

'I've put the kettle on,' she said, fussing at having a visitor other than Louise and Bill though Bill visited less now the garden was manageable without him. She pointed to her snug two-seater, then wondered whether the two-seater was appropriate, but Maja already sat down. Her weight pressed down on the seat cushions. Her long legs sprawled out in front of her, her trainers rested on the edge of the coffee table shelf.

Too late, she realised Maja was sitting directly opposite the fireplace; Maja faced piles of ash and debris from the last time Judith lit her fire and a curling wallpaper seam gaped open, yawning, on either side of the exposed chimney breast's brickwork. *Such a mess*, thought Judith.

The mouth of her bag, not zipped, opened up as she dropped it on the sofa next to her, revealed its contents, exercise books, paintbrushes, and an overstuffed pencil case. 'Do you paint?' Judith asked, nodding towards the paintbrushes poking out, ignoring the chocolate bar.

'My favourite subject at school. The only thing I'm good at,' said Maja.

'I'm sure you're good at a lot of things.'

'Netball but I'm never picked for the team.'

'Why not? You're certainly tall enough,' said Judith.

'Not been picked, ever… you know how it is.'

'I'm sure your turn will come.'

'Maybe,' Maja said, her voice a whisper.

'I used to like playing netball. Always a goal shooter or goal attack. I also paint,' she said. Maja nodded and Judith, losing her nerve for a moment, said instead, 'Do you drink tea?' and the kettle whistled, shocking them both.

'Coffee, two sugars. Actually, one sugar. My mum always puts two,' she said, laughing, and Judith caught her looking up at the silvery lacework of a cobweb hanging from the old defunct spot track, the light fitting disconnected but still hanging there. She hoped to get a tradesman to come and sort out the ceiling and put up the new miniature chandelier she had bought during one of her antique-shop rambles.

'I need an electrician.'

'My dad used to fix electrics. He taught me a lot.'

'And another thing you're good at then.'

'I can do it for you if you like. I know how. It's easy. Two wires,' said Maja.

'Really? Would you do that for me?'

'I need a step ladder though,' she said.

Judith placed Maja's coffee on the table, sat down at one end of the sofa, slowing her breathing, and straightened out her long skirt with one hand. 'You, okay? You look thoughtful. Will your mother mind you fixing the light for me?' she asked, and she took a slurp of her tea.

'Yes. No. I mean… no, she won't.' Maja seemed to be grappling with something. Judith, with her experience of teenagers, all waistless figures, and baggy sweatshirts, though sadly not her own, sat and waited.

Eventually, Judith broke the silence. 'What else do you like doing when you're not in school?'

'Physics and painting,' she said. 'And ring netball. I was the number one scorer in Poland.'

'You must be good. Physics was never my thing at school. But did you know I used to be an art teacher? I have so much stuff here,' she said, waving in the direction of her art materials. 'Come by any time and use what you like.'

'Any time?'

'Yes. I'm always here pottering around.'

'I will come and fix your light.' She took a swig of her coffee and got up.

'You do that. See you soon… any time,' Judith said, a little sad note of disappointment creeping into her voice that Maja was leaving so soon.

***

For four days on the trot Judith tried to find the motivation to paint but to no avail, not even a hint of inspiration visited, her muse away entertaining someone else.

'Why are you so grouchy?' asked Lou on their morning walk.

'That girl, Maja. She said she would come and fix my light, but she hasn't come back.'

'You of all people should know what kids are like.

They say things, then forget. She probably said it to get away from you.'

'What do you mean?'

'You can be quite pushy when you have your teacher hat on,' said Lou.

'I haven't had my teacher hat on for months.'

'You might not see it, but your teacher persona has never left you. It never will, Judith. And that's a good thing. A whole life of teaching. You don't want it to shrink from you, leave you unmarked, an empty ghostlike shell.'

'Lou, you're not doing a good job of cheering me up today.'

'Sorry. But it's true. You can't shake off what makes you *you*.'

On the fifth day she heard the creak of the garden gate, and being early, expected to hear the postman's familiar steps coming up the path. Peering out the window, she was surprised to see Maja. She had become accustomed to seeing her hunched-up frame clumsily mooching about the village but seeing her approaching Chrysanthemum Cottage made her smile though she wondered why she wasn't at school.

'It's a teacher training day,' she explained, chewing through a packet of cookies, crumbs collecting on the front of her sweatshirt. 'And Mum didn't want me wasting the day.'

'So here you are,' said Judith.

'I told her I was going to the library.'

'Not that I condone telling lies, but you can borrow some of my books on the great painters. That will make me feel better about you being here.'

'Thank you.'

'I'm guessing your Mum won't be too displeased if you tell her you borrowed the books from me.'

'Maybe not.'

'Bill passed by yesterday and left his step ladder. Do you think you could fix that light?'

'I need to turn off the power at the fuse board first.'

'I can do that,' yippeed Judith, clapping.

As Maja looked through Judith's meagre toolbox Judith made coffee for her and within an hour the old lighting track was dismounted, and the new antique candelabra was shining a beautiful golden glow across the room.

'You are so clever! Thank you. Now let me pay you,' said Judith, scrambling for her purse in the bottom of her shopping bag.

'No, it's okay. Mum says we must always help others and it will come back to us when we least expect.'

Maja chose one book: *A Biographical Dictionary of Artists*. It was a huge, doorstopper of a book and too big to fit into her bag. 'I will take good care of it, thank you Judith.'

'Keep it as long as you like.'

After that, Maja passed by most days on her way back from school and even at the weekends. Judith and Maja's friendship blossomed, slowly, like blossom petals unfolding and basking in the summer sun.

A quiet camaraderie developed between them and seeped into the fabric of Judith's routine, and she liked the girl. They talked about the great artists and looked through Judith's collection of books and art magazines. Maja was smart, a great raconteur and Judith enjoyed her tales of life back home.

'You don't shine talking about life here the same way as when you talk about Poland.'

'Poland was easier… no one made fun of me at school. I wasn't too fat, everyone wanted me on their team. I had good friends.'

'And now?'

'The other day a brother and sister in my class said I looked too big to be in school.'

Judith thought about this. 'Oh, take no notice. It's just jealousy. Tall, strong girl, like you. Who else is tall in your class or year group? Hang out with them,' said Judith. 'It's perfectly okay to be who you are without judgement from bullies. Honestly.'

'One girl is my height, maybe even a bit taller. She's in my art class but she usually sits alone. A loner like me.'

'Then join her next time. You might be surprised to see how pleased she is to sit with you.'

'Maybe. She might think I'm being weird.'

'And she might welcome having some company,' smiled Judith.

They painted for a couple of hours; Maja with rough, angry swirls and sweeps as if all her doubts and frustrations were reflected upon the page. Judith, in contrast and finally finding her creative inspiration restored, painted with soft careful strokes. Judith painted her mother's prize chrysanthemum featured in a Women's Institute magazine article from all those years before. She mixed and dabbed and added yellows and browns and ochres to her palette until the paint colour was exactly right, matching the exact colour she had not realised she had held in her mind all these years.

Maja had a YouTube channel blaring out loud; a wild tune with some foul language but Judith refrained from complaining, surprisingly welcoming the noise, and enjoying her company more than she had imagined. She watched Maja as she relaxed more, swept her brush across the canvas, now almost covered in dark, black strokes. And then her technique changed. She applied two lines of colour on her palette and dipping the tip of her brush in water she added splurges of pink and orange and then yellow in smooth loops. The effect was magnificent.

'That's so…'

'Not what you expected,' she said, looking younger than her years and less sure of herself.

'Surprisingly good and yes, unexpected.' Judith heard Lou's voice at the porch. 'Come in, we're busy painting,' she called out to her friend.

'Oh, hello,' Lou said.

'I need to go. Thank you,' said Maja, grabbing her backpack and dashing off.

'Stay, Maja. Louise is a good friend.'

'Don't leave on my account,' said Lou, bewildered.

'It's late. Bye,' she called as she swept out of the living room, the porch door banging behind her a few seconds later.

'She's a bit on the shy side,' said Judith, tidying away some of the brushes and pushing the easel to one side of the room. 'Let's put the kettle on.'

'You didn't tell me you were painting again,' said Lou, unable to keep the accusatory tone from her voice.

'I thought I'd give it a try. But I keep thinking about my artistic talent… where did it come from, Lou? Mum wasn't artistic.'

'Maybe not with paint but she was creative. Look at her garden, how much effort she put into it.'

'Maybe, I don't know.'

'And you've studied art, you've taught art. It's not always nature which gives us our talents. You've worked hard to be the artist you are.'

'But when I was little… what about then?'

'We're all different. At least you have found some inspiration at last.'

'But where does that come from?' asked Judith again.

'If not your mother's genes, something has worked its magic and inspired you to paint again.'

'It just kind of happened. Maja inspired me to try again.'

'That does surprise me,' said Lou, pulling a face.

'I think there's more going on with her than we know.'

The following day, Maja appeared at Judith's door. 'From my mum,' she said, pushing a Tupperware container into Judith's hands. 'They're Polish.'

In the kitchen, Judith opened the lid and smelled them. Little puff pastry cases filled the box, bowties oozing with a jam-like filling and dusted in icing sugar. 'They look like mini-Danish.'

'They're called *kolaczki*. My grandmother used to bake them at Christmas but Mum bakes them every week.'

'I suppose it's her way of connecting to home,

remembering. Funny how food can evoke fond memories and pull at our heartstrings. Is she still alive, your grandmother?'

'No, *babcia* died. Covid got her. We never got to say goodbye.'

'I'm so sorry, Maja, but it's good that your mum has something so special to remind her of home,' said Judith, recalling her own regret at not being there to say goodbye to her parents. 'Do you want to paint today?'

'Yes, maybe. There's just something I need to…'

'What is it, Maja?' asked Judith, her heart suddenly heavy.

'I don't know.'

'Tell me. I feel there's something you want me to know. Tell me what it is.'

'I don't know how.'

'I find the best way is to just spit it out. So go on. One, two, three…'

Maja swallowed and took a deep breath. 'I'm so lonely. I force myself to go to school every day. The bullying is…' she said, the sentence almost springing from her mouth and then just as quickly she seemed to regret it.

Before Judith could respond, Maja burst into tears, grabbed her phone, and charged, as fast as lightning, out of the cottage. The cottage's door, wide open behind her, like a gaping hole which desperately needed to be filled.

Chapter 12

For the next two days, Judith ate the pastries, for breakfast and as a mid-morning snack: the buttery flakiness melting on her tongue, all the while her thoughts filled with Maja's parting words.

Maja did not return to Chrysanthemum Cottage and Judith wondered whether she would. Patience, however, had taught Judith well. Maja needed space, and on the third day, her clumsy footsteps clip-clopped along the path.

Judith swung open the porch doors and stepped back to let her in, her heart racing with relief on seeing her.

'There's so much I want to say,' Maja struggled.

'I'm listening,' said Judith.

Judith sat very still, her hands in her lap. She nodded ever so slightly; years of teaching had taught her to be self-controlled, not to prompt. She didn't say anything. She watched Maja. She fiddled with the ties of her hoodie, pushed her hands into the front pockets. She rounded her shoulders as if wanting to hide, as if closing in on herself, making herself smaller, would stop her from talking.

Judith waited. The ticking clock seemed to get louder, the cat flap sprung shut behind Jasper who trailed in and pushed up against her feet, nuzzling her ankles, meowing for her to pick him up, his heart-shaped nose bright. She gently nudged him away and eventually he sidled off to the kitchen where she heard him crunching on the last of the tuna and cheddar cat biscuits in his bowl from breakfast. She made a mental note to buy some more but instantly forgot when Maja spoke.

'My mother tells me not to be so sensitive, but I can't help it. I used to have so many friends in Poland. My cousins, neighbours. But now all we do is sit at home and Mum bakes all the time.'

'She's certainly a good baker.'

'That's part of the problem.'

'How so?'

'I want to be careful what I eat but how can I when Mum is pushing cakes and pastries towards me? I want to lose weight, but she keeps feeding me. She thinks I'm still her little girl, someone else and I can't be who she wants me to be anymore. I'm older. I want to have my own life. I want to fit in again like I used to.' There was a desperate note of urgency, despair, in her voice, almost pleading to be understood.

'I hate to be the bearer of bad news but everyone in the village notices you Maja. Your attire does rather make you stand out,' she awkwardly added but softly, hoping to ease her pain a bit.

'I feel like I cannot make a life away from my mum.'

'Have you ever told her how you feel?'

'No, not really, but it's always on my mind. I don't have any friends and all I do is eat.'

'Speak to your mum. Tell her what you've told me.'

'I can't. She won't understand, will brush it off. She will hate me, think I do not appreciate her, and I can't have her hating me.'

'Have you tried?'

'No,' she answered, unable to meet Judith's gaze.

'Do you think your teachers know how unhappy you are? Have you spoken to them about the bullying?'

'Everyone thinks I'm some sort of misfit, an outcast. I really like the boys in my class. Prefer their company to that of the girls. The girls stare at me like I'm unimportant, irrelevant.'

'I'm sure that's not the case. They're being cautious. Girls have a lot more than boys to be cautious about though, sadly, that's changing. Boys get bullied too.'

'Maybe. People always judge me.'

'People will always judge people. When people feel threatened, whether through their own ignorance or prejudice, they will retaliate the only way they can. Angry. Mean. Cruel.'

'What should I do? I try to ignore them. Sometimes I name call back.'

'Show them who you really are. Find those who like you, support you.'

'It's so hard,' said Maja sullenly.

'It is and remember that there will always be people

who don't like us. What we have to do is make sure we like ourselves first. Once we work on ourselves, we can work on creating the right time and place for others to like us too.'

Maja listened intently.

'What about the girl in your art class?'

'She has been away sick. I am so lonely. I am so fed up with the name-calling, the snidey comments.'

'I know. Those people unable to honour their own humanity will be unable to honour anyone else's. This, sadly, is the problem with hate-filled bullies, they are so blinded by their own pain and rage that they project it onto others they perceive to be weaker or less important than themselves.' Maja stared back at Judith, then fiddled with her fingernails. 'So,' she continued, 'your best bet is to avoid them and if you can't, find an ally, preferably bigger and stronger, to stand by you. Someone who will speak up for you when you feel you can't, someone who will magnify your voice. In my experience people only judge those they understand the least.'

'What experience? You live alone in a cottage.'

'You're right, I do live alone. I'm a lot older than you. But I had a life before Chrysanthemum Cottage. I was an art teacher for over thirty years. I've seen many young people battle with all sorts of demons... supported them to make the transition into adult life after having to deal with the most challenging, sometimes traumatic, situations. And do you know what they all had in common?'

Maja shook her head. Judith could see her fighting her emotions; her hands now clasped together between her knees, her knuckles white with tension.

'Gumption. Attitude. Belief. But also: Self-doubt. Fear. Loneliness. Anger. Confusion. But they all found a way. They all turned things around and came out smiling. I'm not saying it was easy, some of them lost friends, some gained friends, others realised they were bigger than their fears. And they all thanked me for showing them it was worth it, worth doing what they wanted, to do the right thing for themselves. All it takes is one person to accept who you are, and the rest will slowly follow.' Judith paused. 'People are like sheep; they tend to follow one another so if one person says you're okay, they all agree and do the same. And believe me this village, and your school, isn't all that different from anywhere else in the world.'

Maja sat contemplating; her forehead furrowed in thought. 'Will you help me?' she asked eventually.

'I'll do whatever you need me to do.'

'How do I tell my mum I am being bullied? She will blame herself.'

'You'll find a way. Just remember she loves you. She wants you to be happy.'

'Your mum didn't.' She said it so matter-of-factly that Judith couldn't deny it. It shocked her hearing it from someone else and thought carefully before replying.

'That's not what I said,' she said, eventually. 'I meant my mum didn't show me love. But she cared for me. Clothed me, fed me, made sure I was safe.'

'I'm scared. I don't want to let her down, make her worried. I should be able to look after myself.'

'And she doesn't want to let you down either. She

loves you. You've got this. You deserve to be happy.'

'I sometimes wake up and I'm full of the dreams I've had. Of being popular like I used to be in Poland, playing netball, surrounded by my friends, laughing together. I miss being me, the one with lots of friends. I might as well be invisible now,' she said with downcast eyes.

'And you will. You won't always hide behind your oversized hoodie, and you're not doing a great job of making yourself invisible,' Judith smiled.

'I know,' Maja half smiled. 'Mum has worked hard to build her reputation, to fit in here.'

'But this is about you.'

'Mum and me, we are one,' she said simply, and a stab of regret came at Judith. She had never had that relationship with her own mother; whatever Judith did it had never been enough, but she also wondered whether Maja's relationship with his mother was a healthy one, but this was not what Maja was seeking her support with.

'What a waste of time,' her mother had said, walking through the door after the end-of-year Parents' Evening at Judith's school. 'The only teacher who praised you was the art teacher in her paint-splattered overalls and nicotine-stained teeth. You had better pull your socks up, Judith. Whatever will I tell the other mothers when they ask?' And Judith had gone to bed with a heaviness, with shame, yet not quite sure why she had to be ashamed of being so good at drawing, expressing herself with chalks and paints.

She wished she had said something and made her mother see how wonderful her work was. But she could see, now, how it was not Judith's fault what her mother saw or didn't see, but her mother's own. Judith had been a child.

She took a deep breath and shook off the shroud of regret. 'My dear Maja... I think you will find a way to be as popular as you were, and as well-liked as your peers.'

Maja took a deep breath and blew out gently through her open lips. 'My grandmother said my great grandmother was like me. Never raised her voice. Always a bit of an outsider. Before she died, she told me nothing was ever greater than us other than God, that I could do anything if I was brave enough.'

'Your grandmother sounds incredibly wise indeed.'

'She had such a stern voice. A stern look too. She sometimes frightened me with her strong words, her fight. Why can't I be more like her?'

'Strong is good, but it doesn't have to be loud. Strength can be quiet, unseen. It can get you to where you want to be along the quiet lanes, you don't always need to be racing along a motorway.'

'You make this sound so easy,' Maja said.

'I've learnt in life that things are only as difficult or as easy as you perceive them to be. It's about our reactions to obstacles. It's about our attitude.'

'You're wise too. *Babcia* Maja would have liked you.'

'Be brave, Maja. Give yourself wings and fly. Go in search of your dreams and you will find eternal happiness. It's a quote I read somewhere,' Judith said, noticing Maja's expression of confusion.

'Great quote,' she eventually laughed.

'So how are you going to approach this new you?'

'One of the first things I'm going to do is set up an

after-school netball team. I need to stand up and show everyone what I can do. Show them a side to me I like and am confident about. I'm a good netball player. I'm really good,' she said. 'Then I'm going to make friends with the girl in my art class.'

'Good for you!' said Judith, hoping Maja would approach this with the confidence she needed to make it happen. *Saying and doing it were two different things. Intention needed to be backed by action.*

'And I might try and speak to my mum about all the cooking she does.'

'One of the happiest times of my life, and I suppose one of the most challenging, was when I was sixteen, about your age. And I struggled a lot with how my parents reacted to my artistic eccentricities— my nude modelling for the village art class and my big ideas to be the next art phenomenon, but I'm glad I pursued my dream.'

'You posed nude?' Maja snickered and then composed herself, embarrassed. She then quietly asked, 'What did you do to persuade them?'

'I didn't. I simply carried on doing what I was doing, away from here until I was able to confidently be myself. But you don't have that option. You have to stand up to bullies. Maybe if I'd stayed…' said Judith as she trailed off and she felt the downward pull of her mouth but continued. 'Sadly, my parents didn't experience my success firsthand. In the end, though they never said, I want to believe they became quietly proud of my career, the art I created. They even framed and displayed my art before they died.'

Judith pointed to the wall behind the sofa and Maja turned to look at the triptych piece of art. The colours, muted behind the glass, danced in the pale sunlight; the fluidity and hues gentle but alive and Judith hoped their positivity spoke to Maja.

'As easy as that?' Maja eventually said, emitting a deep sigh, her cheeks coloured.

'You have to escape the unkind, hard-shelled chrysalis of your own making, keeping away, keeping yourself to yourself, while protecting you, has imprisoned you too. You have to set yourself free; like the butterfly,' said Judith.

They sat companionably as if they were friends of old and something in Judith skipped and jumped. She wondered whether this wasn't her call, yet knew that as a teacher and educator, she had untold experience of dealing with bullying issues and friendship breakups. A tiny voice inside her told her to be cautious, not to fan the flames. She didn't want to encourage the girl to become more aggressive. She had been forced to leave the village once under a shroud of shame, she didn't want to face the same exile again. She mulled it over and over until she convinced herself she was doing something good here. She was setting her three magpies free; 'Three for a Girl,' she said to herself and let a smile slide across her lips.

'Thank you. But I really should go now. My mum will wonder where I am, and she'll be getting hungry. We always have breakfast together.'

'Of course. And here is the sewing. She will understand what I'd like her to do with it,' said Judith as she handed

Maja a canvas bag.

Before closing the door behind her, Judith gave Maja a hug, stepped back and squeezed her arm.

Inside Chrysanthemum Cottage, Judith nestled into her father's armchair. Jasper came and snuggled at her feet while Judith sipped her lukewarm tea. Despite the coolness of the drink, her heart was warm.

A sudden thought came to her, and she ran out to warn Maja it might not be easy, not to expect immediate change, her black shrouded figure already a dot at the end of the road. She called but her voice carried on the summer breeze, got caught in the trees. She didn't hear and she didn't shout a second time.

Chapter 13

She pulled out one of her unfinished canvasses and painted with *The Sound Of Music* CD playing a little too loudly to call it background music. She lost all sense of time and space and didn't stop until her stomach rumbled in protest at not having stopped for anything to eat. She had fobbed Lou off that morning saying she had things to sort out and had avoided leaving the house for their customary walk. She felt bad lying, but painting was what she had to do so it wasn't a complete lie.

While Judith painted, she thought about Maja, and acknowledged her yearning for Maja to be happy and hoped the girl would find a way back to the happiness she so obviously had once had in her life. She considered the girl Maja wanted to be, surrounded by friends, playing netball, being popular, fitting in. A friendless child lived a lonely childhood, which sadly led to a lonely path in adulthood too. She wanted it to be different for Maja.

Judith knew what that was like; trying to keep away from a community, distancing herself from the waffle clouding her head. The inevitable feelings tugged at her own heart; intangible, invisible yet pulling her in thick and gooey like tar, and she tried to shake them off.

She took out her sketch pad and reached for her set of pastels. She popped open the tin and took out a piece of grey chalk. With the pad on her knees, her back propped upright by two overstuffed cushions, she began to make sweeping lines across the page, rather like the arches of a rainbow but all crossing each other at different angles.

She used light strokes and heavier strokes; some of the contours unfolded as faint lines while others appeared more dominant and aggressive as she filled the top half of the page with dozens of sweeps. She used the tip of her finger to smudge some of the lines into each other, to soften them, to draw them out wider across the page. She held the chalk on its side and filled the art paper with solid wide lines. The contrast of the lines began to build a picture of sorts… a rainbow of lines, a sky of strands, a sun of rays.

She imagined each curve representing a life within the village. Some remained apart and distanced from each other while others entwined many times. She wanted to focus on the big picture; the details would come. She had lost sight of who she was to be since retiring but the simple shapes beckoned her, seemed to come alive on the page, and Judith felt her heart jolt with joy, patterning out a rhythm, lazy ripples and energetic slashes, which she welcomed.

Her jumbled thoughts and feelings were being

interpreted through the chalk in her hand. She was more than an artist; she was a designer, a problem-solver, a thinker, a life manipulator and above all she was a compassionate human being. She had to find a way to help Maja out of her invisible days; Maja was ready to face her bullies and say hello to the world as a stronger, independent teenager.

She looked down at her board… chalk dust, tiny particles making up solid lines, creating a whole picture for all to see. That's what we all are, she thought, tiny fragments, different but the same. She considered the tiny fragments which everyone has and manipulates to find a way of portraying, putting forward their best selves, and living their best lives. She would focus on the bigger shapes first and the small details would shine through. The first shape had to be the focus. The minutiae would fall into place. The interpretation would have to be the individual's.

She took a piece of white chalk and held it loosely, bouncing it up and down across the page to create a spattering of tiny snowy flecks, punctuated dots and then, with an ochre and a burnt orange pressed hard on the page to make a more solid mass of colour. Fire. Energy evolving. Energy rising. Energy burning.

She knew what she had to do. She now had a reason to visit Maja's mother and maybe, in time, have the conversation with her that would allow her mother to support Maja the way she needed to be supported. *Being a single parent, so far away from home, must be difficult.*

The scratchy scrape of the garden gate's hinges interrupted her thoughts, and she sat up a little straighter listening to the sound of the footsteps on the path. She recognised them; it was Lou. She put her chalks back in the tin and closed it gently with a click; she laid her sketchpad on the sofa and heaved herself up to answer the door. Before she got to it, Lou had knocked her habitual rat-a-tat-tat and bustled in.

'Good morning.'

'Lou. Is everything okay?' asked Judith.

'Of course, it is. Why wouldn't it?'

'Because you're here.'

'I'm here because I wondered where you were. I waited at the fork in the road, and you never came. Then I saw your message.'

'I went out early.'

'I know that much.'

'Maja came over for a chat,' Judith said.

'I thought you painted together. Don't you talk all the time?'

'Not properly,' said Judith.

'What did you talk about? Why are you being so secretive? Does she know who the magpie postcards are from?'

'No, nothing like that. Life. Choices. Making the right choices for ourselves.'

'Have you been telling stories again?' teased Lou.

'Made-up stories are the ones which tell our truth, the truth we wish we could say out loud, but which stir from their rocky beds.'

'That sounds deep.'

'I've made mistakes, Lou. Too many to dwell on yet I wonder how my life would have been different had I just made different choices, written a different story. Stood up for myself.'

'How?'

'My relationship with my mother might have been different. If I'd talked to her, asked her to explain.'

'Explain?'

'There was always something amiss. Something which haunted her, plagued her and I think it was something my father did.'

'Anything your father did has rightly remained between them. You can't take on their troubles and make them your own.'

'I guess not,' said Judith, a sigh of remorse leaving her.

'There's no point in regretting the past, Judith.'

'You say that, but something feels strangely unfinished, like there's something waiting in the wings for me.'

'Wings? Ha-ha! You mean magpies?'

'Ooh, I see what I did there,' laughed Judith and continued, 'You're right. Regrets steal our happiness.'

'Did the girl actually talk to you?'

'She did. And there's a lot more to her than meets the eye.'

'I wouldn't say that's exactly the problem. Not very much meets the eye other than her awful baggy clothes, her sullen expression.'

'You'll be surprised what is waiting to be revealed under those clothes.'

'What did you talk about... exactly?'

'All will be revealed my dear Lou and, in the meantime, I'm going to have a cup of tea so please join me. I have crumpets too,' announced Judith, successfully moving the conversation away from Maja.

'You're spoiling me. How can I refuse a hot buttered crumpet?'

Louise filled the kettle and set it on the stove. Judith popped two crumpets under the grill and placed her cow-shaped butter dish filled with a square block of butter onto the table with two mismatched side plates and two bone-handled butter knives.

'I picked these for you too,' said Lou, taking out a small posy of wildflowers and herbs tied with parcel string from her shopper.

'They are delightful, truly. Thank you, Lou. You're a good friend. I'm lucky to have you.'

'Don't go all soppy on me,' said Lou. 'You know I can't stop blabbering once I start.'

'I'm not far behind you. I've become a mass of emotional atoms the last few months.'

Judith placed a crumpet on each plate and Lou made the tea. She smiled as she stirred two heaped spoons of sugar into Judith's mug.

'How you have the most gleaming white teeth after all the sugar and red wine you consume is beyond me. Definitely one for the nature versus nurture argument,' said Lou.

'Not sure, my dear Lou. Both Mum and Dad didn't have particularly white teeth; Dad's mouth was full of fillings and Mum complained all the time about her overbite and tooth pain, used to give her headaches.'

'We are all a beautiful concoction of our ancestors and what we choose to show the world.'

'That's deep. You've been overthinking. More likely I use the same toothpaste as the vicar. His teeth sparkle.'

'Maybe. And have you received another postcard?'

'Three for a Girl.'

'And what does that mean? Do you have any ideas?'

'All will be revealed in good time.'

'Patience is your virtue not mine,' said Lou, sighing deeply before taking a bite of her crumpet.

'Unless you're doing crosswords.'

'Unless I'm doing crosswords,' laughed Lou.

'Anyway, on this occasion you probably won't have to wait too long,' winked Judith as she topped up their cups from the pot.

'And I noticed your sketch pad's out. Painting something new?'

'A scribble with my chalks, but yes. My creative mojo has been revitalised and I'm beginning to feel like my purpose has found me all over again.'

'Painting, purpose, and passion. Lucky you,' said Lou.

Chapter 14

Being a weekend, the village green teemed with children playing rounders and untamed boys playing football, their voices shouting and screeching at top volume, excitement shaking the leaves in the trees, ripping the air. Judith imagined a happy, boisterous Maja playing her chosen sport, uninhibited, no threats of name-calling flying at her, passing the ball, shooting, and scoring the winning point.

In the distance, Judith glimpsed all sorts of paraphernalia erected on the grassy plot: pink fairy castle pop-up tents make-shift dens and brightly striped parasols. A handful of adults, who had in typical British fashion stripped off the minute they saw a single ray of sunshine, lay on their backs with eyes closed resisting the mid-morning glare.

They decided to walk in the opposite direction instead. Taking the short-cut through the overgrown, ramshackle cemetery of St Barnabas, they sat on one of the worn benches shaded by the branches of the huge walnut tree. Harry and Charlie were leaning against the tree with a couple of other boys.

'Hey, I want a word with you boys,' said Judith, but they scarpered when they saw the women approaching. 'Smoking, the little blighters,' said Judith. 'Look at all these cigarette ends.'

'What did you want to say to them?' asked Lou.

'To keep away from Maja. I saw them the other day shoving into her as they got onto the school bus. Told them to stop being so immature.'

'Don't get involved, Judith,' said Lou and changing the subject said, 'Can't quite believe this tree is almost two hundred years old.'

'Standing taller than the both of us,' said Judith.

Opposite them, rows of tombstones, too weathered to decipher any of the inscriptions, faced them like a row of exhausted soldiers unable to stand straight.

'It's always good to walk and talk with you,' said Judith. 'Thank you for persuading me.' But Judith, full of suspicion, wondered whether her friend had an ulterior motive, wanted to talk to her about something else, and Judith, always waiting for her secret to be discovered, felt her heart ticking like a time-bomb. She didn't want to talk about that... not now, not ever.

'You're welcome. We needed to walk off our crumpets.' Judith stared at Lou, waiting for her to say something more. 'What? Crumpets have calories.'

Judith, relieved to see her friend was not about to broach her most embarrassing secret of her adult life, relaxed her shoulders and gazed at two squirrels who chased each other across and around the gravestones until they scampered into the foliage beyond, disappearing from view.

'How's your Ashleigh?' asked Judith.

'Always working. Barely has time for a phone call let alone a visit. But she's doing well. Promoted for the second time in as many years.'

'She should make time to visit. After all, she only has one mum.'

'She may on my birthday. That's seven weeks away. I'm going to have a little party for her.'

'She should be organising a party for you, Lou.'

'It will be for the both of us. Say you'll come. She'd love to see you after all these years.'

'I'd love to. I'll bake a Victoria Sponge. I'll make it extra special for you since you'll be celebrating.'

Lou tried to hide her angst, but Judith was well aware of her flaws as a baker. She always rushed which resulted in flat, heavy cakes with soggy bottoms. She stubbornly didn't sieve or fold in her flour, believing it to be a waste of time. Her impatience always got the better of her; opening and closing the oven door countless times and rushing to ice the cake before fully cooled.

'You're a darling. Not sure who else I should invite. But I've seen Kerry twice this week. She had her make-up on, and she smiled at me for the first time in weeks, months even. I was so pleased to see her out and about. She's finally found her... what's it the youngsters say? The word you use... pojo.'

Judith laughed out loud, 'You mean mojo, Lou. Mojo.'

'Yes, that's it. She's such a pretty little thing. Hiding away like she did was no life for her. I suspect Paul is feeling the benefit of her new positivity. Bless them both. Such a lovely couple. I'll mention the party to them next time I pop into the pub for a bottle of wine.'

Judith smiled. 'Thought you'd given up the vino.'

'Medicinal, Judith… medicinal.'

Chapter 15

Judith was on edge. She wondered how Maja was fairing. She had not crossed paths with her for a few days. She wondered whether Kerry was still painting and if she was enjoying the advantages Judith assured her that she would experience by expressing herself through art.

'I might pop in to see her this afternoon,' she said to Jasper who was curled up on the hearth; the warmth of the sun in that spot always made him sleepy.

'Hello, Judith,' greeted Paul, a wet cloth in his hand, his reflection mirrored in the shiny bar top. He continued to wipe the stubborn fingerprint smudges on a couple of tumblers and a faint lipstick smear on the rim of a wine glass.

'I'm here to see Kerry if that's okay.'

'Go on through. I'm guessing she's in our bedroom,' he said, putting the glasses on the shelf and then arranging the beer mats along the bar. 'I haven't been allowed in for days now. Been sleeping in the spare room. Think she's having a reshuffle… you know after…' Judith nodded and reached out to pat his hand. He was in turmoil too. The men often got left behind after a miscarriage and she wondered who he turned to for support.

As she climbed the stairs to the eaves at the top of the house, each tread creaked underfoot, each one seemingly a little louder than the last until she reached the little square landing, slightly out of breath.

She expected the bedroom door to be closed but it was flung wide open, the sunny day filling the space with a bouncing light which reflected off the wall mirror of the tiny square landing.

'Kerry. It's me, Judith. I wondered how you're getting on.' Judith took a moment to get back her breath and settle the wobble in her legs before walking into the room. What she came face to face with was beyond words and she was instantly brought to tears. 'Kerry?'

'Judith, sorry. I didn't hear you. I was rummaging around in the back of the walk-in wardrobe. What do you think?'

'It's incredible. It's absolutely beautiful.'

'Really?' Kerry asked, her eyes shining, a tremor in her voice giving away her taut emotions.

'It's so original. What a wonderful mural. And the yellow… it's glorious.'

'It makes me smile all day long.'

'And reminds you how life can still be incredibly bright and happy and full of joy,' beamed Judith.

'It's taken me a long time to climb out of the darkness,' said Kerry, her eyes brimming with tears.

'But you've done it. You're so strong and brave, Kerry.'

'I didn't think I'd ever feel happy again.'

Judith, fighting her emotions, coughed to clear the squeak of a crying voice building in her throat and said, 'Now tell me about it… all of it. How did you create such a beautiful wall?'

'Before I started, I did a bit of spying on you.'

'Spying?' The room temperature seemed to drop to zero degrees and a shiver ran through her. Judith willed her heart to slow down. *Had Kerry found out her secret?*

'On your old college website. All the art you created with your students.'

Judith felt the heat spreading red across her chest and up her neck and face. Had Kerry seen anything else? If Kerry knew, would she tell anyone?

'And then I began with what I had. You know all the little things around the house which represented Paul and me and the baby. And me pregnant. Paul took so many photos of me with a bump it was difficult to ignore them, and I didn't want to anymore. They showed me life was happy then and that our baby made me so happy even if it was only for a few weeks. I cried a lot after you left me that day and the days after that. And then I woke up and decided to do something. I played around with a kind of 3-D wall of love and hope. It evolved. It came to me out of despair.'

'I love it,' beamed Judith, gaining her confidence, relieved Kerry had not uncovered her secret.

'Really? You don't think it's too… I don't know… too childish?'

'There's nothing childish or immature about the mixed-media effect you've created.'

'That means so much coming from you. And thank you for helping me see more clearly. I know now, I'm still here and I can go on living without suffering guilt or staying broken.'

'And Paul?'

'I've not had the courage to show him. Not yet.'

The two women hugged, and Judith felt a pang of loss for her own child, but this wasn't about her it was about Kerry.

'Have you talked to him? Don't hide the words inside you, Kerry. Songs not sung; canvases left blank. They eat away at you.'

'Not yet. I couldn't find the words. But I will.'

'Love and hope. It's pretty amazing. Really, it's incredible,' said Judith, looking back over the decorated expanse of wall.

Judith took in the tiny fragments of broken glass and mirror shards; yellow fingers reaching outwards from the top left-hand corner of the wall, glinting in the light like a beaming sun. Each sun ray created by an eclectic collection of photographs, fragments of fabric and ribbons, images from magazines, cinema tickets, bits of letters to hospital appointments and check-ups, baby scan images spoke a million words but only one emotion: Love.

Paint effects with wide bold brush strokes as well as pieces of lace and hundreds of buttons covered the space. The design was incredibly uplifting and so poignantly personal and raw. Judith struggled to hold it together and, in the end, cried. Kerry gave her a tight hug, gulping back her own tears.

'I kept a video diary of what I was doing each day,' she said pushing away. 'Episodes of me at night, in this bed… sleepless hours twisting under the duvet. At other times wanting to feel close to Paul but not knowing how, so I wore his shirt knotted at the waist and talked to him while I painted. Some of it is a bit rambling but I wanted to remember the feelings I went through as I unfolded myself and breathed in life all over again.'

'Your loss left a hole with jagged edges in your life and in Paul's life. Healing takes time.'

'There are so many traces of us as a family of three here. I wandered from room to room, penny-coloured skies touching the walls, touching tangible objects to make my intangible ghost of a self-real again.'

'Invisible things have worth too, Kerry. You're so brave,' said Judith, touched by her poetic words, her personal narrative.

'And so stupid too. I allowed the grief to consume me. Welcomed it, enjoyed wallowing in self-pity.'

'There are no rules to grief. And I know you weren't keen initially but it's such a cathartic thing to do… like a living diary,' said Judith, her arm extended towards the wall in a sweeping gesture.

'Judith, you saved me. And saved my marriage. Without all this I would have disappeared indefinitely, and I think Paul would have lost his patience… left me.'

'Paul loves you. He's a good man. He's also had to go through this remember.'

'I know that, but I couldn't deal with his feelings on

top of mine but now… well, let's say he's been the most patient man I have ever known or loved. I thought he was going to leave me…'

'What are you going to do with the recordings?'

'I'm not sure yet. But the right idea will come.'

'What about a podcast… you know a kind of support network for other parents who have lost their babies and have nowhere to turn.'

'To show them there is hope and there is life after miscarriage,' said Kerry.

'That's beautiful. It's amazing. And if you need help with setting it up and doing the tech side of things, I know someone who is brilliant. I think they'd be happy to help. It'll keep them occupied over this long dragging summer.'

'Do I know them? Will you ask for me?'

'You do know them, but you won't recognise them, perhaps not at first. But I will ask, of course.'

'Thank you, Judith, and…' Kerry sniffled and tried to compose herself, 'without you, your Mary Poppins bag of tricks and your belief in me, I would never have done this. Not like this and not now… maybe not ever.'

'Timing's everything.'

'This was the right time. Thank you again.'

'You're very welcome, Kerry. You deserve to be happy, and happiness breeds more happiness,' said Judith as she stood up, wiping away the tears which filled her eyes.

'And one more thing,' said Kerry. 'I'd like you to be here when I show this to Paul.'

'I'd be honoured. I'll even buy a bottle of champagne to celebrate this next phase of your life together. Stronger and as one.'

Chapter 16

On her way back home, Judith walked with a spring in her step. She bunched up the layers of her skirt in one of her hands and lifted it to her knees in an effort to cool herself. Paul and Kerry would be okay, and she knew in her heart their journey together would be a happier one. They deserved happiness and peace, and she swung her canvas bag like she used to back in her school days, the swoosh against her skirt a rhythm which helped her keep her momentum all the way back to Chrysanthemum Cottage.

Three afternoons later, Judith put on her sturdy walking shoes but not without some frustration. The inner sole of the left boot, unstuck after years of wear and tear, kept scrunching uncomfortably towards her toes and she struggled to hold it in place and push her foot in at the same time. 'Oh, I do hate this growing old malarkey,' she said, out loud.

Within fifteen minutes she found herself knocking on the door of Zuzanna and Maja's house. The front door painted a glossy admiral blue contrasted beautifully with the brass knocker shaped like a fox.

Judith heard a muffled movement inside and whispering voices. She bent down and pushed open the letter box. She peered in and called, 'Hello. It's Judith.'

She saw a frail-edged shadow behind the kitchen door at the end of the narrow hallway and noticed a pair of flip flops at the bottom of the stairs. A brown, tan bag hung over the banisters.

A figure approached the front door and Judith steadied herself as she straightened back up.

The door swung open, and Judith blinked and blinked again.

'Hello.'

'Hello Judith,' said Maja and she leaned in and gave Judith a kiss on the cheek.

Judith hesitated a split second, taking in the young fresh-faced, smiling person before her. 'It's so lovely to see you Maja,' she said, noticing her renewed demeanour. 'Is your mother home?'

'She is. Please come in,' she said, stepping aside to let her pass.

Judith wiped her feet on the door mat which "welcomed" her and proceeded down the hallway to the kitchen where Zuzanna greeted her with a clumsy hug and not two but three kisses, one after the other on each cheek.

'Judith, I hope you come by.'

'Lovely to see you too Zuzanna and of course it's

lovely to see Maja smiling too,' said Judith, following Zuzanna into the small, square kitchen.

'Yes Maja,' said Zuzanna and then, her eyes filled, and a stream of tears flooded her face. 'I sorry. I feel emotion.'

'Please, don't apologise. It's a terrible thing, bullying. But I can see Maja is looking and feeling better. More confident.'

'My Maja, you make her so happy. Thank you.'

'Oh no, not at all. It was all a matter of timing, like most things in life, we have to be ready to not only talk about change but put all that talk into action, to make the decision to do something. To say enough is enough.'

Maja looked at Judith from under her long lashes and characteristically shoved her hands into the pockets of her red knee-length sweater dress, the frilled hem and long balloon sleeves adding detail which Judith thought were fun, girly.

'I feel alive again. Like me again. The excitement of better days coming my way make me want to scream but in a good way,' Maja laughed.

'That's just how it should be. Let your passion for life and it all has to offer consume you,' said Judith, and a lightness filled her. *Her own life was filling up too, with love and joy and good things.*

'Please, sit,' said Zuzanna, pulling out a ladder-back chair, painted a pastel grey, from under the kitchen table, gold bangles jingled at her wrists, her skin white, delicate, under the metal bracelets.

'Thank you. But I wasn't planning on stopping.'

'You have time? We talk… please.'

'Of course, but I'm no expert. I gave Maja a helpline

number which deals with bullying. You're not alone,' said Judith, nodding her head as Zuzanna blew her nose and wiped the fresh tears from her eyes.

'Yes, I feed Maja too much. I know this now. It is how you say? Our culture, our lifestyle and I was holding onto my homeland through the foods and tastes. I will cook less now,' she laughed hesitantly and disappeared back into the hallway. She returned with Judith's bag.

'My sewing. I wondered how you got on with it.'

'All done,' said Zuzanna, looking relieved to be talking about something she felt more confident about. Judith felt a little embarrassed at the sight of her bag; Monet's Water Lilly Pond now faded with years of summer usage but then noticed, with a surge of delight, the stitching around one of the handles, which had unraveled to reveal the rough inner edge, had been repaired.

'You've neatened the fraying handle,' said Judith. 'Thank you so much.' She pulled out the two garments and marvelled at how nifty a job Zuzanna had completed.'

'I be guessing you fix this yourself, no?'

'Maybe. But I've been so busy with…'

'It's okay, I understand. You want to come here and check on Maja. She tell me you speak to her. She tell me you wise and clever. I say thank you to you.'

'Honestly, I only did what any thoughtful person would do. She is lovely. She deserves to be happy. You both do. I am so pleased for you both.'

'In Poland such a thing not happen and after hard life in London I am happy to be here Judith. We are both. I compensate for too much with cooking, cooking, cooking all the time. Maja, she eat to make me happy.

But she unhappy. I want to as well make sure Maja is happy.'

'Traditions are important. What you create today based on your happy memories of yesterday will also become memories for Maja in the future. Happy memories are what she will treasure the most,' said Judith.

Zuzanna looked towards her child and in the shifting light of the midday sun their eyes locked and appeared bluer than ever, and Judith felt a little conscious of intruding on such a poignant and beautiful moment between a mother and her daughter.

'*Kocham Cie, mamo*, I love you, Mum.'

'*Tez cie kocham,*' said Zuzanna back.

'You both deserve some happiness,' said Judith, coughing back a tickle of emotion.

'And as well you, Judith.'

'I'd like to also say I have a little project for you. That's if you'd like to take it on,' she said, turning to Maja.

'A project for me? What is it?'

'Let me tell you all about it. I think you'll love it.'

Maja listened intently, her eyes wide with obvious excitement and enthusiasm for the proposed task. 'I will give it a go, yes. No school on Monday morning. Teacher strike.'

'I know what you're thinking Zuzanna,' Judith said as she stood on the doorstep. 'You think she is going to slip away from you now... grow up too quickly... new friends, new hobbies, but she won't. She will become a young woman and an adult, but she will always be yours. In finding herself, she is returning to who she always was.'

Chapter 17

At home in her garden, the muted clacking of Judith's bamboo wind chimes scattered the birds, sending finches and sparrows fluttering and hopping from one spot in the garden to another. Judith, pottering around, stopped to wipe the trickle of sweat from her brow. She thought about all that was happening in the village over the summer and the next few weeks and decided the mysterious delivery of postcards had to be someone's way of encouraging her to be more sociable and useful.

"One for Sorrow" had been actioned as had "Three for a Girl." And of course, Kerry and Paul were solid again, the couple they used to be but stronger, their bond closer than ever because of their shared pain and loss.

Her gardens, both front and back, were an abundance of vines clambering up porch posts, roses twining across a rickety old arbour, the beds overflowing with fragrant herbs and other organic edibles. Judith's cottage garden was a personal and embracing space; bursting with summer colour, and its happy clutter complemented the character of the small cottage and the confines of the tiny lot as well as her quirky, friendly personality. Traditional cottage plants filled every space, old-fashioned hollyhocks and delphinium, iris, hydrangea, catmint, and pinks as well as roses and chrysanthemums.

'I wonder whether the next card will follow soon?' she asked herself as she dug a hole large enough to transplant her baby seedlings into the ground. She brushed off her knees as she stood up and discarded her gardening gloves, leaving them atop one of the bags of fertiliser with her hand spade and her rusty watering can.

'Hello.' Judith heard Lou's excited voice from the other side of the fence.

'Lou. Hello.'

'How are you?'

'You're just in time for a cuppa. I'm gasping. I've been gardening for an hour or so, and the sun's surely scalded my legs through my trousers.'

'Let me put the kettle on while you get cleaned up,' offered Lou. 'I've been baking this morning, my old mum's scone recipe, so I thought I'd bring a couple over for us to enjoy together.'

'If only I had some clotted cream and jam.'

'Don't worry Judith. I've brought some with me.'

'Give me five minutes to change out of these muddy trousers and we can indulge.'

Upstairs Judith slipped out of her clothes and dropped them into her linen bin. Just as she shimmied into a blouse and pleated skirt, she heard the clank of her letter box.

She rushed to her bedroom window but didn't see anyone. In one direction a woman was pushing a pushchair towards the play area and in the other a small group of children played football on the street: kicking their ball against the rustic stones of a low retaining front garden wall. She imagined the sweet smell of the trailing catmint and white climbing roses and leafy grapevines scrambling up the porch's posts, while pots overflowing with kumquat and rosemary flanked the steps at the top of the short garden path. The children far too involved in their football competition had clearly not approached the cottage.

Judith ran down the stairs as fast as her lower limbs would take her. There on the mat lay the expected fourth card. 'Just as I thought,' she muttered.

'You, okay?' called Lou from the kitchen.

'Did you hear anyone a moment ago?' asked Judith as she walked into the kitchen holding it close to her chest as if afraid it would disappear as quickly as it appeared.

'No. What's that? Is it another card?' Lou's eyes searched Judith's face and then spied the card in her hand. 'Oh, Judith… this is so exciting.'

Judith lowered herself into one of the kitchen chairs, straightening the overstuffed seat cushion underneath her. 'Better than another gas bill,' said Judith, sighing.

'What does it say?' asked Lou as she pulled a chair closer and sat down.

Judith rested the card on the raffia place mat in front of her, brushing away the crumbs from breakfast. 'I haven't looked yet.' Lou said nothing and waited, working her hands in her lap. Judith turned it over and gasped with joy.

Lou snatched it from the table and beamed, 'Four for a Boy,' she read out loud with a twinkle in her eye.

The fourth magpie card, a soft dove grey, speckled all over with a sprinkling of steely spatters and splodges, depicted the faces of four adult-looking magpies and, of course, the words "Four for a Boy". Each little visage had the most intricate detail etched into it, gaping beaks, and eyes the darkest black like beads of jet.

'Whoever this is, they are so good with a brush,' Judith said as she bit into her scone, cream, and strawberry jam squidged over her upper lip. 'I wonder where this will lead?'

'Such cuteness,' squealed Lou as she poured the tea from the pot, minding not to drip tea down the knitted tea cosy.

'It's got to have something to do with a boy, or a man... now who could it be?'

'Well, there's the church choir. That's made up of four men... and they're always bickering about something or other... complaining about each other,' said Lou.

'But they're always present, standing proud, in their white choir robes and singing the chosen hymns at the tops of their voices every Sunday morning.'

Lou gave her a look. 'How do you know that?'

'I've seen them filing in. It's amazing how far I can see from my bedroom window.'

'Proper Miss Marple, you're turning into.'

'I wonder,' said Judith. 'But whatever I'm meant to do will present itself to me and I will intuitively know. And until then I'm going to enjoy this scone. Lou, you are such a wonderful baker. You really should bake for the tea shop. They'd be honoured to serve your scones alongside their famous cruffins on their afternoon tea menu, I'm sure. All those tourists passing through would love them!'

'I can't imagine trying to keep up with their trade. Two coaches pulled up last week. Japanese tourists in droves. Like ants rushing around in their little groups,' said Lou.

'Just a thought…'

'Thank you but I do think you're rather biased… especially when your own baking skills are so…'

'Less developed…' laughed Judith, finishing off her friend's sentence and spattering a few crumbs before taking another bite of the flaky delight.

'I was going to say basic,' said Lou.

'You're too kind. I'm certainly no Mary Berry or Julia Child in the kitchen but I do enjoy well-cooked food… flavours and sauces and divine ingredients all make for a perfect meal,' Judith said, knowing all too well exactly what her baking skills amounted to.

'We can't all have the same skills. Look at you and all your wonderful art and your beautiful garden. I can't even grow all year-round perennials,' said Lou, taking another slurp of her tea.

'Darling Lou, bake for me anytime. I'm happy to be your guinea pig.'

'Cheers to that,' said Lou and they both lifted their mugs, chinked them together.

'So have you heard from Ashleigh?'

'Yes, she's going to come home for the weekend of my birthday. She says she has a surprise for me.'

'A surprise, eh? What sort of a surprise? Has she

bought you a special gift?'

'Oh, I doubt it very much. She's never been one for extravagant presents.'

'No gifts wrapped in sheets of wrapping paper and ribbon curls?' said Judith, remembering the pre-made bows her mother used to use for her father's Christmas and birthday gifts.

'I'm rather hoping it will be an announcement of some sort. You know like she's met the man of her dreams and she's getting married or she's going to be a mother.'

'Not asking for much, then?' laughed Judith.

They both sat companionably for another twenty minutes or so and after washing up together, Lou, shivering against the late afternoon's drop in temperature, borrowed one of Judith's cardigans promising to return it when they met the following morning for their customary walk.

Chapter 18

'Thank you,' said Maja, standing tall, her chin out and her shoulders back. She wore a pair of green leggings and a matching crop top. She stuffed the loaf of bread, the slab of cheese and the punnet of tomatoes into the plastic bag, took the change and walked out of the shop, her head held high and a smile plastered across her face.

'What a polite young lady.'

'Who was she? I've not seen her before.'

'Actually, you have. But you haven't seen *her*,' said Judith.

'You're talking in riddles, Judith. Whatever do you mean?'

'That's Maja... the Polish girl.'

'Always sullen and uncommunicative?' asked one woman, with a confused expression.

'The one who hid behind dark shapeless clothes?' asked the other.

Judith nodded, waiting to see their reactions.

'It never is.'

'It is. She's beautiful, isn't she?' said Judith.

'Well, yes–yes, she is.'

'And really rather clever too. She's been helping me with something. Something very special,' said Kerry, who caught the tail end of their conversation as she walked in.

'Who would have thought?'

'She has the most striking eyes. Eyes I'd not noticed before.'

'Well, I never…'

'It's amazing what a little confidence can reveal,' said Judith and before anyone could say another word she paid for her shopping, uttered a clipped good day, and walked out of the shop, the tinkle of the hanging doorbell echoing a much-cherished cheery chime behind her.

Chapter 19

Outside, Maja was waiting. Judith ambled over towards her, full of inexplicable joy, her heart full. Maja joined in step with her and as they walked past St Barnabas Judith gave thanks for all that was good in her life.

'Judith,' said Maja, almost unable to contain her joy. 'I've got some news!'

Judith stopped and turned towards her.

'Hello. I've been thinking about you and how you're getting on. I'm glad you waited for me.'

'I know. Sorry. I should have come and seen you sooner. I have some news.'

'You sound much happier. How exciting.'

'I have made a new friend. Her name is Charlotte, and she came to my house after school yesterday.'

'That is the best news, Maja.'

'And there's more. Charlotte is a school prefect, and she has proposed a new after-school netball club for anyone who wants to join. The majority voted for it and so it will be on the timetable next term.'

'My oh my. You have been busy. Such good news.'

'I am so excited, Judith.'

'Maja, you are amazing, and everyone will see it now. The clouds have lifted, and the sun is shining down on you.'

'I feel it too,' said Maja.

'A new start. New beginnings. They always feel a little strange, but this is good news.'

'Yes, I hope so. I feel like the clouds have parted and the sun will shine always on me.'

'And so it should. You have been through so much. You deserve happiness. You deserve love and lots of it.'

'And you?'

'Me?' asked Judith.

'Yes. Are you happier now. In this village. With new friends.'

'Oh, Maja. What a thoughtful girl you are. And yes. I am finding my place and my place is finding me.'

'I am glad.'

'And I am so glad for you too. And your mother. How is she?'

'She is happy too. She tells me that I am a part of her, and she will always be a part of me.'

'That's a beautiful sentiment,' said Judith, wistfully, longing for a typical mother-daughter relationship.

'Thank you, Judith. I will come and see you soon,' she said, and she skipped off down the road, flying ahead of Judith. 'You will have to come and cheer me on when we play our first match.'

'I will,' called Judith after her. 'And send my regards to your mum.'

Chapter 20

'I'm getting chilly too,' said Judith to Jasper. The pot of clotted cream and the homemade strawberry jam still adorned the middle of the table. She twisted the lid back onto the jar and covered the pot of clotted cream with cellophane before refrigerating it.

She pulled the woollen throw from the back of the sofa over her and snuggled down with her book: *Life after 60: time to dream and hope*. It had been one of her retirement gifts from all the staff at the college. Until recently she hadn't given it much of her time, expecting it to be full of baking and yoga. But actually, it was an absorbing book with beautiful photographs and daily inspirational mantras and ideas for making new friends and building a new life away from the confines of an overtly familiar career and safe work routine.

Once she began to browse its pages, she soon became engrossed in its practical tips on how to enjoy herself and make the most of her time. Before long, she was struggling to read as the daylight faded into a slow-diving sunset, deep pinks, and lilacs on its tail, and she leant over to switch on the side lamp.

She stretched out her legs and crossing them at the ankles put them up on the multi-coloured patchwork pouffe, the leather soft but cold to touch. She had lagged it back from a backpacking holiday to Morocco in her early twenties. She had taken a gap year after graduating with a first in a History of Art degree.

As she flicked through more pages, she realised she was no longer bored in the village. Life was less busy and quieter, especially in winter, but with the summer months more and more tourists visited, and she was filling her time easily. She got used to her daily routine with Lou and the longer days of July and August had kept her occupied in the garden. And now, of course, she had the postcards. She put the open book face down on her lap and stretching her arms above her head, she rested her tired eyes.

Unsure how long she had slept for, Judith woke with a start. 'Oh, my goodness.' She jumped up as the book slid off her lap and clattered to the floor. 'I must have nodded off.' She had only meant to close her eyes for a few seconds. She glanced over at the clock on the mantel. 'Half past eight?'

She shifted in the sofa, her neck, and shoulders stiff from falling asleep in an awkward position. She got up and locked the kitchen door and pulled the lock across the front door before drawing the curtains in the sitting room. Jasper looked over at her from his basket in the kitchen. She hadn't fed him this evening. She unwrapped the chicken slices she bought especially for him and emptied the pieces into his bowl.

'Sorry, Jasper. Guess I was more tired after all the gardening than I thought. Night-night old chap.'

She retired to her bedroom, slipping into her long nightdress, and brushing through her long hair with her faded yet intricately embroidered brush which had belonged to her grandmother. The bristles still ran through her locks with such a velvety smoothness; like a princess getting ready for bed.

She was about to turn out the light when she remembered the fourth card. She tiptoed downstairs and brought it back up to bed with her. With the faintest blue glow of the moon highlighting the card she switched on her bedside lamp and studied it more carefully. The four images had mature faces; perhaps Lou was right about the choir. *But what did Judith have to do with the choir.* Judith rarely went to church and didn't cross paths with any of the four men who sang. She propped it up against the brass base of the lamp and flicked off the switch.

That night Judith dreamt she was swathed in a long white robe. Her hair was cropped short around her ears and neck, and she was singing with the four fat magpies on the postcard at the front of the church. Their raspy chatter echoed around the empty nave as another four magpies flew in through the main doors, circled the pulpit three times and swooping low they each pecked at something bright. They quickly flew out the way they came in, their wings not flapping but rather stretched out as they soared and glided, following each other in a pattern, their beaks holding onto golden letters. They quite unusually flew back to a nest where their mother was waiting and spilled their treasure, spelling out her middle name: ALMA.

'Do you know where your middle name came from?' Judith asked Lou as they walked.

'Of course. Bethany was my great aunt's name. She didn't have any children of her own and her sister, my grandmother, insisted mum and dad chose her name to make her happy. She lived until she was one-hundred-and-one years old. Got a letter from Queen Elizabeth she did.'

'Why the sudden interest?'

'Because I have no idea where mine came from. I never thought to ask, and I don't recall my parents ever telling me.'

'Probably a relative, and most likely one of your grandparents,' said Lou, puffing as they trudged up an incline. 'Though back in those days no one without money could pursue a creative career.'

'You could be right. I just feel like there's a secret there.'

'You're just getting carried away because of the postcards, all that mystery.'

'Maybe,' said Judith, but she wasn't totally convinced. 'And last night I had an odd magpie dream.'

'Too much red wine before bed,' laughed Lou.

'You're probably right,' said Judith and she chuckled along too.

Chapter 21

Judith woke later than usual and as she raised her head from the pillow her head swayed with nausea. She had an awful headache. Her dream still played on her mind; she remembered it in fragments and felt her long hair; it was still there splayed across her shoulders. She propped herself up and glanced at the postcard. 'You've a lot to answer for,' she said and closed her eyes protecting them from the slither of persistent sunlight peeking through the gap in her curtains and promising it to be another hot day.

Her house phone and then her mobile phone rang from somewhere downstairs; she didn't have the energy or the inclination to find out who it was, so she turned her back to the window and buried her head under the pillow to block out the glare.

She lay there for another half an hour, maybe longer and, when she heard the phone in the sitting room ringing once more, she decided it was time to get up and get on with her day, though she let it ring off, unable to muster the energy to run and answer it. She swung her feet onto the Turkish rug, bought in Istanbul on her honeymoon. The market trader had kissed her hand, a flamboyantly romantic gesture, and had serenaded her with sweetly plucked notes on his tambur. She smiled at the memory.

She perched at the end of the bed concentrating on stilling her pounding head. She slipped into her kimono. She shivered against the silky cool fabric as it nestled on her still bed-warm skin and tied it around her waist. She took a hairband and pulling it up and over her forehead she smoothed the velvet bandeau over her hair.

She made her way downstairs and as she entered the kitchen Jasper appeared, weaving in and out of her legs, almost tripping her up. Judith picked up the kettle, filled it, splashing water everywhere, and set it dripping onto the Aga. She filled Jasper's bowls each with fresh milk and some chicken pieces. Within seconds he purred with satisfaction as he tore at the wafer-thin pieces.

By the time Judith buttered her toast and finished her morning cuppa, the caffeine livening her senses, the morning light had dipped behind a grey blanket of low-lying clouds.

'Just perfect.' Judith, conscious of complaining, splashed the hot soapy water carelessly as she washed up her breakfast dishes. 'I need a bubble bath. Now where is that bath-time pamper set from last Christmas,' she asked Jasper as she rummaged around in the back of the sideboard, cursing herself for not having yet sorted through what was in there. After taking almost everything out from the cupboard she found a screwed-up gift bag. 'That'll do,' she said, pulling out a bath bomb. As she tried to stuff everything back, she caught sight of a brown envelope she didn't recognise. She almost stopped to have a look at the contents. *It would be old documents, gas bills, employment contracts, and the like of her father's. He seemed to keep everything. She didn't have the time to look now.* She stuffed it back in with everything else, not giving it another thought.

Jasper surveyed her from his hearth-side position. Judith stuck her tongue out at him and then ambled through the kitchen to the tiny downstairs bathroom. The bath filled slowly, and the fragrant bubbles kissed the curled lip of the roll top bath. She threw her bath sheet over the gold towel rail above the rusting radiator and slipped out of her kimono and underwear. She was still shaking.

She lowered herself into the almost scalding water, wanting to disappear, wanting to escape the strange emotion enveloping her. The frothy eucalyptus bubbles filled her senses, and she sank back into the bath. She propped up the paperback poetry collection she most often read while bathing on the wooden book holder she'd found in a flea market many moons ago. Though it was morning she wanted to create an escape. She tried to light a candle and after five attempts she managed to get the long match to ignite. Too much condensation in the air had dampened the match head.

The bathroom door squeaked, and Jasper wandered in; a feline ghost materialising in a fog of steamy vapour. He settled on the bathmat and closed his eyes; the laziest cat she had ever come across. The fact she only ever knew one other cat didn't matter; he was still totally slothful.

As the bathwater cooled and the steam dissipated along with her headache, she noticed how grubby everything looked. *When was the last time she gave it all a thorough clean?* She had no idea; the vanity unit drawer was half open. Packets of paracetamol, toothpaste, tweezers, nail clippers, and a razor she hadn't used in weeks, spewed out. A faded flannel hung limply over one of the bath taps. A couple of shower caps sat on an old wooden milking stool; they had faded from the brightest fun colours to the jaded colours of a retired art teacher.

The basin taps, both caked in stony-green limescale, built up over the years, dripped intermittently in a kind of singsong pitter-patter leaving a tear-shaped stain on the sink. Judith sighed. She turned on the bath's hot tap and the pipes shook in the walls as if murmuring in agreement with her.

She picked up the candle and brought it closer to her nose breathing in the smooth patchouli and vanilla essence as it burned. She placed it back on the windowsill and ran her fingers over her legs, relishing the creamy bubbles softening her skin, wiggling her toes. The steamy condensation lulled her senses and unable to concentrate on reading, Judith simultaneously closed her eyes and the book, leaving her finger between the pages as a marker. She drifted into a hazy lull, the cottage's now familiar groans and creaks a welcome gift of added comfort. Suddenly the bathroom door flew open.

'Oh my God,' she yelled, crossing her arms over her chest, and sinking into the bath, the book disappearing into the frothy bubbles with her, shivering against the tepid water.

'Judith. Thank God you're okay,' screeched Lou.

'Of course, I'm okay. Why wouldn't I be, okay?'

'When you didn't answer the phone or the door, I let myself in… and Paul's with me.'

'Hello, Judith.' Paul, his cheeks colouring with embarrassment, gave Judith a wave.

Lou turned round to usher Paul out the narrow door. As she did so, she slipped on a pool of deflated bubbles. She lost her balance, fell back and splash landed on top of Judith in the tub. Her arms and legs waggled and kicked like a spider having a convulsion. She spluttered, the bubbles coating her face. Judith held onto the side of the bath to stop herself from being submerged under the weight of her friend.

'Oh my,' panicked Paul and he grabbed Lou by the arms and tried to pull her out of the bath. Chaos prevailed for a few hectic, drawn-out moments until eventually, sitting in a wet heap on the bathroom floor Lou broke down and laughed. Her clothes were dripping and ever conscious of how she looked she tried to sort out her short hair which stuck out in spikes and at funny angles.

'Are you okay?' Paul asked Lou, looking bewildered.

Judith indicated to him to turn around and she stepped out of the bath. She wrapped the big hotel-size towel tightly around her. 'She's fine. It's nerves. This rather brings a new meaning to three's a crowd,' she said and then she burst out laughing too, chuckling so much her cheeks ached.

Lou managed to get onto her knees, puffing from the

exertion, and leaning on the side of the bath eventually got onto her feet without too much trouble.

The bathroom floor was covered in soapy water and Judith's book, the pages soggy and disintegrated, fell apart when she fished it out of the bath.

'Guess I won't be finishing that.'

'Guess not,' said Paul, his face desperately trying to hold onto a serious expression.

Judith and Lou looked at each other, stunned, until Judith asked, 'Tea anyone?' and they all broke into uncontrollable laughter.

Chapter 22

Judith in a yellow ditsy-print sundress, Lou in a borrowed pair of jeans and a T-shirt with the words "Stay Trippie Little Hippie" across a psychedelic rainbow and Paul still looking ashen, sat around Judith's metal table on wooden mis-matched chairs on her tiny back garden patio.

'This has been quite a morning,' said Judith as she sipped her Earl Grey.

'It certainly has,' said Lou, stifling a giggle. 'Who would have thought. I only wanted to bring your cardigan round after borrowing it.'

'Poor Paul. We've scarred you for life,' said Judith. 'So sorry.'

'No, not at all. And as long as you're both okay. I really should be getting back.'

'Of course, you go ahead and get on with what you have to do. Thank you for checking up on me and I'm so sorry Lou wasted your time. See you soon.'

'As I said, not a problem,' he said.

When Judith heard the creak of the latch on the gate and was sure he was out of ear shot, she gave Lou one of her looks. 'That was certainly eventful. What on earth were you thinking?'

'I panicked.'

'Really? I would never have guessed.'

'All those postcards and you living on your own.'

'You're right. I'm sorry... I don't mean to belittle your concern or your friendship. You really are a gem. But honestly those postcards pose no threat to me.'

'Then why say I was wasting Paul's time? How embarrassing. Makes me look like a right idiot.'

'Well, you have been a teensy-weensy bit of one.'

'What have you decided about the fourth card?'

'I don't know. I'm a bit stumped,' said Judith as she shook away a shiver, her arms embracing her own body. 'I mean it could be something to do with the men's chorus, but I'm not convinced. So far nothing else has come to mind but I'm sure something will present itself to me given time.'

'Who could it be? And why are they sending them?'

'It doesn't matter. It's probably all and nothing,' said Judith, but she could hear the bristle in her response.

'Your expression tells me otherwise,' said Louise.

'It's not the magpie cards. It's the dream I had.'

'What sort of dream?'

'It was jumbled. Magpies flying around the church... four of them and I remember my middle name in it so clearly: Alma.'

'You'll work it out. You always do. You're so clever, Judith,' said Lou proudly.

'Stop it. Look how clever I am at those crosswords. Not,' she laughed. 'But thank you for believing in me.'

Judith brushed the rosemary to release its scent, the almost-too-overwhelming smell instantly filling her nostrils. Lou reached out and squeezed her hand. Judith squeezed back. They both sat a while with their thoughts. The earlier cloud cover had cleared, and the blue skies looked hand-painted in contrast with the distant almond-blossom pinks dotting the skyline.

A tiny field mouse appeared from behind a plant pot, its scratching sent Jasper screeching. Jasper, in fright, vanished behind the candelabra fronds of flora and fauna. He looked at the little rodent through half-open eyes, as if toying whether to pounce, and closing his eyes it was obvious he decided it wasn't worth the effort. *He wouldn't be able to catch it if he tried.* The mouse looked as if it knew this and wiggled its ears as if to say, 'You can't catch me.'

Judith wondered whether she would ever catch whoever was posting the cards and then thought it didn't really make a difference. They had somehow given her a purpose and she was grateful, though a little curious.

Chapter 23

Judith sat at the long bar alone, though within the next hour the tourists were sure to fill the bar, with their chatter and clicking of their camera phones as they captured evidence of the old pub's interior to take back home with them. The clock, wedged between two wall shelves above the optics, struck an hour before midday. Though too early in the day, she was enjoying her glass of merlot, which went some way to calming her nerves.

Part of her anxiety stemmed from Paul seeing her half-naked in the bath only a few days before and part stemmed from wondering whether being a part of Kerry's beautiful art unveiling should remain a private moment between husband and wife. Paul and Kerry had gone through so much, the healing needed to come from each other.

'What's my wife been up to?' asked Paul.

'That's not for me to tell. But I'm hoping you'll

appreciate all the effort she's put in… it's been a labour of love for her, for you.'

'That I don't doubt. She loves deeply, does my Kerry.'

Judith was taken aback by his words for a moment and a little part of her wanted someone to know her like that, to understand her and love her, flaws, and all.

'Okay. I'm ready for you… for both of you,' announced Kerry as she appeared in the doorway leading to their living quarters. 'Come on then,' she said. She pulled Paul's arm and, throwing a towel down onto the bar, he turned and followed, her dress floating behind her in a sweep of coral as she rushed ahead, her eagerness infectious.

Judith pressed down on her churning stomach; excitement tinged with a tiny bit of angst. Kerry had put almost every breathing waking moment into this mural and wanted Paul to love it; to feel its healing powers and to see the love and hope it encompassed. She followed them both up the stairs and waited as Kerry blindfolded Paul with one of her silk scarves.

'Kinky,' said Paul, as Kerry adjusted it, knotting it tighter, making sure he was unable to see at all.

'Stop it,' giggled Kerry, 'And in front of Judith too.' Turning to Judith, she said, 'He's no shame, honestly.'

'Judith and I are more familiar with each other than most,' laughed Paul.

'Oh, stop,' said Judith. 'I will never live it down. Lou has a lot to answer for.'

'Paul did tell me, but I was hardly myself. But I do remember. I was listening Paul,' she said.

Judith smiled and shook her head, 'Anyway, let's

not bring that up again. And don't mind me. I was once young too, you know.' But despite her sing-song voice she fought a dragging sensation which tugged at her age. *She was old, older than she was and older than she wanted to be.*

Kerry pushed open the bedroom door and guided Paul into the room. She then gestured to Judith to come in too. The bedroom smelt overwhelmingly of paint and glue for a second and then the summer clematis packed Judith's senses as it wafted in through the open window; the thin lace curtains billowing in the breeze.

Kerry took Paul's hands in hers and swallowed, 'So, before I show you what I've been up to I wanted to tell you how much I love you. I know things have been hard, often unbearable since we lost our baby.'

Judith fought back the tears as she listened to Kerry, so full of emotion and a raw naivety she hadn't noticed before.

Paul nodded as she spoke, massaging her hands in his, and his shoulders relaxed as Kerry continued. 'I wanted us to have something to make us smile and remind us of the happiness we had during the few weeks we were a family of three.'

He reached up and pushed a digit under the smooth edge of the scarf; Judith watched as a tear trickled onto his cheek; he wiped it away with the pads of his fingers, sniffed.

Kerry hesitated, then released the scarf. Paul stood still and unblinking, staring at the bedroom wall.

'You did this?' he asked, unable to take his eyes off the artwork. Kerry nodded, too emotional to speak. 'I don't know what to say. This is amazing. You're amazing.'

Paul pulled Kerry into him and hugged her tightly. Judith looked away, being present at such a personal moment felt intrusive. 'I love you my darling and this will always make us smile first thing in the morning and last thing at night, for the rest of our lives.'

'Do you like it?' giggled Kerry nervously as she wriggled away from him only to have Paul pull her back into a big bear hug. 'Like it? I love it. And I love you. I always have and I always will.'

He reached out, one arm around Kerry, his other arm shaking, as he ran his hand across the collage: a mural of bright colours, photographs and recorded memories.

He blew out through his mouth when his hand rested over the picture of Kerry and him laughing on the swings, Kelly's bump obvious under the T-shirt which stretched taut across her tummy. 'We have so many happy moments to be grateful for,' he said, swallowing.

Kerry finally extricated herself from Paul's arm and held his hand in both of hers. 'I couldn't have done it without Judith, so Judith,' she said, leaning over to the side of the bedside table, 'this is for you to say thank you for all your patience, and for everything you have done for me... for being such a wonderful teacher, and mentor, and most of all for being the friend I didn't even realise I had.'

She opened the top drawer of the polished mahogany chest and handed Judith a flat parcel, about ten inches by ten inches square, wrapped in delicate white paper. 'Open it,' she urged, her hands wrapped around Paul's again, her fingers intertwined with his.

'You're most welcome. But you did all the hard work,' said Judith. 'This is your energy, your love.'

She unwrapped the package, tearing at the thin tissue paper, and the sheets fell to the laminate flooring with a quiet whisper. She turned the canvas around and gasped.

'Kerry, thank you so much.'

'I know how much you love Jasper and your garden.' The simple childlike portrait of Jasper and Kerry had beautifully captured the contrast between his scowly face and the summer colours of Judith's garden in bloom through the garland of flowers adorning his head.

The light seemed to shine from each flower head giving Jasper an angelic quality, bringing a smile to Judith's face and then a huge belly laugh.

'Oh my… Kerry, you have captured his look perfectly. I will treasure this always and I will treasure our new-found friendship even more. Thank you.'

She gave Kerry a hug and squeezed Paul's shoulder. She walked out of the bedroom with her canvas and rushed down the stairs before her heart burst with emotion; Paul and Kerry had found each other again and had found life again too… a new life different to what they had planned but full of renewed hope.

She strolled at a leisurely pace towards Chrysanthemum Cottage. Through Paul and Kerry, she had also stumbled upon a new kind of life too… one with hope, love, and friendship. She shaded her eyes from the shimmying dip of the sun, a great bronze coin behind the tops of the trees and did a little run, and a skip, as she continued towards home. The air, filled with birdsong and heavy with clematis and fragrant roses in bloom, tickled her senses and she thought she may not be able to contain her torrent of joy. She gave herself a little shake and smiled. Today was a good day and one she would remember for a long time to come. The little card, "One for Sorrow" had extraordinarily incarnated real-life joy.

Chapter 24

'Oh, I almost forgot. This was lying on the door mat as I came in.' Lou pulled out a postcard from the deep pocket of her tunic… "Five for Silver",' she said as she handed it over to Judith.

'I can't say I'm surprised.'

'Neither am I. But it's still as strange as ever,' said Lou.

'I've come to look forward to receiving them,' Judith said, glancing down at the image, taking in every detail, the brushwork, the colours. 'And the artwork is just as incredible as on the other cards. The work of an experienced, talented artist.'

The postcard depicted the faces of five magpies, each holding a silver coin in their beak. The brilliance of the silver paint shone out and Judith ran her fingers over the layers of paint so carefully applied.

'This is so exciting. It's a trail of sorts and it's certainly livened things up a bit round here… summer seems to be dragging and the plans for the Summer Fete are being thwarted by one obstacle after another. People are set in their ways, never wanting to change anything…'

'Me, you mean?'

'No, not you… everyone else.'

'By everyone else you mean the priest and his posse?'

'The committee, yes. The grey-cloud brigade. But I'm going to find a way to liven things up on the day. Throw in a little party confetti and summer sunshine of my own. I was too agreeable all my life working for the council and it's high time I shook things up a bit and listened to my instinct,' Lou said, handing the postcard back to Judith.

'Good for you. If you need me on board with the organising, as long as it doesn't involve anything illegal,' winked Judith, 'I'm here.'

At the next planning meeting, Lou was ready with her clipboard and pen. Judith came along to provide a little extra support for Kerry.

'Kerry, you're a natural,' said Judith, surprised at Kerry's persuasive manner. 'Your soft voice and your calm, concise response to the opposing questions fired at you worked perfectly in your favour.'

Kerry had certainly done her homework and Judith felt a swell of pride as she sat amongst the committee in the semi-circular arrangement in the church hall.

The proposed addition to the Summer Fete created a stir, but in the end Kerry and Maja's winning argument, without giving too much away, convinced the coordinating team. Finally, by ten o'clock, and with a few of the older members too tired to pour rain on anything more, simply nodded their agreement, or perhaps because they had almost drifted off to sleep, Kerry, and Maja, got the approval they hoped for.

Beaming with pure happiness Kerry hugged Maja tight. Judith felt her excitement the same she would a bolt of electricity. Kerry rushed over to Judith and gave her a huge hug.

'If it hadn't been for you, I would never have done this.'

'It was in you all along; it just needed a little coaxing.'

'You certainly came at the right time,' said Kerry.

'Kerry's Truth: Life After Miscarriage, deserves to be a success. You deserve to be a success.'

'You've helped me find a new reason to live, a new purpose… and Judith, you might not have realised this, but I think you saved my marriage.'

That night, Judith thought about Kerry and her marriage, how it had come back from the precipice, and felt a little jolt of pride in having helped her. She quietly wished her a long life ahead, full of adventure and full of discovery.

Chapter 25

'I wondered whether you'd be ready,' said Lou. Leaning on the garden wall to keep her balance, she bent one of her legs at the knee and kicked it up behind her as she adjusted the buckle on the side of her wellington boot.

'You know me too well, but today I was up early.'

'Too excited, eh?'

'I thought I'd bring a couple of sketch pads and pencils, keep us occupied. I may just find some inspiration,' said Judith as she approached Lou; her bulging tote bag digging uncomfortably into her shoulder. She adjusted it and twiddled with the ends of the scarf she had tied around it. With a small old-fashioned picnic hamper in one hand and a bottle of red wine in the other, Judith's house keys jangled against the glass bottle as she kissed Lou good morning.

'I've grabbed the latest crossword competition, my bumper crossword edition and a pack of cards.'

'Lou, you know I'm no good with words. I'm sure I must be dyslexic.'

'All the more reason to think about words,' said Lou but Judith sensed her friend was teasing her.

'Have you room for this?' Judith handed over the wine and after moving around a few items in her cooler bag Lou found a space for it. She forced the zip round the two front corners, until it was fully closed, and Velcroed the handles together.

'So much stuff. Look at us. Glad we decided not to bring the camping chairs.'

'We'll be fine on the picnic rug, though I'm not sure once I'm on the ground what with my arthritis I'll be able to get back up again.'

'Maybe we should have brought our camping chairs,' said Judith.

'I'm sure we'll manage,' laughed Lou. 'It's going to be a beautiful day.'

'The weather girl said highs of twenty-four degrees apparently.'

'Good job I grabbed my sun cream.' Lou tapped her jacket pocket, her face lit up by her boastful yet cheeky, bright grin.

They set off on their country ramble and within fifteen minutes reached the end of the first part of the narrow, muddy footpath. Lou stung herself on a wild patch of nettles as she swung her arm back and forth rather too enthusiastically and then stepped into a pile of fox poo reaching for the dock leaves to treat the burning. Judith tired early on and though she didn't say anything to Lou, she was pretty fed up with all the cheery hellos and good morning greetings from other ramblers and fellow hikers; her jaw ached from all the smiling. No one was usually this friendly, so she failed to see why walking encouraged people to invade her quiet thoughts with far too much enthusiasm than was necessary.

'Come on,' Lou beckoned, ducking her head to crawl through a sizeable gap in the field's hedgerow. Judith pushed through the perimeter, pulling her art bag behind her, her hair matted, nearly breathless.

They crossed the field following unseen trails, the grass smooth and shimmering beneath their feet, barely speaking, their heavy breathing tapping out a rhythm; the bumpy ground was on an incline. Huge rolls of hay scattered across the field like buttercream-filled Swiss rolls and Judith imagined the farm hands hauling bale after bale, their exhausted bodies shining with sweat under the burning sun. In the distance, a church steeple rose majestically above the treetops and a speckled spatter of sheep grazed lazily; the top fields gleamed in a patchwork of greens in the blazing mid-morning sun.

Close by, blackbirds and finches and sparrows hopped from bough to bough and chased each other through the tree branches, singing their chirpy tunes. A single magpie's chack chack chack call caught Judith's attention and she searched for another but could not see it. 'One for sorrow,' she muttered under her breath.

On the other side of the field, Lou, oblivious to Judith's slowing momentum, had raced ahead at a much faster pace. She swung open a decrepit wooden gate and held it open for Judith.

'I need a drink,' Judith said, wiping her sweaty brow

as she approached, her steps slow. 'The exertion and the heat are getting to me.' She leaned back on the gate trying to catch her breath.

'Almost there,' puffed Lou. 'I can hear the trickle of a stream. Thank goodness I wore my wellies.'

'I'd forgotten what a hike it always is when we go out together,' said Judith looking down at her soft leather peep-toe sandals. 'My feet are beginning to ache now. Where on earth are we going?'

'Not long to go,' said Lou, looking down at her mud-spattered footwear but Judith had guessed Lou was second-guessing their trail.

They followed another path, edged on one side with prickly hawthorn and blackberry bushes, which took them through the stunning ancient woodland this part of the country was famous for, to the far west of the village, and finally it opened out into a natural clearing, partly shaded by a row of three great chestnut trees.

'Here. And it's worth it.' Lou dropped her paraphernalia to the ground and with a sweeping gesture stood back so Judith could survey the view.

'You're right,' Judith said in two short bursts as she tried to steady her breathing. 'It's wonderful. How did you discover such a perfect spot?' She tipped her head back until her neck hurt, taking in the sky overhead.

'Quite by chance and by trespassing across that last field.'

'We trespassed? Lou… you're quite intolerable.'

'No, I'm not. I took a chance and look at what we've discovered. Doesn't this place deserve the company of Ms. Louise and Ms. Judith for the day?'

Lou laughed and unrolled the picnic blanket, patting the ground, discarding a few stones and twigs. Satisfied the area was fairly bumpy-free, she sprawled across the blanket. She huffed and puffed pulling at the heel of her boot.

'Here, let me help,' said Judith, pulling one and then the other with a tug. Judith tried to hold intact her "I'm-not-impressed" expression but failed miserably.

Lou placed them behind her on the ground and proceeded to wiggle her toes. 'Ooh, that's better. Wellington boots are practical but they're so heavy, unforgiving, squidged my toes like you don't know what.'

'That's because you haven't got walking socks on… thick socks to cushion your toes.'

'Ooh, listen to you.'

'I might not do much walking, but I do know good socks make a difference,' said Judith. 'My dad always bought thick wool socks. Swore by them.'

Lou continued with her ankle exercises, rotating clockwise and then anticlockwise and, leaning back on her elbows, looked across the river and beyond to the riverbank, taking in the smooth curves of the pebbles and hard edges of the rocks, of all sizes, protruding from the river's shallowest parts.

Judith followed her gaze. 'We could go for a paddle later,' she yawned and wriggled into a comfortable position.

'Sounds like you need a mid-morning siesta,' said Judith and following her friend's lead she lay down, fanning her fiery hair around her like a lion's mane. She listened to the rustle of the leaves as the fresh summer breeze ruffled the wild foliage around them and the dense nature seemed to come alive. She felt calm, already glad for Lou's invitation even if she had inadvertently trespassed.

She listened to the turning pages of Lou's puzzle book and the click of her pen. She took in the furrowed lines of deep concentration on Lou's face. Lou peered at her over the words arranged in the grid.

'The answer has to be right here... when the clue says as seen in... it's an indication it's right there in front of us.'

Judith smiled, turned onto her side and, cushioning her head with her scrunched up scarf, the sun warming her back, the overhanging boughs shading her head. 'I'd forgotten how leafy it is this time of year,' she said and fell into a welcome slumber, its warm embrace pulling her in.

Judith slept for how long she wasn't sure, but deeply enough to feel disorientated at the sound of Lou's urgent voice.

'Judith, Judith, wake up,' said Lou, shaking her out of her siesta.

'What is it?'

'I can hear shooting,' Lou whispered, an edge to her voice.

'No one will be shooting round–' Judith stopped and listened, as she sat bolt upright. 'You're right. Oh, my goodness.'

'We're going to be murdered and no one will ever find our bodies buried out here.'

'Stop being so melodramatic…' but Judith's hand had flown to her chest.

They both sat holding onto each other, their breathing shallow so as not to miss a sound. Judith tucked a lock of hair behind her lobe and cocked her head. Every little sound seemed magnified in their silence and fear.

'Footsteps,' said Judith and they both peered back in the direction of the trail they'd taken through the forest.

'Someone's coming,' Lou said.

Judith cocked her head, listening, 'And they're getting closer,' she whispered, her heart pounding in her ears. 'What should we do?'

'Let's get out of here.'

They sprung onto their knees and started to throw everything back into their bags. Judith was about to sweep up the picnic blanket from under them when the burly figure of a man appeared from the shadows.

Chapter 26

The man made his way towards them; tall, a dark floppy hat crowning his head. He dragged an amorphous load behind him. One hand gripped the baggage and the other held onto the strap of the rifle slung across his shoulder.

Both women dropped to the bare ground in silence and continued clinging onto each other. Judith clutching the end of the picnic blanket, as if a life raft, in her arms. The shrill kee-kee-kee of two birds of prey shocked them and overhead the birds hovered and then dived into a hole in the highest part of a tree trunk, visible between the upper boughs.

'Kestrels,' said the man. Lou nodded and Judith, too shaken up to speak, gave him a half smile. 'Hello there,' he said in a surprisingly high-pitched sing-song voice.

Lou was the first to answer, 'Hello,' she said. Judith picked up the nervous tremor in her friend's voice and tried to push down her own rising panic, one hand pressed to her throat.

'I'm Matt. The farmland up yonder is mine. What brings you down here?'

Judith started, speechless for a few seconds, a familiar yet long-forgotten tendril of emotion wrapped itself around her. 'Just a lazy afternoon,' stammered Judith and the sudden high colour across her Lou's cheeks told Judith that Lou suspected their trespassing was about to get found out.

'And how d'you get all the way across to this here point?' And there it was. Out in the open.

Judith was sure she could hear Lou's heart thumping over her own and she swallowed.

Chapter 27

'We walked, followed the path from the next village, through the forest and across the f-i-e-l-d…' said Lou, finding her voice but dropping her gaze.

'You both walked across my farmland.'

'Yours?'

'That's what I said.'

'Looks like we may have. We're so sorry,' said Lou.

'I wouldn't have put you down as trespassers,' he said, a smirk creeping out from under his moustache and straggly, overgrown beard.

'We didn't realise. We won't do it again,' said Judith, more assertively than she felt, though her thumping heart, had it been heard, would have betrayed her.

'No? How're you going to get back home?'

'I guess we'll have to find another route,' said Lou, her voice raised a notch.

'There's no other way back so guess you're stuck

here. With me.' Judith and Lou looked at each other and automatically reached for each other's hand. 'You got any food there?' he asked.

'We have a picnic. Why don't you umm, join us? Judith, we have more than enough for the three of us, don't we?'

Judith caught Lou's eye; a conspiratorial moment between them. *Food was always a way to a man's heart, so it was worth a try.*

'That's mighty kind of you both. What do I call you?' Lou introduced herself and Judith to Matt and as he lowered himself onto the ground, landing heavily next to them, Judith noticed two dead rabbits tethered to the load he'd been dragging.

Matt followed their eyes and said, 'Tonight's dinner. Perhaps you'd care to join us?'

'Us?' asked Judith, fighting the familiarity he evoked around her.

'Me and my cousin,' he said, looking behind him where another figure loomed from the shadows.

'Geoff. Pleased to make your acquaintance,' he said, tipping his tweed flat cap in their direction.

'Louise and Judith might be joining us for dinner. But now let's have some lunch. They've kindly offered to share their picnic,' announced Matt. He took off his floppy hat, ran the back of his hand across his brow.

Judith's eyes immediately darted back and forth, again and again, to the mark on his brow.

'Judith, come on,' said Louise, as her friend seemed to disappear into a state, transfixed.

'Yes, of course,' said Judith, pulling her attention away

from Matt.

Judith laid out the picnic blanket again and both proceeded to unpack their picnic, arranging the food: salmon and cucumber sandwiches, the ham and mustard sandwiches, the cheese straws, the pot of locally produced apple chutney, the wax paper parcel of cheese slices from the deli, two apples and two bananas.

'This sure is a magnificent feast,' said Matt, licking his lips.

'Please help yourselves,' said Judith as she handed out plastic plates and cutlery, surveying Matt more carefully. He had a familiar look, something about his eyes, his mannerisms.

The men didn't hesitate and within seconds both were chomping on the sandwiches and crunching on the cheese straws.

'You not opening the wine?' asked Geoff with amusement, laughing, spraying crumbs as he spoke through a mouthful.

'Yes, yes we are,' said Lou and she twisted open the cap and filled four paper cups. 'Cheers,' she said as she tapped the side of each cup with hers, eyeing Judith who, flustered, looked paler than a rising harvest moon.

'What do you two ladies do when you're not breaking the law?' asked Matt, holding Judith's gaze and she noticed his dark unruly curls, the peppering of silver around his ears.

'I'm a retired art teacher and Lou was a civil servant.' Judith looked down and picked two errant leaves from the picnic throw and tossed them onto the earth beyond the edge of the blanket; a breeze cradled them and dropping them again they landed softly in her lap.

'Retired? Surely not. You don't look anywhere near.'

'Early retirement,' Judith corrected.

'Explains the sketch book and pencils,' he said, inclining his head towards them spilling out of her bag. 'I used to enjoy art. Never had much opportunity to paint or draw once I left school. My art teacher wanted me to go to the art club after school, but my dad wouldn't hear of it. Arty-farty-pansy stuff he called it. No boy of mine... he went on and on.'

'My parents were the same, well you know what I mean, but I stood up to them,' said Judith, gathering courage and familiarity in their common topic of conversation.

'No chance... my dad argued in front of the whole class with... now what was her name? Miss Erning about how his son wasn't going to end up wearing pink shirts and standing in front of an easel all day. He needed me on the farm. I left school at fourteen and the rest is history.'

'Did you mean Ms. Irving?' asked Judith.

'That's it. Ms. Irving. She was a looker too. All the boys fancied her... we used to jerk off...'

'Ahem,' coughed Judith and almost at the same time she sensed another familiarity about him.

Lou let out a snicker; her facial muscles twitched against it in an effort to stop.

'My apologies. Anyway, as I said I wasn't allowed to continue my education.'

'Ms. Irving taught me too. I was in class 3B. It would have been 1966. I remember because my aunt, my dad's sister, made her first appearance in Coronation Street and Ms. Irving asked me to get her autograph, 'She'll be famous one day, mark my words,' she said.

'You're kidding me. I was in 4F. A year older than you.'

'Hold on… You're not Matt as in Matthew Doncaster?' A flicker of recognition came to her, a fiery heat warmed her. *This was Matt, her Matt. Her teenage crush.*

'Two younger brothers who were always in trouble for stealing glue from the caretaker's shed,' said Matt.

'Stuck the main doors shut so we couldn't get into school for two days!' She turned to Lou and said, 'They also used to cover themselves in Copydex glue… their legs, their arms, their hands and wait for it to dry and they'd run after the younger girls pretending to be zombies… they were little terrors. Gosh, that takes me back…'

'The very same. And you're Judith… Judith Alma Brown!' Both fell about laughing, Judith a kind of nervous laugh seeing Matt again after so many years. She hoped he was as happy as she felt with the outcome of such a serendipitous moment. *He was so handsome.*

'Gosh, that middle name!' she said.

'I never thought I'd ever see you again.'

'Oh my! And all this time you've lived a few acres and a field away from me?' Judith couldn't believe it and felt thrilled, a soppy teenager high on her first love all over again.

'Am I missing something here?' asked Lou.

'Still here,' he winked, and it sent Judith into a blushing flap.

'You two know each other?'

'We do, yes. Did you know that this woman was a

mean conker opponent? She had such a way of flicking that string.'

'I think I was one of only a handful of girls who dared stand against you,' she said.

'See this here?' said Matt pointing at the scar on his forehead. 'Ask your friend how it came to be here.'

'Judith did that? Now that's scuppered any chance we have of being off the hook for crossing your land,' said Lou in her matter-of-factly but clumsily flirty way.

'No charges to answer to,' said Matt, turning to Lou as he bit into the other half of his ham and mustard sandwich.

'What's all this about being off the hook?' asked Geoff.

'Long story mate. Will tell you on the way home. Thanks for lunch. We must do this again, soon.' Matt got up, brushed off the back of his jeans and bid the ladies farewell.

'Perhaps not like this,' said Lou as she took the plastic plates from them.

'I suppose I should say good to bump into you,' said Judith. 'And if you like art so much you should go back to it, make some time.' She forced herself to speak slowly, but knew, by the way Lou was looking at her, that she sounded unnatural.

'And good to bump into you, Judith Alma.'

'Thank you,' mumbled Judith, discombobulated.

'Between you and me he's done a few things over the years. Perhaps he'll show you one day,' said Geoff. Judith and Matt's eyes met for a fleeting moment, for a second too long, until they both looked away.

'Good luck,' Lou called.

Once both men were out of earshot and out of sight Judith said, 'That was close!'

'And I've got the answer to the puzzle... it's BREACH OF PROMISE,' exclaimed Lou. 'As seen in ja- B, REACH OF PRO MISE-rably failing to meet expectations.'

Judith sat very still, trying to process her feelings, the serendipity of the moment. *That was Matt. Matt of so many years ago.*

'Failing to meet expectations. Extra cunning points for using "MISE-rably",' said Lou, looking proud of herself.'

But Judith was aware she was taking in what Lou was saying. Not for the excitement of solving the clue but because she had failed. She had been miserable. And she realised it had been for the flicker of love which had been extinguished by time... yet something was quickening her heartbeat now... memories of so long ago.

'Judith... I can't believe your school infatuation saved us!' nattered on Lou.

'Nothing to do with your "not-so-obvious" flirting?' said Judith, putting all the enthusiasm she could into her reply.

'Me? Never.'

'But when you put it like that, I suppose it did,' said Judith and, looking round to check the men had gone, she stripped down to her faded ivory bra and knickers and, sliding down the bank, dipped her feet into the water. 'Lucky we weren't half naked,' she laughed and as the cold water made her shiver, her reignited teenage euphoria danced like crazy inside her heart.

Chapter 28

Judith swatted away the midges humming in a halo around her food and then at a pesky fly drunkenly coming at her, the citronella candles doing little to keep the insects away, moths dancing and fluttering around the flames. She finished her evening meal; a steak pasty bought from the village bakery the day before, and a salad of lettuce, tomatoes, cucumber, and pickled radishes. The sun, now a wishy-washy yellow haze, bigger than the sky, seemed to hang suspended, casting long sunrays still strong enough to burn her insipid white skin, her décolletage blotchy red and upper arms sore. The wind chime jostled gently in the breeze, relaxing her agitation, and filled the air with a soothing hollow sound as its bamboo reeds knocked together. Bliss.

She pushed back in her wooden chair, making it creak under the weight of her body and pouring the last of the red wine into her glass, she took a big gulp and licked her lips. She rubbed the smudge of scarlet from its rim. She gathered the heavy photo album into her lap and prised it open, carefully forcing apart the first two tacky, cellophaned pages.

Polaroid photos, yellowed and sticky from years of being pressed together, fell out, the photo corners loose. Memories of her childhood scattered across her knees. She ran her hand over the first photograph; sitting comfortably in the arms of her father. She eased the others apart: a week or two after her birth, tightly wrapped and bundled, she could barely make out her own face, but her father's expression said it all. He had always been proud of her, but too quiet and in the shadow of her mother's wrath to speak comfortably, or openly, of his adoration for her.

She found a stack of unsorted photos, flipped through them: 1989, 1995, 2001, 2005. None of her. She was long gone by then. Losing contact with her father had been one of the biggest regrets of her life, though she had got together with him twice, clandestine meetups and without her mother's knowledge, in a pub, damp and musty, close to where Judith had moved to in the early 80s. He had said extraordinarily little about her mother, apart from saying she sent her love, but Judith knew that to be untrue. They did not meet again after that until her parents' anniversary party, another short-lived, disappointing visit.

The crackle of the next two pages separating sent a shiver up her back. She looked down at the photos, two on one page and three on the next one, overlapping each other diagonally down the page. The pictures, now faded, or maybe that had always been their colour, seemed like they depicted another life, someone else's life, not her life or that of her family.

Wrapped in a beach towel, her lips blue from the cold, another looking straight at the camera proudly showing off her red muffler, a background of slushy grey snow, another with her tongue sticking out stained black from eating half-penny black jacks, her eyes bright with happiness. Her father had taken all the photos. In the last one a shadowy figure in the background, her mother in profile, looked away, as she puffed on a cigarette. Her presence, even now, seemed to spoil the otherwise gentle comradery she had with her father.

When Judith had collected the keys to Chrysanthemum Cottage, she had arranged for a house clearance company to come in and strip it bare. She kept very few belongings: her father's wing chair, an art deco style sideboard, and a blanket chest she used to hide in at the bottom of her parents' bed. She also rescued her father's cushion dented on his empty chair as if waiting for him to return, her three framed paintings on the sitting room wall and a handful of personal possessions Judith got an overwhelming sense of loving, and remembering, as a child. It had not, however, been a heartbreaking or emotional experience; she had said goodbye a long time before and had accepted her life without her parents.

'Sorry I'm late,' announced Lou, stealing her from her daydream. She swept in through the garden gate, shaking the heather and disturbing the bees still gathering sweet nectar from its breaking flowers, the gate swinging back on the latch with a clang.

'No worries.'

'I've brought wine,' she announced, holding the bottle in the air, waving it around. 'Are we celebrating something?' she asked, noticing Judith's open bottle,

'Celebrating? Celebrating what?' asked Judith, closing the album, and slipping it under her seat.

'Forget it. Who needs an excuse to celebrate, anyway? We've got each other and every day is a reason to celebrate,' chimed Lou, as she sat down and pulled out her crossword magazine. 'I sent off the one we completed down by the river. Fingers crossed.'

Judith rolled her eyes and disappeared to the kitchen, promptly returning with another wine glass and a packet of Bombay mix she'd found in the back of the larder; she hoped the snacks were still in date.

'So, what did you want to talk about?' asked Lou, already focused on the grid on the page in front of her.

'Apart from the fact I've been maudlin all day, I wondered whether you might like to get involved in the pub quiz next month?'

'The pub quiz?'

'It's the first one Kerry has organised in over a year. I thought it would be good to show our support.'

'Of course, but you could've asked me that any old time. What do you really want to talk about?' asked Lou, pulling out her crossword puzzle book, reading Judith like only a good friend can.

'I don't know. Life. Love. The universe.'

'You're thinking about Matt, aren't you?'

'No. Maybe. I don't know. I mean who thinks about an old new love at my age?' said Judith, fiddling with the stem of her wine glass.

'What happened between you two?'

'Nothing really… we had a thing, you know messed around together, kissing, nothing more. Then I left,' Judith said, detached, reflective.

'But he was your first one. You think back now and wonder whether you might have had something real?'

'Maybe. But memories always glow back rose-tinted, don't they?'

Judith waited for her friend's usual sassy comment, but it didn't come, and she said, 'I'm too old to start again.'

'Look at this one,' said Lou instead, proffering the magazine. 'Consumes a portion of meat stew, four letters. So clever. Look… EATS. If you look closer, the answer's in there. Consumes a portion of mEAT Stew,' Lou said, circling the word eats to highlight it. 'This next one's easy. Returning from Acre, talked afterwards, five letters. Afterwards, another word for afterwards is LATER There! Got it!'

'How on earth did you get that?' asked Judith, stunned with Lou's brilliant, yet random, crossword abilities.

'The words returning from tells me it's a reverse hidden word clue, with a synonym for afterwards to be found in reverse order among the letters of the remaining words. So, on returning from AcRE, TALked afterwards.' Lou wrote out the corresponding letters in capitals. 'You take out RETAL which when reversed is a synonym for afterwards—LATER.'

'It's too complicated for me, Lou. My head gets all confuddled.'

'You do the next one,' urged Lou.

Judith reluctantly took the puzzle book from Judith. 'Rewrite article for narration, seven letters. I have no idea, Lou. I really don't. My mind doesn't work like yours.'

'Come here. It's just practise. The more you do something the better you get at it. It becomes a habit, and you know how habits take time.'

'I don't have the patience.'

'Got it! RECITAL. "Rewrite…" the letters in the word "… ARTICLE…" giving another word for the word "… narration" that is RECITAL. Anyway, back to your question. Let me see. There's Harrison Ford and Paul McCartney,' said Lou eventually.

'All men with younger wives. You may see it but I'm in my sixties… I'm no spring chicken.'

'Who'd want to marry a chicken anyway? I saw the way Matt looked at you… that wink he gave you.'

'Marry?'

'And you're younger than him…'

'Not interrupting, am I ladies?'

Chapter 29

Both women turned towards the voice and then back at each other. 'You've not forgotten me, have you? Louise, Judith,' he said, tipping his hat.

Judith squinted in the half light of the flickering citronella candle, which was failing miserably at keeping the insects away, already bitten on the back of her knee and her ankle. She stood up, as if to get a better look at him.

'I've come to return this. I'm assuming it belongs to one of you.' Matt unhinged the gate and with two long strides stood in front of them before they had time to stand. Recognition slowly dawned on Judith. Matt looked different; his moustache and beard trimmed, neat. She lost her voice momentarily, taking in his sleeker, younger appearance, his height at least a full foot taller than she.

'My scarf,' said Judith eventually. 'I wondered where

that had got to.'

'It must've been blown away down by the clearing. Got caught up in the trees.' He handed it to Judith. As he passed the scarf to her, she noticed a tiny film of ingrained paint under his nails. *Was it blue? Grey?* A shiver ran through her, more of excitement than of fear. *Was Matt the secret postcard painter?* But then her excitement was replaced with a bubbling panic. It rose within her, a matted foggy grey of confusion and she automatically stroked the soft silk, now snagged with tiny catches in the delicate fabric. Matt stared at her, and Judith, feeling too visible, scrunched it up. Realising what it must look like, the heat rising in her cheeks, she stuffed it under her seat pad.

'How did you find me?'

'Not difficult. When I set my mind on something. Pub landlord always knows everyone, right?' he said, pressing his hands into the pockets of his black chinos.

Judith wasn't sure whether to be grateful to Paul or upset with him for sharing her address with an obvious stranger. But of course, she didn't know how Matt had introduced himself; a stranger or a long lost relative.

'Since you've obviously made a special trip, perhaps you'd like to join us for a glass of wine,' said Lou, avoiding Judith's school teacher look stabbing her like a dressmaker's pin in the eye.

'Why thank you, just the one mind, I've got to drive the truck back.' He took one of the wooden chairs stacked by the garden wall and unfolded it. His legs stretched out long and lean, his T-shirt taut across his chest in a way that you see in the movies.

'Yes, join us,' fumbled Judith, fighting her discombobulation as she twiddled with the ends of her long hair, loose around her shoulders. She disappeared inside for a few seconds, the flip flopping of her flip flops flapping across the floor.

Inside, she took a few deep breaths and thought of her scarf in the tree waving at Matt. *Everything happens for a reason.* On returning Lou and Matt were leaning conspiratorially close, the crossword on the table between them. 'Friend follows child completely, seven letters,' read Matt.

'Let me see... the clue says friend, a synonym for ally, follows or is placed after. Child a synonym for...'

'TOT,' said Matt.

'Got it! TOT and ALLY give us totally, meaning completely,' said Lou, looking proud of herself and getting up pulled her bag over her shoulder and across her chest, arranging the strap so it fell flat over her.

'Where are you going?' Judith asked, returning, and pouring wine into the glass she held out to Matt.

'I've got to go, sorry. Long-standing engagement I can't be late for... toodle-oo. Keep the crossword. I'll pick it up tomorrow. Enjoy your evening.' Lou waved her hand in the air as she pushed through the gate and walked away.

'But you brought the wine...' Judith sat back down, straightening out her long, layered skirt over her crossed legs. 'Not awkward at all,' she eventually said, and an unexpected surge of prickly excitement ran through her, a sense of magic hung in the air like twinkling stars suspended from invisible thread in the night sky.

'Not for me and I hope not for you, we're not strangers.'

'When you put it like that, I suppose we're not, no, but it was all so long ago. And about your land... about trespassing, I really am sorry. Lou can be quite the daredevil.'

'All forgotten, we wouldn't have met again otherwise. Cheers... to renewed friendship.' Matt's toast seemed perfect and inside Judith something fizzed away... like a shaken bottle of champagne she hoped she wasn't going to explode everywhere yet the thought invigorated her.

'You don't mind me coming over unannounced, do you?'

'No, though I don't receive many guests other than Lou and one or two of the villagers.'

'Time for something new then, Judith,' Matt said, his face taking on a mischievous expression.

Judith looked away, embarrassed, unable to work out her feelings, so instead asked, 'You're still up at the farm. Did you get married? Did you have any children?'

'I did but she upped and left me after deciding she was destined for something far posher than being the wife of a farmer. Left the boys, Ryan, and Luke. They were seven and nine at the time.'

'I'm so sorry. That must have been tough for you.'

'Inconvenient, yes. Tough? I don't know that you can get much tougher than running a farm.'

'They were so young. What about school and homework?'

The conversation threw her back to her school days. Her mum never had time for her. No patience and certainly didn't make any effort to help her with her schoolwork. It had always been her father's role, that of homework checker and homework doer. They would sit on the living room floor, the draft coming up through the floorboards around the rug, piles of open books and encyclopedias, heads together until the side lamp didn't give out enough light to carry on. Judith cherished those days.

'Luckily for me, their best friend's mum took them under her wing and, when it was obvious, she could do better than me, I paid her to look after them while I worked. Absolute gem of a woman. She passed last year... pancreatic cancer. She was gone within weeks. God rest her soul.'

'I'm sorry, Matt. And your sons must be young men now.'

'Both got city jobs, one in Bath with Newton & Coles, the law firm, married happily with one daughter, and the other's in Cirencester, gay as they come, but happy, settled, and works as an Educational Therapist, whatever that is.'

'Both did well for themselves. They sound like a credit to you.'

'I did what I had to do, not always happily but we got through. And you?'

'Not much to say really. Left the village,' Judith hesitated. 'As you must remember when I was sixteen, moved to the city.'

'Of course, I remember. How could I not? You disappeared. No word of goodbye. Nothing.'

'I had no choice.'

'I tried to find you. Your parents were no help. My dad

kept saying focus on the farm, forget the girl,' said Matt, his eyes cloudy with unsolved sorrow. Judith could see how hurt he must have been. In all these years, she hadn't really given him a lot of thought though there was always a nugget of sadness in her, unrecognised, ignored, pushed deep enough to not see the light.

'I'm sorry. I didn't know. I just got on with life. I left and did an art foundation course at college and then did my teacher training. I taught for almost forty years, Milton Arts and Drama College and then Willington Secondary School.'

'Impressive. Teaching's tough…' said Matt, composing himself but Judith had seen the vulnerability there, under the surface, swirling, toying with his emotions, a stormy replica of her own.

'It had its moments but, in many ways, it kept me grounded and I was doing something I loved every single day,' she said with a forced tone of normality.

'Sounds like you miss it. What sort of art do you do? Not that I'm an expert but I know what I like.'

'I taught all types, but my own love is for mixed media. Creating art with other materials, not just paint… fabric, lace, plastic, tissue paper, wood, glass… anything really.'

'Sounds way beyond my imagination.'

'Not painting, then?' she asked, unable to hold back her curiosity.

'No, my creativity nowadays only goes as far as what I should have for dinner and can I be bothered to try out a new recipe.'

'I'm the same, cooking for one isn't the most enticing of situations to be in.'

'Perhaps we could have a meal together some time... that's if there's no Mr....?'

'No there isn't.' Judith took in his profile as he shifted to pick up his glass. He looked tidier than when she saw him at the clearing; his moustache and beard trimmed, and a faint waft of old spices took her back to the days when her mother habitually gave her a couple of quid to buy the same scent for her father on Father's Day.

'Your dad likes that,' she used to say to her every year until Judith left and then there were no more gifts of old spice or anything other than a couple of overly festive cards Judith posted on the 12th of December, her mother's tradition, but as the years passed, Judith gave up sending the Christmas cards and, eventually, the messages too. She did, however, keep the bottle she found with the last few drops in it and placed it in her bedroom, after moving back to the cottage.

Matt seemed to wait for more detail, but Judith didn't indulge him and after a couple of seconds of awkward silence he said, 'I better be off. Thanks for the wine.'

'It's Lou you need to thank.'

'It's you who sat here and listened to me going on. See you soon, I hope. Maybe for that meal.'

'Thank you I'd like that... and thank you for bringing back my scarf.'

'No big deal,' he said and as he turned to leave, he rested his hand on her shoulder and she felt her legs trembling, the most beautiful sensation seeping its way into her, and the touch of his hand lingered even after he was gone, a warm imprint on her skin.

As the western evening sky faded into a velvety

blue studded with a galaxy of stars, the moon, full and silvery and round, gleamed like a shiny new coin. Judith, wrestling with her thoughts and feelings, finally cleared the glasses and placed them by the sink. Jasper snuggled in his basket and Judith, after brushing her teeth in the downstairs bathroom, retired to bed.

Her sleep, fragmented and punctuated with strange, half-forgotten memories pushed her into a night of lucid wakefulness and troubled dreams, a concoction of fantasy and reality. The distinct hooting of an owl cutting across the silence of night woke her.

She switched on the bedside lamp and glanced at the alarm clock; it was the midnight-struck hour of three. She swallowed a dry metallic taste in her mouth inducing a nauseous swirl to swish through her. Dragging her feet out of bed, she sat up and reached for her glass, filled it from her water carafe and drank it in one go, the moon slicing a shaft of light across the room. She shook her head from side to side; the water did nothing to numb her palate or dispel the unpleasant taste across her chapped lips.

The owl continued to hoot sending shivers through Judith. The air was stiflingly warm, and she threw open her bedroom window; a slither of cool air stroked her cheeks as she stood there looking out across her front garden and beyond. With no streetlights the half dark wrapped itself around her as she breathed in the summer night air.

Her thoughts wandered to Matt and his visit. *If he hadn't found her scarf, would he have made the effort to seek her out? Did it matter?* She liked seeing him after all this time and she reached up to her shoulder, the imprint of his hand still there, but the moment was spoiled as her thoughts drifted involuntarily to the paint under his fingernails.

Chapter 30

'What happened after I left?' asked Lou with a little too much eager heartedness for Judith's liking. Her head was pounding.

'Yes, thanks for that Lou. Remind me to return the favour one day.'

'Ooh, yes please.'

'Stop it,' said Judith, steam rising in a column as she stirred her tea.

'Come on, what happened?'

'Nothing much. We had a chat…'

'Tell me…' Lou dunked a ginger biscuit into her mug of tea and before she finished chewing, she reached for another and held it suspended over her mug as she waited for Judith to respond.

'His wife left him you know, and his boys… he has two grown up sons… he asked whether there was a Mr. Brown.'

'He didn't. Oh my… he's "into you",' said Lou. 'How do you feel? He's very handsome in a rugged kind of way, he's a Brian Cox. Ooh, I'd let him sweep me off my feet any day of the week.'

'You fancy Brian Cox?'

'I do, but this isn't about me and who I fancy it's about you and Matt…'

'There's no me and Matt, Lou.'

'But you'd like there to be? I saw the way you blushed around him.'

'He's an old school friend, he kindly returned my scarf. I doubt I'll be seeing him again,' said Judith as she twiddled with the ends of her hair.

'But you like him.'

'I hardly know him, not now.'

'His kisses will be the same as the kiss you shared in the school tuck shop. See, I do listen when you talk to me.'

'That was one kiss,' said Judith, not meeting her friend's gaze. 'Maybe two, or three…'

'You're twiddling your hair,' laughed Lou. 'You still like him, after all these years, even if you won't admit it to yourself.' Judith instantly dropped her hand into her lap fighting against her emotions, a yearning to be held by Matt encompassed her.

'Did you notice anything about his hands?'

'His hands? What do you mean?'

'His fingernails?'

'What are you talking about?'

'I'm sure I saw traces of dark paint under his nails.'

'Paint? More likely soil from flexing his muscles on

the farm. All that dirt and grime.'

'Lou! No, it looked blue, dark grey, charcoal. Not soil.'

'Grease?'

'Maybe, I don't know.'

Lou sat bolt upright, as if only just getting Judith's drift. 'Do you think he's behind the postcards?'

'I really don't know. It doesn't make any sense.' But the thought of Matt playing games boiled her blood more than she cared to acknowledge. *Men and games did not sit well with Judith.*

Chapter 31

On her way back from the village grocery store, Judith noticed the vicar standing outside St Barnabas, puffing on a cigarette. He blew the smoke in billows around him, and she caught a whiff of it as it carried on the breeze. Judith caught him staring. She felt intrusive of his quiet time despite the smell of nicotine intruding on her enjoyment of the fresh summer air. It was rare to see him alone; his parishioners were demanding of his time and energy, and she knew how much of himself he devoted to preparing his sermons and religious teachings, though his sense of timing, she had heard, was off, not a punctual man.

When she returned to the village to claim Chrysanthemum Cottage, she had heard some of the parishioners complaining, saying how ungodly-like, so impure, it was to see their vicar smoking and drinking. But Judith, the rebellious Judith, liked the way when he wasn't working, he threw convention out without a care, and she caught herself wondering what else he broke the rules about.

She looked away, intending to walk on, but then something propelled her to stroll over to him. She pushed the gate back, barely attached to the gatepost, a bit too forcefully onto its rusty hinges, the bang punctuated the serene peacefulness. She meandered along the crazy-paved path; dandelions and daisies pushing through the cracked paving and loose concrete, their heads nodding as if in greeting.

'Judith, how are you?'

'I was about to ask you the same thing,' she said more assertively than she felt; the church was always uncomfortable, reminding her of her scratchy Sunday coat, making the back of Judith's neck and her wrists red and blotchy and which her mother insisted she wore, nevertheless.

'Oh, you know...'

'No, I don't. Why don't you tell me? Your thoughts were elsewhere the other night at the meeting and dare I say it, you were rather short, verging on rude. What's going on?' She guessed an odd conversation was about to unfold and for a split second regretted being so forthright.

'How long do you have?' he asked, taking another drag of his cigarette before stamping the discarded butt underfoot.

His reply stumped her. 'Well, if you put the kettle on, I'll have a lot longer,' she said, surprising herself with her bold response, her willingness to be around him.

Judith noticed his reaction: he looked at her as if he wanted to kiss her but instead pressed his hands palm to palm, in thanks, his eyes glistening. She followed him along another meandering path around the church, a neatly clipped lawn sloped downwards to the left towards the periphery closed in by a crumbling dry-stone wall, covered in trails of creeping ivy and patches of furry moss.

She walked faster than she naturally would, trying to keep up with the vicar who moved like a whirlwind through a second gate. The parsonage, an imposing two-storey red brick building with a porch, appeared ahead, flanked with an array of pots and old chimney stacks, geraniums and pansies bursting forth. The porch's orange-tiled roof and tulip-red door clashed with each other yet equally created a bright and warm welcome.

Judith wiped her feet on the exterior door mat which welcomed her with the words 'ALL WELCOME.' Inside the porch, wiping her feet again, she looked down at another mat which said: "Unless God sent you, I'm unavailable." She stifled a giggle, but a note of laughter escaped her.

'A parting gift from the previous vicar. Did you know him? Fabulously great sense of humour.'

Judith shook her head and now inside, it took her a few seconds to adjust to the dimness; the dark panelled walls and old floorboards absorbing the light which came in through the tall but heavily curtained-leaded window in the long, narrow hallway.

She followed the vicar to the kitchen where the dark slate flooring of the kitchen-diner did little to lift the atmosphere despite the lighter tones of the limed kitchen units which appeared rather congruent with the rest of the old traditional feel of the vicarage.

'Please, sit down,' said the vicar. He turned on the tap, the pipes gurgled, and a sudden spurt sprayed his dark shirt as he filled the kettle.

'Blasted plumbing,' he blasphemed and then, as if remembering Judith was present, softened his voice. 'These old pipes are forever playing tricks on me.'

'Don't you have a housekeeper?' Judith surveyed the kitchen with its overflowing bin and discarded take-away boxes and bags on the worktops. The sink seemed to be straining under the weight of all the washing up and a dead fly sat next to a pot of wilting baby daffodils on the windowsill, crumbs of soil littering the surface.

'The long-standing housekeeper retired three months after I joined the parish. Arriving on my own I never saw the point of enlisting help. I quite like my privacy… you know what village gossip is like.'

'You don't need to tell me; I've been there, and it hurts. But that's not what you wanted to speak to me about is it?' Judith fought the niggling untruth about her own situation sitting heavy on her chest. *Was the vicar about to reveal her secret? Had he found something out?*

'No, it's not. Firstly, I wanted to say thank you to you.'

'Thank you? To me?'

'Yes. You've done wonders with Kerry. And I know you've helped Maja and her mother with the ordeal of…' his voice trailed off.

Judith relaxed. *So, this wasn't about her.* She breathed with relief.

'Kerry's come out of herself and though she didn't give me the details, she came to see me and told me how she has found faith in life again. She apologised for not attending my Sunday morning services, saying you've been instrumental in her recovery. Her words were, 'bringing me back from the cliff's edge'. I'm sure she wouldn't mind me sharing that with you. You are very dear to her.'

'She's so young to have suffered such pain, Vicar. She and Paul deserve to have a second chance at life... as does Maja. We all do.'

'Life chances, that's what I wanted to talk to you about. And please call me Lee.'

'I'm not happy discussing anyone in the village with you.'

'No, not at all. I wouldn't ask you to break anyone's trust. But you seem to be quite the problem-solver so I'm hoping you can solve something for me. Here's my predicament...'

Chapter 32

'My wife and son want to come and live in the village with me.' He paused as if to let his announcement sink in, but Judith saw it was to build his nerve to carry on speaking now that he had started.

'You have a wife and son?' Judith prompted him.

'A wife, yes. And a stepson.'

'Why aren't they with you already?'

'It's complicated and I don't know how my flock will react.'

'I'm guessing how they always react, with malicious gossip and pointing fingers one minute and then taking holy communion the next.'

Lee nodded, reddening. Judith knew her comment was getting his cassock in a flap.

'My wife, Megan, is Tom's mum. She had Tom out of wedlock. She was only sixteen and dropped out of school, leaving home when her father gave her an ultimatum:

to have the baby adopted or move out. Anyway, she struggled being so young and with no proper support. She wanted to keep him, but social services got involved when she was sleeping rough with the newborn. I supported her through her ordeal. I stepped in as her responsible adult and she was housed and got the help she needed to find a job and take control of her life.'

'The poor girl. Parents can be so harsh, unthinking,' said Judith, her own mother's treatment of her tainting her thoughts, which pulled her back to a place she didn't want to go. She had long before forced herself not to think about that time.

'I had little to do with her or the baby after that until she decided to have Tom christened and brought him to my church. She had grown up a lot.'

'Having a baby does that, I'm sure.'

'She came back more mature, responsible. She tried to walk away but wanted to hold on at the same time.'

'That's the mind at war with the heart,' Judith said, almost a whisper.

'We spent a lot of time talking, often sitting at the front of the church, cup of tea, biscuits if I had any, while Tom slept in his pram. We enjoyed each other's company, clicked as they say, and within a few months we declared our feelings to each other and got married.'

'But you're not married anymore?'

'We are, and happy despite Tom's misdemeanours. They both live in the next village. Tom did some sort of musical apprenticeship, sound engineering, production, and he's working in a music studio now, acoustics and that kind of stuff. Setting up the odd gig.'

'Riddle me this and riddle me that. Sorry, am I missing something here?'

'Tom's been in prison for the past three years for ABH. He was released, five months after I was offered the parish here.'

'God's timing is not so great, right?'

'No and I don't want my parishioners thinking I've been hiding something from them.'

'Even though you have?'

'They all assumed I was unmarried, childless, and I didn't correct them. As time went on, the opportunity to tell them didn't present itself.'

'I see what you mean. Dishonesty. Shame. Embarrassment.' Judith had, in the past, always made little time for church in her life. She instinctively decided she wasn't going to let Lee off the hook, but despite her words she inwardly admitted she liked him and wanted to help.

'Yes alright. He's only twenty. He has his whole life ahead of him. He made one mistake. One mistake which the judge used to make an example of him.'

'And you're worried about being judged too?'

'I suppose, yes.'

'What did he do?'

'He got mixed up in a gang, a street gang. He didn't know what he was getting involved in as naïve as that may sound. It started off as a laugh, nicking cigarettes and booze, he was seventeen.'

'Any parent's worst nightmare. I'm sorry,' said Judith, shifting in her seat, an all too uncomfortable familiarity bringing out her empathetic side.

'I never lied intentionally but once everyone assumed I was unmarried. I'd really like it if you could help me, help bring everyone round.'

At home, drinking the last of the red wine Judith had opened the night before with dinner, her alcohol-induced thoughts drifted to Lee; not only his situation but to him. It wasn't like her to be drawn to a man of the cloth. But there was something about him, she felt at ease with him and at the same time that discombobulated her.

He was certainly in a pickle but perhaps there was a way to smooth out the bumpy edges. Jasper jumped onto her lap, and she spilt a little wine on the couch... it spread slowly, soaking through the fabric until it left a dark red stain like an old wall map on the lumpy cushion.

It reminded her of her own deep shame and that which had coloured Lee's face as his hands wrung over and over in his lap, his voice shaking, as his secret unfolded.

Judith sipped on her wine as she mulled his proposal over, dabbing a wet cloth absentmindedly at the wine stain. She watched the rest of her mid-week soap. *Help the vicar.* The vicar asking for her help had her questioning whether she was liked enough by the parishioners for her voice to make a difference. She hardly ever attended Sunday services. Didn't attend at all.

She needed something to bring his family together and the village. There was only one event that could possibly do that, and Judith clapped with delight, the sharp clap frightening Jasper drifted off to sleep, curled up on the sofa with her. He nuzzled his face into the back of her knees as she sat sideways. She patted him gently, his little snores comforting her.

'Sorry, Jasper,' she said, jolting in her seat, emitting an excited whoop. 'I think this is my "Four for a Boy" magpie mission.'

Chapter 33

Days in the sun had brought out a sprinkling of freckles across the bridge of Judith's nose and across her cheeks. She dabbed at them with foundation, but no amount concealed them, so she gave up. She ran a pink lipstick over her lips and smacking them together she slipped her smart linen jacket over her summer dress and grabbed her straw hat at the last minute.

The climbing country roads, taking them away from the village, were quiet with only a supermarket delivery van and a tractor rumbling along ahead of them. The farmer kindly pulled into a furrowed layby to let them pass and Lee, in typical country fashion, beeped his horn in thanks while the delivery driver overtook and sped off ahead.

'Nice car,' said Judith, taking in the smell of the leather interior and the scent of the air freshener.

'It was my father's. He used to exhibit at the classic

car shows up and down the country and when he died my mother, not interested in its upkeep, gave it to me. She knew nothing about cars and engines. More interested in her own hobbies.'

'It's surprisingly comfortable even for my old bones.'

'I had it reupholstered.'

'Do Megan and Tom know I'm coming with you?'

'Yes, and Megan's already grateful for your help.'

The vicar turned on the radio, a tune crackled into life over the airwaves, and they sat in quiet companionship for the rest of the journey. The vicar sang along to the songs he knew and hummed to those he didn't. The euphonious tones of her own father's singing voice, deep and clear, drowned Judith's senses. Her mum, ever the domestic goddess, kitted out in her customary floral pinny and matching head scarf, standing at the sink, yellow rubber gloves squeaking with the liquid soap suds in the washing up bowl. Her dad would spring up behind her, always singing and circling his arms around her waist as she merrily splashed him with soap suds.

'Get away, you soppy sod,' her mother used to say but Judith knew she didn't mean it. Her mother's curves moulded perfectly into her husband's, they would suddenly merge into one shape, one form and, Judith watching on the sidelines, would become invisible. Her mother didn't smile much for her, but she always smiled for her father.

As Judith got older, she recognised the petty jealousy yet never understood it, hoping it was something else, something less destructive. Her mother relished having her father's attention. Judith's father lavished Judith with love and affection throughout her childhood but her mother always seemed to intervene, cut their bonding time short with a clipped, sharp tongue: 'Time for bed, Judith… Go and do your homework, Judith.'

Perhaps that's why her mother never tried to persuade her to come home after Judith ran out. She had wanted him all to herself again. The realisation landed with a thud in a solid heap in the pit of her stomach and Judith squeezed her eyes to stop the tears from falling. Even after all this time it hurt; it hurt so much her insides knotted and her chest felt tight with the strangling emotions which rose within her, and she rested her hand over her beating chest.

Judith desperately shook away other slim fading memories threatening to drag her into an abyss of pain and focused instead on the fields of lavender, rapeseed, and wheat as their colours whooshed by in a blur on both sides of the road; a rolling screen in front of her. The music's slower tempo beat in unison with the car's low hum and made her eyelids heavy. She took off her hat and placed it in her lap. She leaned into the padded headrest and within minutes, lulled by the car's movement, fell into a gentle half-sleep.

'Judith, we're here,' whispered the vicar, shaking her arm gently to rouse her.

'Gosh, I'm so sorry. I haven't been sleeping too well lately.'

'That's okay. Your snoring wasn't too distracting.'

'My goodness,' said Judith, flustered.

'I'm joking. You only fell asleep fifteen minutes or so ago.'

They got out of the car. They were parked in a cul-de-sac, and Judith walked a few steps behind Lee, watching his shadow dance across the pavement ahead of her. He promptly took out a set of keys and unlocked the door to a newly built townhouse, with a tiny square front garden.

'Megan? Tom? I'm home,' he called out, placing his keys on a strip of beach hanging on the wall above a small, highly polished console table.

'In the kitchen,' called a soft female voice. 'Tom's still working. He should be here soon.'

'So pleased to meet you,' said Judith, shaking Megan's hand.

'Sorry, I'm covered in flour. Thought I'd bake some muffins but I'm not sure they're going to rise,' she said, nodding towards the oven. 'I forgot to add the baking powder.'

'They smell delicious,' said Judith, balancing on the kitchen stool, placing her handbag on the worktop.

She watched as Megan wiped the flour from her hands onto a tea towel, its corner singed. She wiped down the kitchen surface she'd been working at with a damp sponge. Judith already liked Megan not only because she appeared to be as messy a baker as herself but because of her friendly and unassuming manner.

'So, you're going to help us relocate to the village with Lee?'

'Not physically, not with my creaky bones, but I'm hoping to smooth the way, with Tom's help. Has Lee filled you in on my idea?'

'Yes, and Tom's excited about it. He's a good boy really. He's turned his life around and he's paid the price for what he did. Surely people will see that.'

Tom appeared in the kitchen doorway. 'Hi, I'm Tom.'

Tom's muscly stature seemed to swallow up the space in the tiny kitchen. He stuck out his hand and Judith shook it. His handshake was strong, and his hand felt sand-paper rough in her soft fleshy palm.

'Hello Tom. Pleased to meet you,' said Judith and she genuinely felt glad to be there.

'I'm guessing you're all talking about me?'

'Well, not directly, but about you moving to the village with your mum,' said Judith and then addressing Megan and Lee said, 'It will take time, but they'll come around, even the stubborn ones, the judgmental ones, will welcome you all as members of our community… eventually. They won't be able to resist Tom with what I have in mind.'

Judith explained her idea in more detail and by the end of it Tom had been persuaded. Between them, they hatched a practical, workable plan to win the affection of the villagers, and especially Lee's parishioners, Megan made a pot of tea and one of filtered coffee. She carried them over to the small dining area of the kitchen on a wooden tray and offered round the muffins which had predictably sunk in the middle.

As Megan emptied the tray of its contents onto the table, Judith noticed a faded print of a magpie on the base.

'That's pretty,' she commented, running her hand over her face in agitation.

'Lee's mum painted it as a birthday gift. She's always loved magpies.'

'Is she an artist?' asked Judith, leaning in to have a closer look at the design.

'She's incredibly talented. Magpies feature in most of her work. Kind of her signature,' said Lee.

'Does she live around here?'

'Not far. She's stayed pretty local all her life. Roots and all that.'

'Lee says you used to teach art. Where does your talent come from?' asked Megan, seemingly steering the conversation, which made Judith all the more suspicious.

'Yes, retired now, though I still like to paint when the muse finds me.'

'How's the muffin?' asked Lee.

'They taste so good,' said Judith with a full mouth. 'Who cares about the dip in the middle. You could use that as a selling tool... a "fill your muffin dips with" approach... strawberry butter icing, Nutella cream or lemon curd. I'd eat them all.'

'Ingenious, creative and entrepreneurial,' said Lee, between mouthfuls.

'Do you think so? I'd love to but always feel so inadequate when I see the likes of all those master bakers on *The Great British Bake Off*.' Judith nodded, declining to mention her own lack of baking skills, and a sparkle lit up Megan's eyes. Judith saw a flash of determination there, the same she'd seen in Tom's eyes, and she knew her plan would work.

'You can bake a tray or two for the Summer Fete, see how you get on.'

'Really? That would be great. Thank you so much,' said Megan, but Judith noticed Lee shrink into himself, his earlier enthusiasm quashed, which left Judith a little suspicious, but she couldn't work out why.

'These really are quite delicious,' said Judith, taking another bite, breaking the awkward silence. Megan beamed across from her and Lee squeezed Megan's hand.

'That's a great idea. We need as many goodies as possible. And anyway, we can't expect the vicar's wife not to contribute to the biggest event of the year, can we?' said Lee, seemingly shifting the darkness which had creased his face only seconds before.

***

On the way home, clutching the proposed stage set up and rigging Tom had already worked on, Judith and Lee chatted amiably. The temperature had dropped, and the fan of the car heater whirred in time with the vibrations of the car's tyres as they rolled over the road.

'With my sermon on Sunday to pave the way do you think people will start talking and wondering?'

'Almost definitely. I know I shouldn't criticise but if there's one thing I know, about your parishioners, it's that they like a good gossip. Let them stew for a couple of weeks, reveal the project and they will gladly welcome the addition to their fete. Once underway you'll be able to set them straight. What can they possibly say after that? They won't reject him or his generosity, not when it benefits them and the village. It's a win-win. I promise.'

'I have to accept and believe in the benefit of your standing in the community. It's been hard fitting in. I know they think I'm too young and inexperienced, but I do like being here. It feels right and once Megan and Tom are with me…'

'It will feel like home,' said Judith, a stab of envy swallowing her up as she realised, she wanted it to feel like home for her too, and though it did more and more there was still something missing.

Chapter 34

Judith slipped into the back of St Barnabas unnoticed. The Sunday service had already begun, and she sat down, the pew rickety under her weight. She recognised the majority of the congregation from the backs of their heads: Paul's thick black hair, Kerry's soft mousy waves sitting on her shoulders, the familiar pink head scarf of the village's gossiper, the woman whose silver-grey hair was always tied in tight chignon at the base of her neck...

'I was talking with one of our own community, earlier this week, she doesn't frequent church, but she is a wise woman,' Lee looked up from the pulpit, almost instinctively, and briefly met Judith's gaze before looking back at his sermon. Judith felt her cheeks colour, hoping no one would recognise the person he spoke about as her. She looked up and observed Lee, how he leaned onto the pulpit and paused for effect, creating anticipation amongst his audience. The daylight exaggerated his authority as it bounced through the stained-glass window, casting a rainbow of brilliance around him.

'Think back to when you were at school writing or drawing and you made a mistake, what did you do? It's easy to answer, isn't it? If, like me, you rushed things and wanted to finish your work quickly, you would have made many mistakes. So, you used the eraser on the other end of the pencil. God's forgiveness is not too different to the eraser you used,' he said, holding up a standard drawing pencil. He pointed to the little pad of white rubber on the end, the ferrule around it glinting in the light.

'God's forgiveness is a lot like this eraser. We all make mistakes, and God is always ready to forgive us, if we ask. And just like this eraser removes the mistakes we made with a pencil; God's forgiveness can remove our sin when we do something wrong. We all make mistakes, me included. I could stand here and fill the whole morning with a list of my mistakes, accidental, unintentional, some foolish, yet mistakes all the same.'

Judith watched as some of the congregation looked at each other, leaned into each other and whispered. She knew they were already asking what mistakes their vicar had made and who knew about them.

The vicar opened his bible and read, '*Matthew Chapter 18, Verses 21 to 22.* Then Peter came to Jesus and asked, "Lord, how many times shall I forgive my brother when he sins against me? Up to seven times?" Jesus answered, "I tell you, not seven times, but seventy-seven times." But you know, some of us have made many mistakes, perhaps too many to remember or to count. So, look at this pencil.' He held a second pencil up in the air and pointed to its worn-down eraser.

'What do I do if this is the only pencil I have? I can't erase my mistakes anymore. I'm going to have to live with them. I have to have an eraser. In fact, can you imagine if you had to live life without an eraser? What if your teacher didn't allow them?' He paused for effect, wiped his brow, and continued.

'But I have a bigger question for you all today, my question is this: what if God didn't allow them? But we all know God's not like that at all. God's forgiveness is not like that. When we do something wrong, we can ask God to forgive us and because of Jesus, He will erase our mistakes and we can start over again, and again, and again. Unlike these pencils, God's eraser never wears out,' he said, raising his voice a touch for emphasis.

'Just as God forgives us over and over again. Jesus taught us that we should forgive other people their mistakes, over and over again.' He put down the pencil and looked around at the faces looking back at him.

'Let us pray, Dear Lord, thank you for forgiving us… and forgiving us… and forgiving us… and forgiving us again. Jesus, help us to remember that we all make mistakes and that if we ask you to forgive us, you will erase our mistakes and make us clean again.'

The choir sang the opening hymn.

'Now let us sing "The Joy of Forgiveness",' the vicar's voice announced, and the congregation all stood; a shuffling of feet, creaking of the old, worn-down pews, and the sound of flimsy pages turning, filled the church.

The organist began to play, and everyone sang.

Judith had no hymn book to follow in the back row, so she mouthed the few words she remembered and just moved her mouth to the majority she didn't. She listened to the out-of-tune voices always to be found amongst the parishioners and the extra loud voices which overpowered and drowned the others. A strange but comforting sensation filled her.

The small church hall, octagonal in shape, with tall windows, each with an iron sconce on the wide stone windowsill, quickly filled to the brim with parishioners; tea was served by the church committee every third Sunday in the month. Judith smiled and chatted briefly to a few of them and then wall-flowered into position at the edge of the room, watching and listening.

'Do you think he's heard about Betty's grandson?' asked one lady as she filled her plate with three sandwich triangles filled with ham and two chocolate digestives.

'I'm thinking I should come clean about that little scrape I had with the post box...' a man with a wiry head of ash-grey hair was saying.

'Patsy, I want to say how sorry I am about what I said about your rose bushes. They are beautiful and I was being mean. I was jealous. Of course, you don't buy that ridiculously expensive rose fertiliser. I should never have accused you of doing that.'

Judith continued to ear-wig on the conversations around her, sipping her tea from the white polystyrene cup, as she stood by the back wall of the church hall. Her ears pricked up at the mention of the vicar, finally, and she smiled.

'I guess our own vicar must have something he wants

to be forgiven for.'

'He's only human.'

'It depends on what it is. I've always wondered why he's not married, handsome man like that.'

'Maybe he has a lover.'

'Oh, no. He looks too loyal to be involved in some illicit relationship.'

'A wife we don't know about?'

It worked. Part A of the plan was underway, and Judith allowed a little smirk to dance across her lips.

Lee had taken some persuading, believing he was using the sermon in an underhand way, but Judith was quick to point out how many of his congregation would benefit from the teachings on forgiveness and how this might just work in his favour.

'Judith. Whatever are you doing here?' asked Lou, juggling her hot beverage and a piece of marble cake in one hand, her rolled crossword magazine under her arm.

'I attended Sunday service this morning,' said Judith, taking the magazine from her.

'What are you hiding?' Lou gave her a suspicious look while offering Judith a bit of cake which had broken in half in the paper napkin wrapped around it.

'Nothing,' said Judith, shaking her head. 'Stop looking at me like I've got something terminal.'

'That's it!' Lou screeched and then crouched behind Judith to avoid the stares.

'For God's sake,' said Judith, through clenched teeth, and then calmed down realising her mistake too late.

'The answer to that blasted clue. Sorry God,' she said, her eyes raised towards the ceiling, and then carried on in a half whisper. 'A seven-letter word. Judith, you're brilliant. Final parts concealed by one minister after another it's TERMINI... minisTER MINIster. The answer's hidden in the two words one after the other. Why didn't I see that before?'

'Lou, really?'

'Sorry,' said Lou and then changing the subject, 'Why didn't you come and sit next to me?'

'I was a little late. I didn't want to disturb the service.'

'I need to apologise to Ashleigh. We rowed last time she called,' said Lou, more sombre now.

'She'd have forgotten by now,' said Judith but, realising her mistake added, 'But of course it's good to forgive and ask for forgiveness.'

Lou stifled a giggle then and they both nodded their heads in agreement.

Chapter 35

'So, you think it's working?' Lee asked Judith a few days later.

'It's certainly got everyone talking and asking questions about you… I heard more than one person mention the word wife not only on Sunday but again in the post office and in the butchers.'

Lee ran his hands through his hair and then fidgeted with his dog-collar, pulling at it, as if trying to cool himself. His kitchen was stiflingly warm despite the two sash windows extended fully.

'So, Part B of our mission is going ahead?'

'Yes, why not?'

'Okay. Megan has messaged. She's already on her way and will be here in about half an hour.'

'Busiest time of the day and tongues will be wagging when she's spotted walking towards St Barnabas. Greet her at the gate and make sure you kiss.'

'I won't have any problem doing that.'

'I'm sure you've missed her. It can't have been an easy decision to leave her, especially with Tom coming out of custody.'

'No, it wasn't but it's what we both decided was best.'

'And the tea shop has agreed to trial her muffins?'

'Yes… it really is a Cup of Happiness indeed and it's all thanks to you.'

Judith finished her tea and got up to place the mug in the sink. The dustbin had been emptied since her last visit, but a piece of paper had slipped part way under the kickboard. She bent to pick it up and the distinct logo of Winsor & Newton caught her eye.

'Thanks, Judith, for all your support. You've been marvellous about all of this.'

'Not at all,' said Judith, pressing the little paper scrap between her fingers and slipping it into the pocket of her dress. Her heart thumped. She couldn't wait to leave and did not stop at the gate with Lee who was in position waiting for Megan to arrive.

The school bus had pulled up and piles of sweaty children clambered off, relieved, like Judith, to be out in the open. Parents milled around just as Judith had predicted and she looked on as they greeted their offspring with open arms, ice lollies and cool bottles of drink.

Chapter 36

'You're being ridiculous.'

'Am I? He's one of the few people who knew how hard I was finding this retirement business. He knew about my pastoral duties at school.' Judith had left the vicarage and gone straight to Louise's, feeling discombobulated, and not for the first time in Lee's company.

'Because he's, our vicar. He wouldn't mislead you like that.'

'Why wouldn't he? He's…' Judith stopped herself from blurting what she knew of his guilty secret and instead said, 'he's only human.'

'He's our vicar and your friend. He's probably ordered it for one of his elderly parishioners or for the art classes.'

'What art classes?'

'In the church hall… he's trying to build his flock… a volunteer runs them. Older than us, apparently,' laughed Lou.

'Ha-ha. I read about them in his last newsletter. Sorry. I'm tired.'

'What you need is a glass of wine.'

Lou retrieved a bottle of red from the dresser and poured two generous measures into wine glasses. Judith sipped slowly, savouring the smoky walnut notes, while Lou opened a bag of salt and vinegar crisps and a packet of roasted peanuts. Judith watched her as she struggled to split the bag but they both laughed when she sent peanuts flying across the room.

'Blasted arthritis,' Lou blasphemed.

Lou's mobile pinged and she shared the image of the vicar in an uncompromising embrace. Judith hadn't loitered to witness people's reaction around her but, gathering from the photo flying around, the vicar kissing a woman never seen before, had created a stir.

'At least it's not another blurred image of that flasher everyone's talking about,' said Judith.

She knew the photo of the vicar kissing a woman would create a stir but the imagined excitement, from her plan's successful outcome, was not forthcoming.

She felt impassive with the other matter still on her mind. *What was the vicar doing with an order from Winsor & Newton? Those paints were expensive, used by those who took their art seriously, painted professionally.*

At home, undressing for bed, Judith wondered whether Lou was keeping something from her. She hated doubting her friend, but surely an art teacher would bring all the materials needed for art lessons with her. She'd have an endless supply of everything. She brushed her hair and with each stroke combed her fingers through the soft wavy strands.

'Guess I'm not being totally honest with Lou either…
oh what a mess,' she said to Jasper who waited impatiently
for her attention. She scooped him up and stroked his fur
before gently putting him down on an old tartan blanket,
once used for summer picnics and now reserved for him
at the foot of her bed.

Chapter 37

Judith, pottering in her front garden, heard a commotion: running footsteps, raised voices. She put down her watering can and wandered out into the street, wiping her hands on her mother's old garden apron, one of her mother's many prizes won over the years in various local gardening competitions. Looking towards the village green she saw Ian gesticulating wildly to a group of flustered parents and excitable guardians, children milling around him. The school bus driver seemed to be amid the melee; she recognised his high-viz gilet and black cap.

'Harry and Charlie have gone missing,' puffed Lou, disappearing as quickly as she had appeared. Judith, lagging a few feet behind her, ran to where the school bus was parked.

'How could you not have noticed they weren't on the bus?' Ian was screaming at the bus driver who was full of panic. 'You're always the first to complain about them.'

'That's not helping. Let's phone the school,' suggested Judith as she approached them, firmly back in teacher mode and quietly relishing the control. 'Maybe they had an after-school club or decided to go to a friend's house.'

The call to school couldn't confirm anything concrete. The caretaker agreed to do a sweep of the main building and grounds. Finally, fifteen minutes later, he called back assuring them the school was empty and the headteacher who had already left for a meeting at the council offices had been notified of the boys' failure to reach home.

'I have to find them,' wailed Ian. 'That flasher still hasn't been caught. I need them home with me.'

The adults hurriedly dispersed with their children not wanting them to witness Ian's anguish. Some of the older kids suggested where the boys might be but none of them recalled seeing them after the end-of-day bell rang. The adults still milling around split into groups of two and three and left in the direction of an area to search.

'Judith and I will take the old path behind St Barnabas and down to the woods,' said Lou. Both women raced home and gathered what they needed. Ten minutes later, they ventured out into the woods holding their torches, a blanket each just in case, and a basic first aid kit.

'I don't know why you didn't let the men come in this direction,' said Judith, struggling on the uneven path. 'Honestly, Lou, you just don't think sometimes.'

Her friend opened her mouth and closed it as if about to say something but had thought better of it. The further into the woods they walked the dimmer it became under the canopy of trees. The overhanging branches, dry splitting limbs reaching out like forest ghosts, cast dark shadows across the narrow and twisting path. With their senses on high alert Judith jumped and flinched at every snap and whoosh. Judith shivered as the temperature dropped; the deeper they went, the thicker the wooded area became choked with brambles.

'It's not so pretty out here when you're on edge,' said Judith.

'No, but we're together. If we don't find them, someone else will. They probably missed the bus and decided to take the scenic route home.'

'Kids lose track of time. It's easily done.'

'I hope so,' said Lou.

'It wasn't that long ago they both disappeared into the woods looking for magic mushrooms. They're a handful.'

'And they got into trouble for it. They just don't listen,' said Lou.

'They're just inquisitive, adventurous,' said Judith, as she navigated a fallen tree across their path. She peered down at its branches reaching out like torn limbs with bony fingers, dappled in lichen, palest green upon the weathered bark. Behind her, there was a thud.

'Ouch,' Lou yelled. She lay sprawled across the detritus; half covered in fallen leaves and branches, bark, and stems, all in various stages of decomposition.

Judith dropped her rucksack and knelt down next to her, inspecting the hot swell already pushing against her trainers, around her ankle. 'You've twisted it. Oh, Lou... here, let's wrap the blanket around you, you're shaking.' Lou looked pale and clammy; a vulnerability there not witnessed by Judith before.

'Help me up,' demanded Lou eventually. She stands and waits with bated breath as if waiting for all her joints to settle.

'I don't think you've broken anything.'

'I can't walk on this anymore,' said Lou, her words coming in breathless gasps. She lowered herself onto a mound of earth pushed up by the protruding roots of a tree and hitched up her skirt. Her ankle was swollen and stiff, red, and hot to the touch.

They had no choice but to abandon the search, and even more so because the daylight was quickly fading, the forest becoming darkly foreboding.

'What are we going to do?'

'I don't know. This arthritis is wearing me down. I'm so sorry. I'm such a fool.'

'Stop that talk. Let's rest up and try again in a few minutes.'

As they sat together, Judith closed her eyes and the sounds of the woods closed in on her like a suffocating haze. Snaps and cracks and gloomy-thick rustling, as insects and animals moved about hidden from view, added to her growing unease. What if they didn't find the boys and what if she and Lou stayed in the woods all night? What if something worse happened?

'Lou, there's something I need to tell you.'

'Now's not the time for stories, Judith.'

'It's something which happened to me, in my thirties, after my divorce.'

'Don't go over old ground. It doesn't change anything and always makes you feel worse.'

'But I want to tell you something, something serious.'

'You really do pick your moments,' said Lou, wincing.

Just as Judith plucked up the courage to reveal her secret Lou cried out in pain, and then again in shock as they heard something. The moment was lost. Judith jumped up waving her torch in a wide arc from left to right and back again in front and then behind her. The crunch of running footsteps echoed around the small clearing.

'We've gotta get out of here.' Judith's voice came out in a high-pitched panic. 'Come on, up you get, that's right, and lean your weight into me.'

The veiled darkness closed in around them like a wizard's purple cape and though Judith tried to support Lou she stumbled under the weight of her, toppling over too, but a tall tree stopped her fall, as she reached out to it.

'Hold on, stop,' said Lou.

Judith pricked her ears. 'A voice. Hello!' called out Judith. 'Hello. Help, help!'

'It had better not be that flasher!'

From the shadows a figure appeared making them both recoil in fear, their sharp senses making them as overly sensitive as each other. Judith's heart banged against her ribcage.

'It's me, Geoff.'

'Thank goodness,' said Judith, her heart still pounding. She let out a sigh of relief, sensing his smile in the semi-darkness.

'Judith? What are you doing all the way out here? What happened?'

'Geoff, thank goodness. Lou's hurt herself. She's too heavy for me,' said Judith.

'I weigh less than you,' Lou managed, gritting her teeth through her obvious pain, and then contorting her face into an anxious smile.

'Sorry, Lou. You know what I mean.' They both smiled at each other, the knowing smile friends keep for each other.

Geoff wasted no time. He took over from Judith, hauling Lou onto her feet carefully and though disappointed at abandoning their search, Judith also sensed Lou's relief to be going back to the village. She smiled inwardly at seeing how her friend's whining had ceased and Lou seemed extremely at ease in such close proximity to Geoff.

Judith explained their reason for being so far out in the woods and as they came to the opening, leading them to the back of the church grounds, Judith heard the faint cheer of voices.

'They must be home,' said Judith.

'Thank goodness for that,' said Lou. 'Now please get me home. This damsel in distress is in dire need of a glass of wine.'

Chapter 38

'I've made you a ham and pickle sandwich and here's a shot of brandy for the shock,' said Judith as she fussed over her friend. Propped up on Judith's couch with two pillows and a warm blanket over her, the colour had slowly returned to Lou's cheeks.

'I'm sorry. I can be so clumsy sometimes,' said Lou, nibbling at the sandwich, eating all the crust first.

'Don't apologise. Lucky for you Geoff turned up when he did.'

'What's that little smirk for?'

'You did look rather comfortable in his arms.'

'I had no choice. I twisted my ankle, or have you forgotten?'

'Geoff's touch will have you healed in no time.'

'He did rather take his time wrapping the bandage around it,' said Lou, letting out a giggle.

'Those boys have a lot to answer for. Taking off

into town like that without their father knowing. Not answering their mobiles.'

'We're all safe now,' said Lou dreamily, reaching for the abandoned newspaper and turning to the puzzle page.

'Cooking equipment taken back from heiress I tormented, ten letters,' said Lou out loud.

'You need to rest,' said Judith, taking the paper from her. 'Taken back from "hEIRESS I TORmented". Let me have a look,' Judith said, but totally stumped for an answer she passed the newspaper back to Lou.

Judith watched as Lou scrunched her face in concentration, thinking. 'It's ROTISSERIE,' said Lou, but without her usual excitement.

'You're lucky Geoff came along when he did,' said Judith.

'At least my brain's still working.'

But Judith's mind was elsewhere. 'Geoff and Louise. Louise and Geoff. Has a nice ring about it,' said Judith, taking a bite out of her own sandwich.

Lou threw one of the cushions at her. 'You're being quite intolerable,' she said, but Lou was smiling.

Chapter 39

Judith fussed over her hair, usually slick and straight, today it frizzed, and static possessed it, sending it in all directions except flat against her head. In the end she took a wide velvet hairband and swept it up and away from her face. Everything irritated her. She was unable to keep her hand steady to apply her eyeshadow and after two attempts washed it off. She smoothed a quick sheen of foundation across her skin, coated her lips in a cherry red lipstick and smacking her lips together put the lid back onto the stick.

She glanced at herself in the hallway full-length mirror. Maybe she was overdressed. Perhaps the pair of black trousers would be better. She peered back into the bedroom, clothes piled haphazardly all over the bed, the floor. She dashed back in and scooping them all up she dumped them in the bottom of the wardrobe. She caught the sleeve of her father's jacket in the door; the jacket she couldn't bring herself to throw away even though the hole in the pocket meant her loose change disappeared into its lining every time she wore it. She would sort the clothes out later, tomorrow, maybe never.

Surprisingly, despite the on-off-on-off one-woman fashion show she was ready before Matt's pick-up time. She fiddled around with the cushions, her long skirt swishing as she moved around quickly. She rearranged the nic-nacs on the mantelpiece; finding anything to fill the excruciating forty minutes she still had to wait. Jasper, picking up on her nerves, meowed and missing his litter tray, peed on the kitchen floor, sending an ammonia, stale-like odour into the air.

'Now's not the time to be messing around, Jasper,' said Judith. Squeegeeing the urine, she deposited the wet mop outside her kitchen door, leaving it ajar in the hope the smell would disperse before Matt arrived.

Panicking, she dashed into the bathroom, grabbed the vanilla-scented toilet spray.

'This'll do the trick, Jasper. What will Matt think if he comes in and smells cat pee everywhere?'

Nerves on edge, she shook the sofa cushions again, plumping them, and tidied the pile of magazines in the corner of the sitting room. She fiddled with the hand-painted pottery and carved dolls above the mantelpiece and the woven basket on the dresser. She picked up the pot of dusty pot pourri which didn't smell of orange and cinnamon anymore and emptied it into the hearth. She licked a finger and rubbed at the coffee stains on the coffee table. Failing to remove the marks she wet the corner of a tea towel and rubbed more vigorously.

She stacked her art equipment behind the sofa; part of her wanted to keep it all out, scattered, a prick on her conscience to persevere until her own creative mojo returned but mostly because it reminded her of the impromptu painting session, she'd had with Matt earlier in the week.

But it felt good to have some resemblance of order in the tiny house with its low ceilings and thick walls… she had changed her bedsheets too and had laughed as she got tangled in the duvet when usually she would have filled with frustration; a heat had whipped around her as she imagined lying in bed with Matt. She had never had anyone in this house… and not for a long time.

'Coming,' she shrilled, rather too high pitched, when she heard a rap at the porch door.

'Hello,' said Matt and Judith felt the colour rise in her cheeks as he looked her up and down. 'You look incredible.'

'Thank you. You look nice too,' she said, a tiny tremor of nerves in her voice. She hoped he hadn't noticed.

'You had a tidy up? Hope it wasn't for my benefit?'

'Just whizzed around, you know,' said Judith, trying to play down the obvious effort she'd put in; Matt visiting in the evening, even for a few minutes, felt more intimate, close.

'Not nervous, are you?' and he held out his hands to her.

'Maybe, a little.' Judith felt as if his big hands were wrapped around her whole being, not just her hands.

'Don't be. It's just dinner.' Judith gave him a half-smile. 'Ready?' he asked, letting go and stooping as though he distrusted the low ceilings.

'Yes. Keys, pashmina, handbag,' she said, breathing in the woody scent of his aftershave.

Judith toddled down the path, careful her heels did not get caught between the path's slabs. Matt opened the passenger door for her and waited for her to get into the car. She gathered her velvet skirt, sweeping the waterfall of fabric over her arm so as not to get it trapped in the door.

'I've booked a little Greek taverna, on the far side of town. I hope you're hungry because their meze keeps on coming.'

'Love meze. Some of the best food I've ever eaten was in Cyprus.'

'Greek olives, hot pitta bread, halloumi cheese, sea bass.'

'Delicious. I'm sure to love it. Cyprus is a beautiful place. I really should go back.'

'You're sure to like it then. The place is traditionally done up and we can dance too. Do you remember that boy Nick at school? My best friend? His family was from Cyprus. His cousin owns this place.'

'Will Nick be there?'

'No… he sadly passed away two years ago, and it wasn't the cancer that got him in the end... damn Covid. I've never cried over anyone like I did for him other than for my parents.' He visibly swallowed and Judith sensed his pain. 'Couldn't even pay my respects with all the restrictions at the time.'

'I'm sorry,' said Judith and she reached across to his hand where it rested on the gear stick. She cupped her hand over his where she left it; the warmth of his hand warming her palm.

'Don't be. He suffered for too long… in and out of hospital, chemo, radiotherapy… in the end he at least died in his sleep in his own bed at home. Surrounded by his family. There was no way they were going to let him go alone. With his family to the end… best way to go.'

'Life has an odd way of testing our strength and then snuffs the life out of us. We can drink to Nick tonight.'

'We can drink to Nick, and us, and life, tonight,' said Matt. He drove at speed, the trees either side whooshing past, a green smudge against a darkening blue sky. He swerved to avoid a fiery red fox in the road, everything stood still for a second, Judith tightened her grip on his hand on the gear stick.

'Hello, Mr. Fox,' breathed Matt and they continued more slowly. Judith kept her hand on his for the rest of the journey and imagined her heart beating in time with his.

Chapter 40

Nick's cousin, Demetri, welcomed them with genuine Cypriot warmth and hospitality, hugging Judith and giving her a kiss on each cheek as if reuniting with an old friend. He quickly showed them to a round table by the open bi-folding doors, overlooking a pretty cobbled courtyard strung with a net of glittering stars against the dimming night sky.

'To us,' toasted Matt as they chinked their filled glasses.

The first course arrived; shiny black olives, purplish-red beetroot steeped in olive oil and garlic, potato salad drenched in an olive oil, lemon and fresh coriander leaf dressing, butter beans in a tomato and onion sauce, warm pitta bread and of course houmous, tzatziki and taramasalata.

They both tucked in, and Judith was surprised at how uninhibited she was; she ate with a ferocious appetite which matched the growing excitement coming from the long table, clad in helium balloons announcing a sixtieth birthday celebration, on the other side of the restaurant. She relished the tastes and smells of all the small plates served, and she enjoyed Matt's easy conversation, despite having to raise their voices to be heard over the increasing volume of the other patrons' group celebrations.

She laughed too loudly at his jokes, and she listened intently to his tales of life as a farmer. When their knees touched under the table she didn't move; relishing the electric bolts his knee on hers sent through her.

'Thank you for coming out with me. I thought I'd messed it up by the river. I was so abrupt, rude. But when I realised who was there in front of me… well… I couldn't believe it.'

'You have a right to protect your land.'

'Come and dance, up, up,' said Demetri, pulling Judith and Matt up from their seats. Laughing, they joined in the dancing, making a circle by holding the hand of the person on either side of them and kicking up their legs. They flew round and round, the rushing air from their dancing caused the raffia-clothed water jugs and earthenware pots hanging from the ceiling to sway gently. Sepia-toned black and white photos on the far wall whooshed past like an old cine movie and Judith thought she recognised one of the faces smiling out at her from behind the glass. A waiter pushed his way into the middle of them, dancing in the midst of them with one, two, three and then a pile of four tumblers balanced on top of each other in a tower upon his head. The music, totally infectious, filled Judith to the brim with a happy sensation and she looked at Matt, opposite her in the ring, and laughed.

They fell into their chairs, both breathing heavily; all that dancing was hard work. She stood up and had a closer look at the framed photo; it was Matt and Nick. She remembered him now. She went to say something to Matt and thought better of it, not wanting to spoil their high-energy mood. She sat back down and reached for Matt's hand, as he pulled at his tie and undid his top button, cooling himself.

'Matt, thank you for tonight. I loved it. What a gentleman Demetri is too. Next time I will bring my jingly coin skirt so I can join in the belly-dancing.'

'You do that,' said Demetri and this is for you. He handed her a miniature terracotta pot with a painted map of Cyprus on it. 'So that you remember to return,' he said.

'We will,' she said.'

'And I'd like to see you do some belly-dancing. It's good to have such happy company.'

'For me too,' she said. 'It's made me feel alive.'

Matt leaned in to kiss her on the cheek but somehow Judith turned the wrong way, and they met in an awkward brush of lips against lips. Judith pulled away. Everyone would be watching, she walked towards the exit, the tingle of his lips still playing on hers.

'Matt?'

'Francis?' Matt instantly looked edgy, his relaxed posture stiffened, and though he recovered quickly Judith witnessed his awkwardness.

'Thought it was you.'

'This is… Judith… an old school friend,' said Matt simply, in an uncharacteristic fashion.

'I can see,' said Francis with a clipped tone rather like an old school mistress. 'How's Penelope?'

Judith's heart dropped at the words. Penelope? Who was Penelope? She lowered herself onto one of the seats reserved for waiting take-away customers close to the front.

'She's a little better. I will send your best wishes to her.'

'Please do. Tell her I will call around mid-week to check on her, see if she needs anything.'

Francis turned round and walked back to the long table, the noise more raucous than ever, without so much as glancing in Judith's direction.

'I know what you're thinking but let me explain in the car.'

'Is Penelope your wife?' asked Judith, not moving.

'Yes, but we don't live together, we haven't for a long time. She's unwell, she's in a care home eight miles away. We are not together.'

'You told me she left you,' said Judith, her hands working the corner of a folded linen tablecloth discarded on the banquette, scrunching and unscrunching it in a repetitive motion.

'She did. That was my first wife.'

'And you didn't think to mention you had a second wife?'

'I wanted to. I was looking for the right moment, the right time.'

'Well, now's the time Matt.'

Chapter 41

'So, how was the kiss-and-make-up date with Matt?' asked Lou as she dunked her digestive into her mug of tea. 'You're beaming. So, you're back on, seeing each other?'

'I've invited him for dinner tomorrow.'

'Judith. I'm so happy for you.'

'Can I have your recipe for that stuffed chicken… the one with the feta cheese?'

'You really like him, don't you?' asked Lou, pressing Judith for an answer, knowing the answer to her question already.

'I always liked him, perhaps I even loved him. I don't think I ever stopped. But this thing with his wife is complicated, it doesn't sit right with me. That poor woman.'

'The universe works in the most mysterious ways. You need each other.'

'But it's cheating. Their vows, in sickness and in health, don't they mean anything?'

'She doesn't know… she won't ever come out of that place,' said Lou, her voice almost a whisper.

'That doesn't make it right.'

'Who's to say what's right and what isn't? We're human. He's human.'

'We're all flawed. My mother used to say that to me, "You're flawed, Judith. You don't realise it, but I see it all too clearly," and she'd pull on my hair so hard as if making me cry gave her satisfaction.'

'She was a tough one, your mother. Everyone in the village tip-toed around her.' Lou stopped herself mid-sentence. 'Anyway, she's not here now and you're the kindest soul I know.'

'I've invited Geoff too,' blurted Judith, tears threatening to fall but she didn't understand why. *She had accepted her cold relationship with her mother a long time ago.*

'Geoff?'

'It makes it feel less disloyal if he's here too. Please Lou, for me? I know you like him.'

'Now, you're clutching at straws.'

'And he's already asked if you'll be here,' said Judith, avoiding Lou's eye.

'That's very couply, isn't it? Like that's not going to be sending out the wrong message.'

Judith looked at her friend and Lou smiled at her. 'Who said anything about the wrong message,' said Judith through tears of mixed emotions.

'Pass me another digestive,' said Lou.

Chapter 42

Judith cooked in her usual no-frills style not wanting to ruin the fabulous stuffed chicken which was Lou's signature dish and which Lou had offered to bake. No cookery books, no measuring, just a sprinkle, a dash, and a mix. *Judith knew her food always turned out more successful that way, somehow worked so much better.*

Lou arrived shortly after Matt bringing with her the baked chicken dish, wine and after dinner mints. She put the still-warm oven pot on the kitchen counter, the wine, and mints on the kitchen table.

'What can I do?' asked Lou.

'Matt's in the garden. Go say hello.'

Judith continued to dress her salad and listened to Matt and Lou's voices filtering in through the open window, their polite conversation quickly taking on a more serious tone.

'So, you're still married Matt. I'm sorry about your

wife.'

'Yes, on paper… it's a delicate situation.'

'Exhausting too, I imagine.'

'And frustrating and heartbreaking to see her so frail, weak, lost.'

'What's the prognosis?'

'You know what care professionals are like. They say one thing, something else happens, they say something different. I barely take it in anymore. It's too cruel.'

'I guess they're not God.'

'No, and I'm grateful for their care of her.'

'And do you still love her?'

Judith dropped the vinegar bottle on the counter, her heart beating like a skin drum as she waited for his answer.

'I do. But we're not husband and wife in the true sense of what that should be. We have no relations.'

'I see. And Judith?'

'She's always been the love of my life. I just hadn't realised it until I saw her in the woods,' he said and Judith saw him lightly brush his fingers over his scar.

Judith leaned on the counter and squeezed her eyes shut. *Did he really feel like that about her? Was she ready for this?*

Geoff arrived and they jostled around the garden table, the al fresco vibe light and joyful. They all enjoyed Judith's feta cheese and dried fig tart and salad garnished with dandelion flowers and Lou's slow-roasted feta-stuffed chicken.

'What's your secret fetish, Lou?' asked Geoff.

'Lou is a mastermind when it comes to those cryptic

crosswords,' said Judith, panicking at the word secret.

'It's just practise. The more you do something the better you get,' said Lou, brushing away the compliment and not seeming to notice Judith's momentary discomfort.

Geoff's face lit up every time Lou spoke.

'Not sure crosswords are my strong suit, but I'd love to do some art again,' said Matt. 'If you can face spending the afternoon with a messy artist like me again, Judith,' said Matt, winking at her.

'Of course. It would be my pleasure,' she Judith, and inside she melted, not quite believing this handsome man wanted to spend more time with her, despite his troubles and despite the fuss she had made about his poor wife.

Matt kept everyone's wine glasses topped up and Lou made a beautiful toast which left Judith quite moved. 'To friends of old and friends of new, may we always have love and each other in our lives.'

After a pudding of nature's fall steamed pears and vanilla ice cream, Geoff and Lou offered to wash up together and Judith and Matt moved to the sitting room, taking another bottle of wine with them.

'Alone at last,' said Matt, the table lamp with the fringing softly illuminating his dark eyes.

'Not quite,' said Judith, looking in the direction of the kitchen where Lou and Geoff could be heard rinsing the dishes.

'It's been a lovely evening. A marvellous meal,' said Matt, his arms stretched wide across the back of the couch; the small room shrinking further by his larger-than-life presence.

'Washing up done. I'll be off Judith,' Lou said.

'I'll walk you back,' offered Geoff as Lou kissed Judith goodnight.

'Thank you, it's only across the road.'

'I'll see you tomorrow, my dear friend,' she said to Lou, as she got up from next to Matt.

'Sleep well,' said Lou, winking at Judith.

Judith and Matt stood at the end of the path and watched them walk off together.

'Always the gentleman,' said Matt as he waved goodbye and turned towards Judith.

The watery moonlight danced in the night sky above and Judith looked down, swirling her wine around the glass she still held; her heart beating a little too fast.

'Can I kiss you?' asked Matt. Judith hesitated. 'I've been wanting to kiss you since that kiss we had in our teens. Do you remember?' But before she answered, his lips found hers and his arms came around her.

'You remember that kiss?' she asked, pulling away, breaking the moment, trying to quash her awkwardness.

'I do. And since seeing you by the river, I haven't been able to stop thinking about it.'

Judith wiped her brow, conscious of a sudden heat gripping her.

'Did you enjoy tonight?' he asked instead, sensing her agitation.

'Yes, I did. Thank you.'

'Geoff and Lou certainly hit it off,' he said.

'And us? Have we hit it off?' he asked. Edging an inch closer to her, Judith could feel the tips of his shoes up against hers.

'I heard you talking to Lou, outside, before dinner.'

'You did?'

'Yes, I heard what you said. You told her you've always loved me.'

'It's true.'

'How?'

'If you hadn't gone away…' he said.

'But I did. I didn't realise. Had no idea.'

'How would you? We were kids. I didn't know until years later.'

'And Penelope?'

'We made a life. But my love for her was nothing to what I felt, what I feel for you.'

'Shush,' said Judith, and she gently ran her fingers over his scarred forehead.

'It's plain and simple. You've woken me up, with an exhilarating rattle, from a long slumber… no regrets.'

But so many regrets were coming at her, all at once: her strained relationship with her mother, pushing away from her father and running from Matt, the only love she ever knew, though she hadn't known it at the time, too young and too naïve.

'No regrets,' she said, and the night closed in around them.

Chapter 43

'Scrambled eggs and French toast? You're spoiling me,' said Judith.

'And tea the way you like it. Now sit up.'

Judith shuffled up the bed and pulled the duvet over her, tucking it under each arm to keep it from slipping. She steadied the breakfast tray on her outstretched legs.

'Where's yours?'

'Bringing it up now,' he said, and he leaned over and kissed her on the nose.

'I could get used to this.'

A few moments later Matt placed his mug on the bedside table and got into bed next to her balancing his breakfast plate in one hand.

'Me too,' he said, shovelling a forkful of scrambled egg into his mouth.

'So much has happened, we don't have to rush anything. Penelope's funeral was not even two weeks ago. Her family… well, I don't blame them for shunning me.'

'Don't you worry about them. The funeral was the first time I'd seen Penelope's family in years. They never supported her through this, vultures the lot of them. Every single one of them out to see what they can pick at.'

'That's family for you,' she said and looking up at Matt, she saw him crumbling in front of her. She jumped out of bed, abandoning their breakfast trays on the floor.

'Matt, let yourself cry. You're allowed to grieve for your wife,' she said, faltering and holding him in her arms she felt his bulk heaving against her as finally his tears fell. She stayed there, still, her arms wrapped around him until she began to ache from the weight of him. She gently pulled away. 'You don't have to hide your grief or your love for her from me. I understand.'

She picked up his tray and placed it in front of him. Eat. I'm going to take a bath.'

Downstairs, after bathing and dressing, Judith stood by the kitchen sink, looking out onto her garden. The colours were beginning to change, some flowers were fading, others blooming. 'So like life,' she said, feeling melancholic, feeling the weight of Matt's despair, his guilt, his pain.

'Now, about today…' said Matt, as he closed his arms around her waist from behind.

'We can leave the painting for today,' said Judith, turning to face him, but he couldn't look her in the eye.

'No, let's paint…' he insisted. 'Let's push away from this damn situation.'

Judith set up two easels side by side in the back garden. The space was tight, but she wanted to be inspired by the blooms and part of her didn't trust herself in an enclosed space with Matt. Her heart boomed at what had passed between them and she had to try and still it, otherwise she was sure to blurt it out like an immature teenager after their first date. She also wanted to be outside when she told Matt what she had done only a month before.

'Ready for your art lesson?'

'As ready as I'll ever be. I'm in good hands,' he said, pulling her to him, kissing her.

'And things are good between us?'

'More than good, amazing,' he said. 'And I'm sorry about before. Penelope... her going so suddenly, it's affected me more than I thought it would despite knowing the end was inevitable.'

'Don't apologise. She was your wife. I respect that. I respect you for standing by her all these years. You're a good man.'

They spent the morning painting, Matt surprisingly focused. For a big burly man, he painted with delicate, feather-light strokes but with an energy, Judith observed, which seemed to bubble and fizz. Judith kept stealing sideways glances at him; taking in his posture, his expressions as he painted, his air. He produced a beautiful garden scape of Judith's wildflower garden and at the moment when she imagined him to be near finished, he drew and deftly coloured a quiet, perching magpie.

'What's with the magpie?' she asked, curious, suspicious, her mind racing, her heart thumping.

'I don't know. One for Joy,' he said.

'What does that mean?'

'It means, one for joy. I don't know. Despite sadness, there's always something to be grateful for.' He hesitated and then said, 'You're my joy.'

She allowed herself to smile, expelling the tension through a long low release of her breath. He was here with her and that's all that mattered.

After a lazy late lunch of French bread and paté accompanied by homegrown cucumbers delivered by Bill that very morning, Judith's mind whirled with emotions; the two glasses of red wine emboldening her.

'Matt, I respect you and the difficult situation you've been in. And I want to tell you something. But please hear me out before you say anything.' *She had been agonising over telling him.*

'Okay, shoot.'

Chapter 44

It had been one of those days where the sunshine shone too bright and instead of giving Judith hope she despaired at what the outcome may be. She had looked up the location of the home where Penelope was being cared for and after a nervous call booked a visit.

'I'm a cousin. I don't live in the area and I'm visiting relatives,' said Judith, hoping she wouldn't get struck down by the web of deceit she was weaving.

'Penelope would love to see you for sure. But please, bear in mind, she may not remember, may not remember or be able to communicate with ease. She can be very muddled and confused some days.'

'Thank you, yes. I understand. I will see you on Thursday at one o'clock.'

Thank goodness that's done, she said to herself and then promptly climbed the stairs to her bedroom where she pulled out one dress and one skirt after the other before deciding on what she would wear.

She took the bus into the town and then another smaller bus which went as far as dropping her off a short walk from the home. She got off and gripped her handbag tightly. She hauled the tote bag over her shoulder and marched in the direction of her meeting with Penelope.

Judith had rehearsed what she wanted to say, had anticipated how she might feel meeting Matt's wife, thought about their conversation, wondered about the reaction she might get from Penelope, but none of it evolved as she imagined.

On arrival, Judith was prompted to sign the visitor's book and with a shaking hand she wrote out her name, the date and, checking her watch, the time of her arrival.

A young receptionist directed her towards the main corridor which led to the majority of the rooms on the ground floor. Once she arrived another nurse, probably notified via walkie-talkie of Judith's imminent arrival, appeared.

'You're Penelope's cousin? What a lovely day for her to have a visitor,' Iris babbled on. Her name badge was pinned to her uniform. The standard blue and white fabric stretched across her buxom breast which heaved up and down as she walked with vigour along another short corridor. Iris knocked on the door and without waiting for a reply, pushed it open.

Penelope was sitting in a comfy chair facing the tall windows which overlooked the garden. The floor-length curtains, scattered with a bright red poppy pattern, were pushed to the side, and held in position with wide matching sashes, trimmed in a gold brocade. She was bent over a notebook and scribbling, her pencil moving fast across the creamy pages.

'Penelope, dear. There's someone here to see you. I'll leave you to it. Have a lovely afternoon.'

The door quietly clicked behind Iris as it shut behind her.

Penelope didn't look up. She was immersed in what she was writing. Judith looked around the room, unsure whether to say something or just wait for Penelope to notice her. The double bed, with a smooth headboard of alabaster grey velvet complimented the heavy duvet, which had red and grey stripes across it with matching pillowcases. A wedding photo Judith recognised as Matt and Penelope hung on the wall above the bed, its gold-gilded frame somehow too heavy for it.

Two bedside cabinets, in a light cedar wood, flanked either side of the bed. One housed a collection of books, piled neatly in the cubby underneath, a pair of glasses and a bible sat on the top, a long-armed wall light pulled to one side. The other looked like a store for bottles of perfume, a toiletry bag and a spill of lipsticks and eyeshadows sat on the top next to a little bronze statue of Ganesh, the Hindu god of beginnings and a pool of sparkling crystals.

Penelope coughed and Judith looked round.

'Are you going to sit down?' asked Penelope. 'Don't stand there like a statue.'

Judith, not sure what to respond, moved towards the chair opposite, and sat with her handbag on the floor placed next to her, the tote bag on her lap.

'They keep telling me to write things down but it's

ever so difficult to remember it all,' Penelope said. She looked up and her eyes filled with tears. Judith noticed her eyes, the bluest, brightest eyes which shone out of the sunken, dark sockets around her eyes.

'Oh, I'm sure the order doesn't matter,' said Judith. 'It's getting the words down that matters. Then at least you have something to put into order when you do remember.'

'It's like being in that world of Alice in Wonderland,' she said and pointed to the framed print against the back wall. 'She had to adapt, got confused, tried again. Though sometimes I feel I'm going backwards. Silly tears,' she scolded herself, wiping the single tear which fell from her eye.

'I'd be happy to help you if you wish.'

'No, no one is allowed to see this,' she said, snapping the notebook shut and pressing it to her chest. 'And don't think you can sneak a read when I'm not looking.'

Judith, taken aback with her sudden outburst and show of aggression said, 'What would you like to do now that I'm here.'

'Can you comb my hair? And put some eyeshadow on my lids, the blue one, I would like to wear some of that today.'

Judith took the hairbrush from the dressing table and gently brushed Penelope's long blond hair. It was thin and a little wiry, but it fell past her shoulders in white, glistening strands. With gentle tugs, Judith combed the woman's hair, this stranger's locks, and thought of how her own mother would pull viciously at Judith's to the point she had to hold her tears back. This time, Judith let the tears fall freely, tears for this woman with a lost mind and tears for a much younger Judith who had yearned for this love from her mother.

Judith then, popped open the eyeshadow and with the pads of her forefinger smeared the blue across Penelope's crepey eyelids. The blue brought out her eyes, making them even brighter.

'Let's take a walk.'

Outside, with a woollen shawl wrapped around Penelope's shoulders and a pair of canvas slip on shoes on her feet, the blue skies were filling with cotton-wool drifts of cloud and the sun played hide-and-seek behind the tall poplars, cedar, and great oaks. Judith wondered how old the grounds were, some of the trees were easily over a hundred, maybe even two hundred years old.

'Beautiful gardens,' said Judith, patting Penelope's arm gently as she wound it with hers. A feeling of calm and a tinge of sadness filled Judith.

'Beautiful in the summer but sparse and bare in winter,' said Penelope. 'So, how come you're here?'

'I'm a friend of Matt's and wanted to say hello, you know…' Judith's voice trailed off, not sure how to explain, not really understanding herself why she wanted to meet Penelope.

'Hello.'

Judith stayed silent, toying with an explanation, what to actually say to this beautiful woman who was struggling with this awful illness, stripped of her memories, confused, childlike.

'Who's Matt?'

'He's the man you're married to.'

'I'm not married. I never married. Never had children.'

'I'm sorry.'

'I've been lonely for so long.'

'I'm here now,' said Judith, a little lost for words, losing her previous resolve to visit.

'They don't feed me in here, you know.'

'Shall I ask for some lunch? Are you hungry?'

'Did you bring me any fruit?'

'Yes,' said Judith and she hitched the bag, which was slipping, back onto her shoulder and breathed a sigh of relief at the change of subject. 'Yes. I brought all your favourites.' Judith was glad she had the foresight to ask the nurses for her most loved fruits in advance of visiting.

'Cherries, strawberries and kiwis,' she squealed, clapping.

'And lychees,' said Judith.

'And lychees,' Penelope said, licking her lips.

'Shall we sit and have some now?'

They found a bench, partly shaded by an apple tree in full blossom, a cluster of peonies filling the circular flower bed around its base.

They sat together, eating the cherries and the strawberries, some dropped to the ground from Penelope's shaky hands, her ability to grip difficult, but Judith left them there imagining the finches and bluetits, the blackbirds and sparrows would happily eat them. Penelope's face shone in the dappled light and then gleamed wet when a drizzle began to blow their way.

'Probably time to go back inside,' said Judith, packing away the uneaten fruit.

'I want to walk some more,' said Penelope.

'A few more minutes,' said Judith and arm in arm they took another stroll around the grounds, perfectly manicured lawns, clipped hedges, and an abundance of pretty flowers glistened beneath the settled droplets of the light rain.

'I hope Matt is happy. Happy soon,' said Penelope eventually, as she wiped a rain drop from the end of her nose.

'Do you remember Matt?' asked Judith, not quite sure where the conversation was leading and whether Penelope understood who Matt was.

'He's a good man.'

'He is a good man,' said Judith.

'He always loved me, but when I'm gone, when I go from here, I think he can love again.'

Judith pushed the lump in her throat back down and nodded, too afraid to speak, afraid her emotions would get the better of her.

'I hope you enjoy the rest of the fruit,' said Judith and she took the shawl from Penelope's shoulders and hung it over the radiator to dry. She leaned in and gave Penelope, now sitting back in her chair facing the gardens, a kiss on the cheek. 'It's been lovely meeting you.'

'Where's my pencil,' complained Penelope, snatching it from Judith when she handed it to her. 'Why did you take it?'

'You get on with your writing, Penelope,' said Judith and she picked up her handbag and left, letting the door shut quietly behind her. She leaned against it for a second, her heart beating a little too fast, and then she wandered back down the corridor and out into the drizzle again, towards the bus stop.

Chapter 45

'I visited Penelope.'

'I know you went to the care home.'

'You do?'

'I saw your signature in the visitor's book.'

'Why didn't you say anything?'

'I figured you'd tell me when you were ready. So, tell me. What's playing on your mind my beautiful Judith.'

'You're not upset with me?'

'Upset with you? How could I be?'

Judith swallowed, took a deep breath, and began to talk. 'Penelope was lucid that afternoon, far more than the nurse warned me and I'd anticipated. I took her for a stroll around the gardens, it showered, but only lightly and she didn't want to go back inside. We walked until we were almost soaked through with that pissy drizzle.' Judith paused; afraid she was going to burst into tears. 'She told me she wanted you to be happy, hoped you'll find someone after her. It was as if she knew she was going.'

'She never mentioned you to me, nor did I mention I knew you'd been to see her,' said Matt.

'She was very clear in her thinking towards the end of the day. The nurses said she was calmer, more together than she had been for a long time and thanked me for visiting.'

'She said she had been waiting for the day you'd meet someone before she left. She wanted someone to look after you. She wanted you to be loved.'

Matt fought back the tears and nodded, unable to speak.

'She was a brave woman,' said Matt, and Judith sensed his sharp pain of separation, but also recognised the pain in his relief.

'And two weeks later she was gone. So sad.'

'She deteriorated so quickly. The palliative care team was incredible. She died with dignity.' Matt leaned in and hugged Judith. 'I know it's sad but it's also a release. For her. For me. She went with such a peaceful expression, the covers pulled up to her neck,' he said.

'Part of me wonders if I hadn't visited her, if she hadn't guessed who I was, she might have held on.'

'Judith, please. You don't know that. You don't know she knew who you were. Don't do this to yourself, to us.'

'I can't help it, Matt,' she said, and she left the rest of what she wanted to say to him jumbled on the tip of her tongue.

'Let it go, my darling,' he said, and he pulled her into his chest, wrapped his arms around her and let his tears fall onto the top of her bowed head, buried against his heaving heart.

Chapter 46

'Matt stayed the night?' Lou asked, as they enjoyed a rare visit to the village tea shop; a chocolate cruffin for Lou, a lemon cream filled muffin for Judith, Megan's very own, and a pot of Earl Grey between them.

'Yes, he did. It felt right, Lou. You know, here, where it counts,' said Judith, placing her palm over her heart.

'There's a path from the eye to the heart that doesn't go through the head.'

'What are you saying?'

'I'm not judging. I don't know the last time I was intimate with anyone so at least one of us is getting some nookie.'

'Stop it. It's not about that,' said Judith, looking round to see if anyone was listening, but the place was full to the brim with Japanese tourists, licking their creamy lips and jammy fingers, enjoying the traditional tea served by the owner and snapping selfies in different poses and in all directions.

'I'm just messing with you. All I'm saying is you are allowed to have some fun.'

'I told him about visiting Penelope before she died.'

'You did? And?'

'He already knew. Saw my name in the register at the reception desk.'

'Not the best Miss Marple, are you?'

'Anyway, what's happening with Geoff?'

'You always do that.'

'What?'

'Deflect,' said Lou, stubbornness etched on her features.

'You're the one deflecting. Tell me, come on.'

'He's too serious. He's an over-thinker,' said Lou, but not meeting her eye.

'Like me, you mean?'

'No, like men can be… you know, he always seems to be strategising and plotting and fitting me around other stuff.'

'But that's good, no?' insisted Judith.

'I want to be the stuff he's planning other things around. I want to be his priority.'

'It's only been a few weeks, five? Six?'

'Exactly. If I'm not his priority now, then when will I be?'

'Give him a chance.'

'I'm trying but I don't want this to become an ick between us.' Judith gave her a quizzical look. 'You know, one of those things which breaks us apart before we've even had a chance to make anything happen,' said

Lou. 'I read about it in one of those magazine pop-up posts on my phone.'

Judith looked unconvinced but continued all the same, 'I see your point.'

'Anyway, let's get out of here. It's so noisy. Pub? We could share a bottle of wine, sit outside.'

'Why not? See what's happening on our doorstep,' chuckled Judith in a very unlike-Judith kind of way. 'I now know what my "Two for Joy" will be.'

Chapter 47

Judith had been toying with the second card for too long and now it all seemed as clear as a blue sky on a sunny day. Lou and Geoff. Together they also could be her "Two for Joy" and wondered when and how it would work out. She thought about Lou and her hobbies and having interrogated Matt about Geoff's leisure pursuits outside of farming, she hatched a plan and hoped the joy would come to Lou when Ashleigh visited. *If she visited. Perhaps she would have to make Ashleigh's visit happen.*

'Oh, fiddlesticks,' she blurted, her sudden outburst shocking Jasper into moving from one side of the room to the other.

Matt and Geoff arrived together, and by that time, she was in such a good mood she forgot how nervous she had been about seeing Matt again so soon after sleeping together.

Sitting in the beer garden of the village pub, Judith

chatted amicably with Louise, Matt, and Geoff, enjoying the relief of the breeze brought forth by the drop of the sun on the horizon and the closing in upon the evening.

'Matt says you're a sucker for puzzles.'

'Used to be, not so much nowadays. Always working up on the farm.'

'Perhaps Lou can get you back into it. She loves cryptic crosswords. We recently won another prize; an online book voucher.'

'Don't poo-poo it. I've got my eye on a wonderful Bronte collection.'

'Spend it how you like, Lou. You did most of the work. You deserve it.'

Lou gave her a look, then softened. 'No pressure, Geoff. Judith seems to think everyone has the time to pursue their hobbies just because she's retired. I mean semi-retired. Early retirement... oh, you know what I mean.'

'Yes, thank you. Lou,' said Judith with pursed lips, but Lou's comment seemed to go unnoticed by the men in their company.

'We've been lucky over the years. We've managed to grow a more diverse range of crops and rotating the sheep around the farm has eased things. Lambing season is finished now, so our farmers have a shorter day. Plus, our machinery, innovative and new, makes a huge difference to our output and the man hours we have to put in,' said Geoff.

'There's always something. But our team of three for general maintenance, erect fencing and repair our boundaries. That means we can stay focused on the crops and our herds,' said Matt. 'Then there's the crop spraying and the irrigation, but another team of men handles that side of things.'

'Sounds like a big business.'

'It is. Last year we were awarded Soil Farmer of the Year 2020. Covid hit so many businesses but we somehow managed to thrive.'

'What did you grow?'

'Spring onions, peas and potatoes,' said Matt.

'My parents used to take me pea-picking,' said Lou.

'You should come over and have a look. I'd be happy to show you around,' said Geoff.

'I might just take you up on that.'

'I can cook my famous pea soup for you.'

'I will bake some sourdough,' said Lou and Judith nudged her under the table, pressing her thigh against hers while trying not to laugh.

Chapter 48

Judith walked with a light step all the way back to Lou's cottage having gone home to shower and change; she had spent most of the afternoon helping Lou with the party preparations; her ankle still a little sore after her fall.

Judith even managed to rush off to the bakery to pick up a Victoria Sponge to replace the one she had miserably failed to produce. Her previously aching feet from all the standing, and her sore arms from all the stretching to hang bunting and strings of lights, now felt revitalised and she was ready to enjoy the party.

As she neared Wisteria Cottage, classical music grazed the quiet of the evening. Though the notes were beautiful and seemed to sway with the sweet scent of the budding jasmine clambering over Lou's arbour, an unwelcome apprehension waded in and seemed to suffocate Judith's joy; she slowed her pace, tried to shake it off. A feeling of foreboding clouded her thoughts, strangled the space around her. She convinced herself it was fatigue; she had overdone it.

She clutched more tightly onto her raffia-woven evening bag and tilting her chin in defiance she shook away the sudden claustrophobia and walked more forcefully across to Lou's party den. Scented tea candles in an array of glass holders twinkled along the pretty path as they guided her to the front door, the noise from within and beyond getting louder. She didn't bother knocking; the door, propped open with a pair of old wellington boots sprouting ivy tendrils and a burst of purple pansies, invited her in with a warm welcome.

'It's so good to see you,' yelled Ashleigh from the other end of the patio which stretched across the full width of Lou's home. 'And your Vicky Cake is delicious.' Ashleigh pushed past Paul and Kerry and tripped over a stone Zeus' head, covered in soft moss. White wine splashed the front of Ashleigh's blouse and the back of Kerry's dress, who had inadvertently blocked her path. Ashleigh reached out and grabbed hold of Paul's arm to stop herself from landing smack onto the slabs. Words of apology, incoherent, spiked with alcohol, spilled out frothy, insouciant.

'Ashleigh,' Judith said, forcing a smile; Ashleigh had clearly drunk too much already, and her behaviour was not the kind Lou readily accommodated. Ashleigh, oblivious, launched herself at Judith with clumsy force. Judith bumped into someone and turned to apologise. She caught the back of a tall slim man disappearing into the house, a trail of cigarette smoke behind him. A shudder, out of nowhere, snaked through her.

'Thank you for helping Mum. I was un-avoi-a-bly delayed,' Ashleigh said. 'Mum said you did most of this,' she said with a sweeping gesture. 'It looks great. I didn't know you still had it in you, Aunt Judy,' she said, through a mouthful of sponge. 'And Mum told me you both won a prize. She showed me her posh set of new books.'

'Not a problem,' said Judith, not bothering to explain her mother did most of the work and that the dessert was bought from the bakery. 'Your mum's been a good friend to me,' said Judith, trying not to give Ashleigh the once over. In Judith's day it was legs or boobs, not both and Ashleigh's outfit left little to wonder about.

'Mum told me about pea-soup Geoff. You're a secret matchmaker.'

Judith half-listened, edgy Ashleigh was goading her. Judith took a few seconds to pull her eyes away from where the shadow of the man hovered, sprawled across the garden wall. She shook off another shiver. She turned away, forced herself to survey the twinkle of fairy lights threaded in the fruit trees at the bottom of the garden and the glowing Chinese lanterns along the picket fence. A magical atmosphere yet she felt spooked.

'Who's that?' asked Judith, pointing back towards the man.

'Some prick I hang out with and who I'm totally in love with,' said Ashleigh.

'How much have you had to drink?'

'Not enough,' said Ashleigh and she spewed out a monologue of random thoughts.

Judith listened, as attentively as she could muster, to Ashleigh's tales of life in the city; drinking, hungover mornings, too many one-night stands, too many lovers to remember until she met the love of her life. Eventually, Ashleigh moved onto the next person and Judith jostled her way inside. Less crowded than outside, she walked over to the kitchen table and filled the bottom of a glass with the dregs of the last open bottle of wine.

'Red right?' asked a voice behind her.

She knew that voice. She hadn't heard it for years, but she recognised it instantly. Time seemed to slow down, everything around her fell away. It couldn't possibly be… could it? She quickly composed herself, found the strength to smile and turned around.

'Dan.' She faced him, the glass shaking in her hand. His face went in and out of focus: his almost orange sun-lamped skin, brilliantly fluorescent teeth, and sickeningly soppy smile. In this man's presence, everything falls away, her strength, her defences. Without asking, he filled it to the brim with Merlot; red spots, one, two, three, spattered the kitchen rug.

'Here, let me,' he said and cupping his hand over hers he moved the glass to her lips, forcing her to drink from it, his eyes not leaving hers once. 'I know how clumsy you can be. At least you used to be.'

'What are you doing here?' Judith said, swallowing too quickly, choking, swaying unsteadily. The camera flashed in front of her from all those years ago. She blinked, trying to focus her mind on the here and now; she didn't want to go back to his sleazy flat reeking of sex, the mattress clothed in black silk, the sickly smell of cheap vanilla candle wax, her head pounding yet unable to say no.

'I'm Ashleigh's plus one,' he said, an air of defiance there, ridiculing her, teasing her.

'Ashleigh's? How do you know each other?'

'We've hooked up a few times, you know.' He deliberately held her stare, waiting for a reaction. Judith's whole body burned. It burned red and angry.

'Hooked up? You're twice her age.'

'Jude, age is nothing. It's a number used to control our mind, our behaviour. Society's last hold on us.'

'I'm serious. How do you know her?'

'She came to one of my exhibitions. We clicked.'

'Keep away from her.'

'Too late for that. She's totally besotted by me. And me by her… she's very… what's the word… submissive.'

'You bastard!' spat Judith, her eyes boring into him, on fire, noticing an incriminating smudge of scarlet on his lips all too obvious.

'I'm playing with you. Calm bloody down. I've changed… I'm not the person I used to be.'

'Don't give me that. The fact that you're saying it after all this time…' She looked around for Matt, but her vision was blurred. The seconds stretched out, her heart raced, then she spotted Matt.

Judith pulled her hand away from under Dan's and the glass fell, breaking with a violent crack.

'Judith, I didn't see you arrive,' said Matt, seconds later. Matt wound his arm around her waist and planted her with a kiss. When he pulled away, pushing back her loose tendrils with tenderness.

'Someone's getting tipsy already,' said Dan, winking at her. *The bastard. Trying to diffuse the tension in typical Dan fashion.*

'I'm Matt, by the way.'

'Daniel,' said Dan and he extended his hand. 'We used to... teach together,' he said, glancing at Judith who was picking up shards of glass, her hands shaking.

'The college?'

'No, before that. Grove High Sixth Form,' said Dan, lighting another cigarette.

'Lou doesn't allow smoking in the house,' said Judith, her tone full of contempt.

'I'll head off outside. Would hate to upset Louise before she gets to know me.'

'Where's the dustpan and brush?' said Matt.

'No, let me,' said Judith, her spirits plummeting.

Judith disappeared towards the kitchen sink, her heart pounded in her ears, her legs trembled, barely able to carry her. She leaned onto the rim of the butler sink, a sick feeling rose within her and before she made it to the downstairs toilet, she retched into a recycling box of empty cans and bottles. She wiped her mouth with a tea towel and scrunching it up she hid it underneath the recycling.

She looked over at Matt, but he was engaged in animated conversation; Kerry and Paul chinking their glasses with his.

Judith escaped unseen to the little bathroom upstairs. She slammed the door behind her and locking it, leant against it, trying to calm herself. She swished her mouth out with water and rinsed with some of Lou's mouthwash.

She patted her cheeks to reduce the pink blotches of petechiae and made her way back downstairs.

'Let's try again,' she said to Matt, who had swept the last of the broken glass.

Matt filled another glass and smiled. 'So, the Victoria Sponge Cake…'

'Before you say anything else, yes. I bought it. The one I made is at home.'

'You haven't binned it, surely?'

'No, but it's where it will end up. Now what shall we toast to?'

'To us and cake and us,' he said.

Chapter 49

'The party to end the party of all summer parties,' said Lou, sitting by the kitchen table and nursing her head, a glass of water and an empty blister of paracetamol next to it. 'My head hurts and Lord knows where Ashleigh is. She didn't stay here last night. That boyfriend of hers booked a room at Meadow Hall Estate, don't you know it. Flashy, but she seems to like all that.'

'What did you make of Dan?'

'You mean Daniel?' asked Lou. 'Seems okay. Successful... his photos apparently are all over the Sunday supplements, exhibitions.'

'What sort of photos?' asked Judith, her heart missing a beat, a restless force suddenly radiating from within her.

'Portraits mainly, I think he said. 'Black and White. Elton John, Tina Turner, Madonna, Justin B someone...'

'I bet,' said Judith under her breath.

'Ashleigh speaks very highly of him. He's had features in all the celebrity magazines, Oscar-winning actresses and those economy business magazines too, big wigs in the world of finance and venture capitalists.'

Judith nodded, not really listening.

'D'you fancy a walk? Might clear your head,' said Judith. She needed to get out into the fresh air too; suddenly claustrophobic.

'I've got so much to do still. Look at the place,' moaned Lou.

'I'll give you an hour of my time, do as much as we can and then walk. Deal?'

'Only if I can have a shower first.'

'You go. I'll get started.'

Judith unlocked the windows, opening them until their rusty frames creaked, the action setting her own anxieties free. She breathed in the cool notes of early morning, shaking off her restlessness. She unravelled the roll of black bin bags, cut one free along the serrated edge. She shook it open, the bag billowed wide. Judith cleared the morning-after-the-night-before debris. She started with the kitchen, then the lounge and finally moved outside, the war raging inside her adding momentum to her movements.

She stacked three bulging bags by the refuse bins. One bag, split open from the night before, spilled out bottles and cans, dribbles of liquid staining the garden slabs. An insect slammed into the open window and found its way inside for a few seconds, then flew out again. That's how she felt.

Trapped.

Frustrated, fed up and furious.

'Judith,' shrieked Ashleigh as she waltzed out into the garden. 'Don't look so worried. I haven't bust in. Mum gave me a key last night.'

'Jude,' nodded Dan. 'Great night. You look good on only a few hours' sleep.'

'You timed that well,' said Judith deliberately looking at Ashleigh who drifted past her and discarding a paper plate caked with barbeque sauce onto the grass, slumped into a lounger. 'I've almost finished clearing up.' Judith picked up the plate and shoved it into the black sack.

'Time for a cuppa then,' said Ashleigh, up on her feet and waltzing to the kitchen. Judith followed her, leaving Dan outside smoking.

'Ash, love. I know this might sound weird coming from me but be careful with Dan.'

'With Dan? Whatever do you mean?'

'What do you really know about him?'

'What's to know? He's plastered all over the media. He's a star. He's going to be taking photos of William and Kate in two months… you didn't hear that from me, though.'

'Please just be careful. Ask him about his past. His past photographic career.'

'There's no past, no secrets between us. Don't scowl. You'll get those horrid frown lines even Botox won't eradicate.'

Judith realised she was wasting her time. Ashleigh, totally devoted to Dan, would not hear a word against him. What else could she do to protect Ashleigh?

In the sitting room, Ashleigh handed Daniel his mug of

coffee and sat down stretched across him; limbs, tangled like clinging ivy, entangled in Dan's legs, her flip flops dangling precariously at the end of her feet, her toenails painted scarlet.

'Thought I heard voices,' said Lou. The wet towel hung across and around her shoulders, her hair still wet, a trickle of water traced the side of her face and seeped into the crease of her neck. She dabbed at it with the end of the towel.

'Daniel wants us to go for a pub lunch. So, we're here to take you out, Mum.'

Chapter 50

In the end, Judith, persuaded to join them for lunch and not wanting to be the reason Lou missed out on a few more precious hours with her daughter, sat with her back to the wall of the pub's al fresco dining area. Lou sat next to Ashleigh and Dan slid opposite her and next to Judith.

Judith surveyed the comings and goings of the patrons as they arrived, ate, laughed, talked. It was an ordinary day apart from the fact it wasn't. Not for her. She had to make sure Ashleigh was safe. She owed it to her younger damaged, delinquent, desperate self and to her friend Lou. Ashleigh meant everything to Lou. She had to be clever about this, as cunning and as manipulative as Dan.

Paul thanked Judith for a great party and filled them in on the quiz night coming up later in the month and offered them a bottle of house red with his compliments, which they accepted graciously. The conversation between Dan, Ashleigh and Lou flowed as easily as the wine did. Judith, however, sunk into the background and listened, her smile strained and her conversation non-existent, though she nodded occasionally. She stayed off the red, wanting to stay clear-headed and alert.

The ploughman's lunch arrived; four white oval platters and two side dishes of chunky triple-cooked chips and an assortment of relishes and sauces crowded the round wooden table. Kerry served them alongside one of the weekend staff and expressed her thanks for inviting her and Paul to the party. Dan ordered another two bottles of red wine; his generosity construed as vulgar by Judith. He liberally filled Ashleigh's glass.

'You should watch how much you drink around Dan,' said Judith, unable to hold back. 'You never know where the drink might lead.'

'Hopefully more drink and more fun,' said Ashleigh, taking one long swig which drained half her glass.

'I must say you are looking well, darling. Now Daniel, what's your secret to putting a smile on my daughter's face?' asked Lou.

'Money, lots of it and wine,' said Ashleigh. 'The answer is not in pea soup, mum.' Ashleigh pushed a half-laugh and, in that moment, Judith, releasing a pent-up plug of air, could have slapped Ashleigh for belittling Lou's obvious new-found happiness with Geoff.

'No secret,' said Dan. 'Just want her to be happy.'

'To happy,' toasted Ashleigh and swiftly finished her glass, prompting Dan to refill it.

'No, thank you,' said Judith as Dan, leaning keenly too close, tried to fill her glass too; the whiff of cigarettes on him rank, making her nauseous. 'I'm good with fizzy water.'

'Not like you,' said Lou. 'You love your red wine. And this one is quite delicious. And we're not paying for it.'

'I'm starting on a project tomorrow so need a clear head. Thank you all the same, Dan,' she said with all the warmth she could muster.

'More for us,' said Ashleigh.

As soon as the lunch plates were cleared, Judith declined dessert and made her excuses.

'Call you tomorrow,' said Lou and then, to Judith's retreating back, 'And thanks for all your help. You've been amazing.'

By the time Judith walked home, her feet were sore, her heels rubbing on the inside of her shoes, and she felt the start of a blister forming on each one. She kicked off her sandals, rubbing at the marks left by the leather straps around her ankles.

Glad to be home. Glad to be alone. She relaxed on the couch. Jasper jumped up next to her and snuggled on her lap. Judith stroked his warm fur and cried; crumbling and corroded, she cried like she would never stop. The humiliation, the embarrassment, the unkind words, and the photos from all those years ago going round and round in her head like a black and white horror film. *Why the hell did he have to show up after all this time? And did Ashleigh know? Know what a monster he was?*

Her mobile buzzed and she ignored the incoming call. Seconds later a text message came through from him. *Matt would have to wait.*

'Oh, Jasper,' she said, stroking his thick fur. 'What a mess.'

Chapter 51

Two days later, Matt treated Judith to a home-cooked meal which he prepared in her kitchen, quite at home and wearing her apron. Lounging in Judith's back garden after their dinner of deep-fried white bait, roasted potato wedges and his famous own-grown peas, Judith's legs comfortably spanned Matt's lap.

'That feels so good,' she cooed as he massaged her feet and she relaxed for the first time since the party and the dreadful lunch with Dan at the weekend.

'It's meant to be,' he said and then he coughed, as if clearing his throat. Judith tensed a little, recognising the cough as him having something to say. It was one of his little habits she had picked up on. As if he needed to psyche himself up to voice what was on his mind.

'Dan seemed nice,' he said.

'He wasn't. Not sure about now though. Haven't seen him for years. He's been seeing Ashleigh.'

'You didn't keep in touch?'

'No.'

'What was it with you two?'

'There was no "it". What makes you ask that?'

'The way he was around you. He called you Jude.'

'I was back then.'

'Unfinished business?'

'Not as far as I'm concerned.'

'History?'

'Look, can we talk about something else? Or if there's something specific you want to ask me then ask me straight out, Matt.' Judith swung her legs to the floor and stood up.

'Were you together?' he asked, facing her straight on.

'Not in the way you're thinking. Now can we leave it?'

'You were sick after he spoke to you at Lou's party. I saw you.'

'That was the drink.'

'No, it wasn't. What are you hiding?'

'We weren't lovers if that's what's eating you.'

'I'm worried about you. That was one hell of a physical reaction, and not a good one.'

'He was Head of Photography. We were good friends. You know, meetings together, drinks after work, silly messages under the table at staff meetings that dragged on and on.'

'What did he do? What went on between you?'

Judith felt the blood drain from her face but managed to compose herself. 'He was there for me when my marriage broke down.'

'How? Tell me.'

'You know, kept me busy, kept me high most of the time.'

'And?'

'Use your imagination.'

'Just tell me.'

'He took photos of me, made me feel loved, special.'

'He photographed you?'

'Yes.'

'And?'

'And one night we got drunk, he took a whole film of me, posing, not pretty.'

'Posing? Like posing?' Judith saw the tightness in his jaw, the way his shoulders inched up closer to his ears. *She had been reckless, aggressive.*

'Yes. Naked. Full frontal, erotic, pornographic, up close, and personal.'

'Oh my God. Why didn't you tell me?'

'It's not exactly high up on my list of achievements.'

'I want to know you and your life− all of it.' He tried to reassure her.

'How could I throw that into the conversation over a meal?'

'One rule for me and another for you?'

'That's not fair. This was years ago. This is still painful,' she said.

'Did he blackmail you with them?'

'They ended up on some mature housewives internet porn site.'

'What a creep.'

'Said he needed the money. Was desperate.'

'Desperate my arse. The filthy monster.'

'My pupils saw them, it was awful. I lost my job. The Board of Governors suspended me pending an enquiry and then booted me out. They had a duty of care to protect the children and the school from such "highly inappropriate and damaging business". I hit rock bottom, though I didn't think I could get any lower.'

'Judith. I'm so sorry,' Matt said, and he reached over, squeezed her shoulder. 'It's not your fault. You were the victim.'

'I was, but it didn't make it any easier to handle. It nearly ruined me.'

'And Daniel?'

'I don't know. I didn't hang around long enough to find out.'

'And now?'

'And now nothing. They're probably still out there somewhere, on some outdated defunct site. If you looked hard enough, I'm sure you'd find them.'

'You hadn't seen him again until last night?'

'No, I moved out of the area. Cut him out of my life.'

'Were you okay?'

'I wasn't for almost a year. I drank. I partied. I lost all self-respect for myself. And then the job came up at the college, just as I was about to get turfed out of my rented place. The Head of Art job changed everything for me. The Headteacher was desperate, the position had been unfilled for nearly two terms. If it weren't for that little moment of big serendipity, I'd be in a gutter somewhere or in a ditch. I will always be grateful to Mr. Kowalski. All the way from Poland, he was a good man.'

Chapter 52

The hand-delivered envelope, sealed with brown masking tape across the top, felt heavy in her hand. She put it down on the kitchen table. Probably the final plans and advert posters for the summer fete. She would need to look at them at some point but not tonight. Tonight, she was tired; wanted to drift off and escape into a deep dreamless sleep. She wanted to stay there for longer than eight hours, yearning for the hours of separation from reality sleep would bring her.

She took one pill and then two, throwing her head back to ensure the little water she had in her tumbler pushed the pills all the way down. She took a third pill, to make sure. It wedged in the back of her throat, she gagged, but forcing it down she managed to swallow it. It left a bitter powdery residue in her mouth, reflective of her own sour mood and was glad Matt hadn't pushed to spend the night.

She climbed into bed, exhaustion eating at her bones, a deep uncomfortable ache. The pills were her emergency backup, there when she needed them the most, and tonight she needed them. She couldn't stop thinking about the photos and the website and the downward pull they still had on her. Her head hit the pillow; she could smell herself, her hair, on the pillowcase. Outside the evening seemed to fade quickly into night, from phosphorus to pewter, she willed away the inside sounds and smells, and she let herself be pulled deeper. She closed her eyes, the waning light receded until the blurring came and she felt herself sinking.

Chapter 53

The following morning Judith slammed the porch door behind her; it almost caught Jasper in its jaw, but he uncharacteristically scampered out of the way, the door just missing his tail.

'Sorry Jasper. My fault. Go and find a playmate,' she called as she almost tripped over the uneven path, a new-found energy carrying her quickly away.

Judith pounded on Lou's front door, her hand white, clenched into a fist. The leaded glass seemed to bow inwards under the force of her knocking and fearful of it breaking she continued but banged on the wooden frame. It was early but she needed her friend. She needed her more than ever.

'Judith? Whatever's the matter?' Lou appeared, dishevelled, her faded pink once-fluffy dressing gown hanging off her shoulder. Lou pulled at it and tied the belt.

'I'm so sorry. I should have said something sooner, but I was embarrassed, selfish.'

'What are you talking about?'

'Have you spoken to Ashleigh?' asked Judith as she followed Lou's retreating back into the front room.

'She's here. She came late last night, surprising me.'

'On her own?' Judith hoped, though she felt a little unkind, Dan had gone for good.

'Daniel's gone back. She's staying a couple of nights with me.'

'Did she say anything?'

'Whatever's happened? You're shaking.'

'It's a mess. It's a huge mess. I'm so sorry,' said Judith, tears threatened to fall, but she brushed them away with determination.

'What's all the noise?' Ashleigh walked in, barely covered by the crop top she wore, her long legs disappearing under the lace edge which skimmed her slim waist, her hair in a tangled messy bun.

'Sorry, darling. There's some sort of emerg– '

'Ashleigh, there's something I need to ask you,' said Judith as she lowered herself onto the arm of the couch, her energy seeming to suddenly fall away from under her.

'Me?'

'It's about Dan.'

'Daniel? What about him?'

'You don't know him. What he's really like,' said Judith. 'You might want to look at these, Ash.' Judith handed over the envelope, ripped open across the top, saying, 'I'm sorry. He's not a nice man.'

Ashleigh looked at her mum and then down at the envelope. 'What are these?' Ashleigh asked, slipping out the wad of photographs, staring at them one by one, unflinching.

'He's dangerous. A liar,' said Judith, the venom in her voice uncurling from her like poison from a snake's tongue.

'I already know.'

'That he's a liar. Has no respect for women?' Judith yelled.

'No. I said I know.'

'Know what? What do you think you know?'

'All of it. Dan promised he would make it right by you,' said Ashleigh, soaked in desperation.

'Like this? Sending me the photos. Reminding me of how stupid I was? You have to leave him.'

'Hold on. What's going on? Ashleigh? What have you done now?' Lou asked, who until that moment had remained calm but her complexion turned ghostly white as she turned to face Ashleigh head on.

'It was you… the anonymous message via my website… warning me about him. Did you send it?' asked Ashleigh.

'If you read it, why are you still with him?' Judith's voice rose in pitch, panic and anger, frustration and fear consuming her.

'Ash?' Lou's face was riddled with deep frown lines, angst, confusion. 'What are they? Let me have a look at those.' She grabbed the photographs from her daughter, the shiny photographic paper slipped through Lou's fingers and the images scattered the Persian rug in all their indiscreet glory.

Lou and Judith simultaneously bent down to pick them up.

'Don't look Lou. Please. I'm so ashamed.' Judith frantically scooped up the photos, holding them close to her chest.

'What's this? Looks like some sort of contract,' said Lou, looking down at a thickly bound document.

'Give it to me,' demanded Judith.

'A sale… S-xonlegs.' Lou flicked through the document. 'Sold for five million pounds to Mr. Daniel Hertford-Jones of Hertford-Jones Photography and Hertford-Jones Holdings Limited…' Lou read out.

'Please Lou,' said Judith.

'S-xonlegs?' repeated Lou.

'That's the company Daniel made a hostile takeover bid on and has now, finally, bought it outright. It's taken him months of negotiation,' said Ashleigh. 'He's been so stressed by it all.'

'Stressed? He sold compromising photos of me,' said Judith, her voice scratching the back of her throat like a razor. 'Without my permission or knowledge.'

'Photos? What photos?' asked Lou, confusion all over her face.

'He took advantage of me years ago. So many pieces of me are still missing because of him.' Judith felt her features fall in disarray, disconnected, her mouth wilted, her eyes wobbling in and out of focus as she tried to stay present, stay calm, in control.

'Whatever has gone on?' asked Lou, her eyes watery with fear for her friend.

'Here give me that,' said Ashleigh, snatching the document from her mum's hand, she tore the front sheet off. 'You're missing the point. That's his company,' said Ashleigh. 'He's bought the site and taken the pictures off the internet.'

'He's done what?' Judith turned white.

'I have no clue what's going on and one of you had better explain to me or I'm going to freak!'

'No, he's tricking you. It's a cruel joke,' Judith cried. Inconsolable as the tears fell and dripped onto her top, the material changing from a lime green to a deep-sea green… spreading like his lies, poisonous, venomous, toxic. 'He hijacked my life.'

'Can we all calm down. Please,' shouted Ashleigh, hands in front of her, palms up.

'Why would he do that?' asked Judith incredulously.

'Because I'm going to marry him. Clean slate. No secrets.'

Judith collapsed to the floor screwing up the single sheet into a tight ball, her tears still falling, her anguished cries she knew like those of an animal in pain. Lou dropped to her knees next to Judith and held her friend, rocking her back and forth.

Eventually, Judith fell asleep on her friend's lap and did not stir until Lou tried to move from under her to wake her numb arm and leg.

Ashleigh made them a cup of tea and instinctively handed Judith some paracetamol.

'You never told me. None of it,' said Lou.

'It was a long time ago. It's not my proudest moment.'

'I thought we shared everything?'

'We do. We do. It's just I was so ashamed.'

'Look, there's more,' said Ashleigh, flicking through the documents. 'There's a form in here for you to sign which transfers everything over to you.'

'It's too late. He destroyed me with his lies and his greed,' sobbed Judith.

'But he's sorry. Trying to make amends. Dan wants nothing from you.'

'That's because there's nothing more he can take,' said Judith, her voice rising.

'You're not listening. He wants nothing to do with this. He knows he made a mistake. He was young, foolish, ambitious,' said Ashleigh.

Lou gave her friend a sympathetic look. 'Five million. Five for Silver,' she said.

'It's weighed me down for so long, Lou. I'm sorry I never told you.'

'I still have no idea what's going on, but this is more difficult to solve than one of my cryptic puzzles but I'm always here for you,' said Lou.

'Hope you're going to help me up then,' Judith whimpered, a faint shadowy joy emanating from the shadows.

'Nah, might just leave you on the floor. But seriously, could this be your Five for Silver?'

'Five for Silver?' asked Ashleigh.

'Yes!' they both chimed, and a faint flutter of lightness, like a dancing butterfly, found its way into Judith.

Chapter 54

Over the next two days Judith spent a lot of time with Lou and Ashleigh. Gratitude towards Ashleigh flooded from her though she battled with feelings of detachment.

'I don't know how I feel. One minute I feel free. The next I collapse in a heap, crying, unable to process this awful nightmare has come to an end.'

'That's understandable,' said Lou. 'You're like one of those prisoners of war… emotionally frozen. Suffering anhedonia.'

'I won't ask what that means.'

'It means being unable to feel pleasure in something that you should.'

'I'm not a prisoner of my past anymore,' Judith said, mulling over the events that had led her to the most liberated yet numb state in all her life.

'You could sell those now and get enough to travel the world,' laughed Lou.

'No thank you. I'm fine where I am, and life here in the village isn't so bad after all.'

'No more nude-gate,' giggled Ashleigh.

Ashleigh's giggling was infectious, and Judith saw the funny side to it eventually but also recognised her own part played in the unfortunate events which sent her life spiralling out of control and nearly ruined her career. She wondered if her dad ever knew, and a deep shame and sadness filled her, a feeling of emptiness, emotional detachment as she recalled one of their meet ups.

'You can come to me with anything, my love.'

'I know, Dad.'

They had met at the pizzeria close to where she lived; her dad insisted pizza and pasta was a great idea even though she knew he wasn't a lover of Italian food. They had argued about where to eat and in the end, he had convinced her he would have meatballs with pasta without the sauce.

'I've not always been a married man, a dad. Or this old. I've had a life before your mother,' he said, spooning a greasy meatball into his mouth.

'I know that Dad,' she said, embarrassed by the topic of conversation and where it might lead.

'Just saying. And…'

'I'm fine Dad.' She cut him short. 'Just a little tired. School's been full on. There's been a trail of disciplinary meetings I've had to deal with.'

He looked at her and went to say something more and changed his mind. He took another greasy, meaty bite, and instead said, 'Are you sleeping?'

'What's that?' she asked, fighting to hold back a yawn,

trying to make light of her exhaustion. She knew full well the dark rings under her eyes were etched permanently there, a tattoo, a reminder of her stupidity and her ruined life.

'If you change your mind. I'm only a call away.'

'Oh, Dad, I love you,' Judith told him.

They had toasted their father-daughter relationship and had laughed at the Italian waiter who twice brought out pizza with the wrong toppings for Judith.

That was one of the most intimate evenings she had enjoyed with her dad as an adult, and she suddenly missed him and nestled into his chair. His gentle nature and his warm smile. He was a wise man and she realised now how she could have gone to him with anything, and he would have stood by her; stood by her in his own quiet but stubborn way, standing up for her against the world.

'I'm so tired. So tired of all the obstacles, Jasper. Hopefully, this is finally it. That dreadful two-year period, which lasted a lifetime, is now eradicated allowing for the new that is coming. There must be a Capricorn in Aries or a full moon. Whatever it is, I can feel a shift. It feels good.'

Jasper opened one eye in response and closed it again. There was certainly a new vibe in the air; she sensed it keenly, and it seeped through her until it filled her heart with renewed hope.

Chapter 55

The morning of the village fete, a rumble of thunder and a rolling grey of skidding clouds tarnished the watery blue sky as Judith ate breakfast. On the table, as she drummed her fingers with excitement, next to her plate of toast the sixth postcard, "Six for Gold", stared back at her.

Each magpie had a golden medal hanging around its plump neck, the expression on each face one of victory, pride, dignity. The blue, indigo, and black plumage beckoned her to stroke them, the softness real, so lifelike.

She finished her breakfast, gulped down her tea and stuffed the card into her cardigan pocket. *She didn't have the time to think about the card today. Tomorrow… tomorrow she would have a lot more time to ponder its meaning, to think about its underlying message to her.*

***

The group of volunteers standing on the green talked in hushed whispers accentuated with little sighs and tuts, looking up at the billowing greyness, wondering whether the event they had spent months organising would be cancelled. Two women gripped their umbrellas by their sides, and another pulled up the collar of her woollen jacket, visibly trembling against the morning chill.

Running towards them, the vicar's cassock ballooned behind him like a superhero's cape, his white trainers peeking under the hem of the black gown with every step. He stopped, doubled over out of puff, and apologised for being late through his short, sharp breaths. Judith caught Lou pulling back the sleeve of her cardigan to sneak a peek at the time; Lou shook her head from side to side as if to say, 'late again.' Judith smirked. *Why would he change now?*

The vicar gestured palms down, for the crowd of twenty volunteers to hush, shooing away one of the villager's dogs, overtly excited to see him join the group. 'So sorry I'm late.' He spoke in bursts trying to catch his breath. 'Friends, parishioners, the weather seems to be fighting us this morning, but I'm certain the sun will shine for our wonderful fete this afternoon, so please let's go with plan A for now, full speed ahead with setting up the stalls, rigging up for the lights and music and of course, setting up the stage. Not much has changed since our final meeting and here are extra plans from last year if you need them with added notes and instructions,' he said passing the photocopied sheets around. 'Any questions?'

Judith glanced at the regimental list and kept a poker

face knowing how Lou would react reading it.

'Where can I set up the screen and seating for our contribution?' asked Kerry and she gave Maja's hand a squeeze and looked over at Judith who gave them a nod of encouragement.

'Ah, yes, that… thank you,' said the vicar, ushering everyone on, clearly worried about the last-minute changes and the committee's reaction to them. Their resounding past, insistent "no" ringing in Kerry's ears.

Maja and Kerry waited for the crowd to disperse as people created sub-groups and wandered off in their usual cliques. Maja and Kerry took a step towards the priest while Judith hung back slightly with Lou.

'We've thought about it,' said Maja, conspiratorially, and the plan, as it stands, keeps a free area here and here,' she said, holding up and pointing at her own flimsy, bedraggled plan. 'So, we thought we would set up here, adjacent to the bar and coconut shy.'

'And what about electricity and seating?' asked one of the committee members.

'All in hand.' Judith hoped her intervention was regarded as helpful and knew only too well, and with relief, Tom was helping out with this. Lee agreed and she could tell how hard he was trying to keep the prickle out of his voice but the nerve ticking in his temple gave him away.

'We've got that covered, so you don't have to worry about a thing,' interjected Lou too, sensing his frayed nerves and concern about the organising posse's overbearing control over the event.

The priest gave her a side-long look and, nodding his

head, walked off towards the stage area where a group of people were heaving parts of the staging across the green. Furrows of turned up grass, as they dragged the metal platform components one by one, marked the ground.

Once out of ear shot, Lou said, 'I thought he said we could use the chairs from the church hall... okay, let's not panic. We need about thirty to forty chairs. Let's approach everyone we know and ask if they can bring along their garden chairs. We need to borrow as many as we can.'

'Some of them live on the other side of the village, Lou. We can't expect them to ferry chairs over. And so many of them are here already setting up. I don't think that's going to work.'

'What about asking Matt to collect more seating in his truck?' asked Judith.

'Oh, I don't know... taking advantage like that and then being indebted to him,' said Lou.

'Call him. He told me he'd be coming over later so a couple of hours sooner won't make a difference,' insisted Judith.

Chapter 56

Judith was untangling the bunting, agitated, and fighting a niggle of guilt at not running the art stall. She hadn't made much progress with her paintings; not in the way she had hoped and had declined the offer of selling her work. She knew someone had been pulled in to offer arts and crafts though she had not had the time to check out their art, and she had not seen them setting up either. She hoped the artist was not going to let them down.

The cloudy haze of earlier had disappeared to reveal a China blue sky and working in the full sun had made her thirsty. She grabbed her water bottle from her canvas bag and took a long drink surveying the hustle and bustle. She stretched to ease away the twinge at the base of her back.

The village green was a hodgepodge of stalls offering a wonderful collage of homemade and other goods: The "Go Potty" stall was filled with potted plants in an array of terracotta pots and colourful wooden trays, ivy trailing down like a waterfall, the "Pre-loved Books" stall with second-hand books piled high like Jenga bricks also invited you to have a "Blind Date With A Book." Judith wondered what the busy-body committee would think about that little addition to the book stall and suppressed a smirk.

Nic-nacs and ceramics spread across a pretty floral-covered table showcasing pretty pastels and chintzy vintage items. Bunting, spelling out the words "LOVE NICNACS", fluttered in the breeze.

The "Happy Baking" stall took up three tables and displayed a tower of desserts donated by the village bakery. Cakes, with enough butter icing to give you a giddy sugar rush with one bite, thick slices of banana loaf, generous slices of pineapple upside cake, lemon drizzle caked in lemon gin icing and homemade scones with all the trimmings, were sure to tempt even the most careful eater.

Megan's dippy muffins took centre stage and three bowls of filling to choose from promised they would be totally delicious. There was even an area where children could decorate their own fairy cake with sparkly sugar balls, hundreds and thousands, sugar-paper flowers, and cartoon characters. The next stall along, "In A Jam", weighed down with tartan-lidded jars arranged in pyramids, displayed homemade jams, marmalades and sweet fruit chutneys was manned by the women of the local W.I. and, of course, Megan.

Other stalls included framed retro pop posters and the popular helium Disney character balloons. Each stall had electrical leads snaking through the table legs and on to the next stand. One of the locals was on his knees, securing the trailing leads in place with heavy duty tape.

Two men, who Judith didn't recognise and likely had been employed specially for the event, called to each other as they balanced the weight of a huge speaker between them before lowering one, and then the other, onto its base with a gentle thud, securing the amplifiers to free-standing brackets either side of the staging.

The live entertainment drew people in from the surrounding area and amongst the run-up were those professional acts, bringing with them their own fan base. The evening's D.J. attracted the younger generation and teenagers.

In the distance Judith saw Matt walking towards her with long strides and a wave of his hand; his taut T-shirt teasing her with a chest she knew was well-defined. Lou interrupted his gait and Judith watched as Lou gave him a list of addresses; villagers who had agreed to lend their garden seating for the media show. He nodded, and then walked with determination towards Judith. Judith's heart fluttered when he pulled her into him and planted a kiss on her lips in front of everyone.

Judith pulled back and smiled, not daring to look at anyone. 'Guess we've truly confirmed everyone's suspicions,' she laughed.

'That's okay, right?'

'It is, yes,' she said with a smile and leaned in to hug him. He pulled away, tapped her nose with his finger, like a doting father would to his daughter, and shoving the list of pick-up addresses in his pocket he shot off towards his parked truck on the other side of the green.

Judith continued watching him for a few moments, his hurried steps taking him away from her and she felt a stab. *What was it? Love? It couldn't be love, could it?* The speakers, after too many screeches and ear-deafening sounds, crackled into a modern variation of *When You're in Love with a Beautiful Woman.* The organisers cheered and she saw Tom throw his hand in the air in a sign of victory. As she was about to turn away, Matt turned round, their gaze met and in the middle of the busy village green Judith realised she had fallen in love with him. Her mouth slackened, fell open and she quickly turned it into a "hello" as Lou approached.

Chapter 57

Judith spent the remaining hour or so before lunch, with the help of Maja, marking out the seating area with chalk for their surprise event privy only to a handful of people. Two of the village's handymen hammered wooden posts into the grass at the spots marked with chalk crosses and looped thick rope through the metal rings at the top of each one to cordon off the area.

Some distance away, Judith threw down her cardigan, claiming a little patch of the parched green. She sat down facing the full sun suspended in a blue sky. A trail of thin clouds, like the twisted-spun sticky wisps of candy floss spun around a stick, promised a beautiful rest-of-the-day as they sailed away in the lightest of breezes. A pair of sparrows landed a few yards from her feet. They pecked the dry earth and then, noticing a pile of nature's fall apples, busily hollowed out their bruised flesh before flying off, their cheeping notes still singing in her ears, over the humdrum of activity around her.

She closed her eyes for a second and when she opened them her heart missed a beat as Matt strode towards her. He pushed a wide four-wheel barrow heaped with chairs, of all shapes and sizes, secured and bound with a length of green washing line. She watched as the wheels bumped over the grass, keeping her fingers crossed they didn't stumble over a pothole and send the whole load tumbling.

Kerry and Maja called over to a few youths, a mixed group of boys and girls, probably known to Maja from school, and with none of the teasing or name calling of the past they agreed to set up the chairs in an amphitheatre-style semi-circle facing the large white screen. Matt and another villager made another three runs back to his truck and finally the seats were arranged.

'Done,' said Matt, wiping his brow and running his sweaty palm over the front of his trousers where it left a damp smear.

'Rather haphazardly, but at least we have our seating. Thanks for your help.'

'Happy to help a damsel in distress,' he teased.

'Who's in distress? Oh gosh, whatever else can go wrong?' asked Lou.

'Nothing. It's all good. Now stop flapping Lou,' said Judith, pleased to see how Maja was in the middle of a group of friends, smiling and laughing with them. Lou shuffled over and Judith patted the unfolded arm of her cardigan indicating for her to sit. Judith wanted to show her the new postcard.

'No time for sitting, I need to tick off the stands against

the plan and check all the stall volunteers are here. Less than an hour till our official kick off time. And anyway, I'm sure Matt will sit with you. Toodle-loo.' She waved in her signature way and Judith felt herself blushing under Matt's impregnable stare.

He sat next to her and as he folded his legs towards him, his arm grazed Judith's sending a current of electricity through her. She could feel his eyes on her, and she struggled not to look at him but, in the end, he turned her face towards him, his two fingers under her chin.

'Are you okay?'

'Yes of course. And thanks for your help, Matt.'

'You've already thanked me,' he said.

'I want you to know how much I appreciate you.'

'I know that. And do you know what I would appreciate?' he asked with an upthrust of his chin.

Judith didn't answer him, lost in his hazel eyes.

'A weekend away with you. A proper weekend, somewhere nice, somewhere we can talk and be together.'

'We're talking now, aren't we?'

'I mean properly. Just the two of us… you know.'

Too afraid to speak, to reveal her resurfacing feelings, she gently nodded her head, and he took her hand in his and squeezed it.

Chapter 58

The village green was a colourful throng of people; women swathed in soft, shimmery summer fabrics, young girls in daisy print leggings and pink tutu skirts cartwheeled across the emerald lawn and boys in their favourite football-team shirts kicked a ball around, their knees already grass-stained and their faces sweaty. Adults, the young and the old, guiltily licked ice creams, sucked on lollies melting too quickly or tucked into slabs of cake the size of bricks.

Men drank beer served in plastic pint cups and women sipped at their Pimm's and lemonade, swaying to the music, some dancing not caring if they spilled their drinks, laughing, flirting with the music, while they kept one eye on their children.

Judith saw the vicar standing under the great oak tree; its huge trunk adorned with a huge bow. He surveyed them all, a humble shepherd watching over his faithful flock. He caught her eye and waved. Judith smiled, gave him a wave back; genuinely happy for the first time in a long time though she forced away an invasive shiver.

The weather hadn't let anyone down and the warm temperatures lingered on. People continued to dance, their abandonment increasing with their intake of alcohol. They laughed and joked, and the clink of change and the folded notes being posted in the collection tin was testament to a warm and loving community.

Judith had wondered how the collection, to raise funds for the care home Penelope had spent her last few months, would be received. But with her sensitivity and her heart on her sleeve, she had won over the committee and Matt had been overwhelmed when she told him. Judith had also accosted the village's most gossipy women in the village Post Office. Once they had vividly detailed their actual and imagined illnesses and gone on to discuss the obituaries in the local newspaper, she shared that she had known Penelope.

She mentioned the planned fund raising for the care home. They had immediately, and wholeheartedly, offered to "shake" the collection caddies, surprising Judith with the warmth of their generosity. In addition, the W.I. had offered to add twenty per cent of their annual income to the cause. Judith could not have asked for more, knowing how kind and thoughtful the staff looking after Penelope had been.

'I'm going to take a wander,' said Judith, suddenly overwhelmed, tired. She stifled a yawn which came out too loudly.

'I'll come with you,' offered Matt.

'No, you stay and enjoy yourself.'

Judith pushed through the dancing crowd, her feet getting trodden on more than once and a drink of wine splashing over her skirt as someone pirouetted and lost their balance. Eventually away from everyone, Matt pulled her back by the arm.

'What's the hurry?'

'Sorry, I just don't want to stop you from enjoying yourself.'

'Judith, stop. Look at me,' he said, and he waited until she turned to face him. 'What's going on? Don't push me away. I want to be with you. I'm only here because of you.'

'Matt... I...'

Before she could vocalise her thoughts Matt kissed her, with more passion than earlier in the day. 'Don't speak, Judith, my darling.'

He pulled her so tight she could feel the beating of his chest as she rested her head there, could feel his breath on the top of her head as he exhaled. This wasn't how she had envisaged her retirement panning out. She'd outwardly celebrated having time on her hands, being able to do all the things she hadn't had time for while working full-time, but inwardly she had dreaded trying to fill eight or more hours a day, she had feared being alone, feared being unimportant and worthless. Lou and Matt, and the magpie postcards, had changed that: Lou had kept her sane even if the crosswords had driven Judith mad, Matt had come into her life and given her something to look forward to, and the cards had given her something to do. She wrapped her arms around his neck and looked up at him.

'You're my tomorrow,' he said, as if he'd read her mind.

Chapter 59

Judith slipped away, needing to think. She bought two pots of strawberry jam laced with gin, a gardening kneeling pad and chatted with the villagers, all doing their bit, with big smiles. She then turned to go back to Matt when she realised, she hadn't passed by the art stall. The one stall she should most definitely visit. She approached the stall, one of the few which was tented to protect the artwork in case the weather turned, and hesitated as she heard the distinct voice of the vicar inside.

'She's a wonderful woman. Helps the villagers. Has a huge heart.'

Then a woman's voice, 'That doesn't mean she'll accept you. Accept who you are.'

'She's already accepted me, despite not being religious. She's supported Megan and Tom. She has so much love to give.'

'But it might not be so when she finds out.'

'Mum, please. Be gentle, be kind. I know how much she means to you.'

The art teacher, also the stall holder, was Lee's mum? Why hadn't he said anything?

A warm shiver caused her to stop in her tracks. The woman's voice seemed familiar, pulling at her, but why. She bundled in, her arms full of her purchases.

'Not interrupting, am I?'

'Judith, hello,' said Lee. 'This is Alma.'

Alma looked up at Judith and Judith blinked in disbelief. The woman, standing before her, was like her: a mane of fiery orange hair, perfect white teeth, and a full wide smile.

'Hello,' said Judith, hesitating, fighting the emotion in her as she looked from Alma to the display of paintings on the table, magpies. A huge canvas, on a ground sheet, leant against the front of the stall table was filled with magpies. Judith counted them. Seven. She counted them again. 'Seven for a Secret Never to be Told,' she said aloud, staring at Alma.

'I think you know who I am,' said Alma.

'You've been sending me the postcards.'

'I've been waiting a long time for this day. I never thought God would be so good as to bring you back to me.'

'What's going on? Alma is my middle name,' Judith said, staring in disbelief, confused, but not sure why she should feel so.

'Yes, the one connection his family agreed to keep.'

'What do you mean?'

'Let me explain,' jumped in Lee.

'The postcards, they're from you,' repeated Judith.

'Yes,' said Alma.

'Why? Sorry, but I'm confused.'

'I'm your birth mother. And this is your half-brother.' Alma squeezed Lee's arm.

'Judith, say something,' said Lee. 'I didn't want you to find out about me, about Alma, like this.'

'I know it's a lot to take in. I've been following your career and your life, from afar, since the day I gave you up to your father. He was a good man. I was a trollop, a troublemaker, well, according to your grandparents and they didn't want your father to have anything to do with me.'

Judith gazed, unblinking.

'But I wanted you with all my heart. I have loved you every day for sixty-one years.'

'But you didn't keep me,' Judith spat, ill-temper building in her, a crescendo of symbols crashing in her heart and mind, an explosion of bewilderment and hurt and disbelief.

'I grew up in a children's home. I had no family. No support.'

'And now?'

'Now's the right time.'

Judith blinked back her tears, tears of anger, frustration and confusion and ran home.

***

She burst into Chrysanthemum Cottage and tore at the brown manilla envelope; it told her everything. 'Oh, why didn't I look at this earlier?' Judith yelled in exasperation, as she tore at the unopened envelopes concealing tender messages and wishes written in handmade birthday cards. All from so long ago; there were so many, sent all the way up to her twenty-first birthday, all signed "Love you always, Alma". A sense of betrayal strangled her, she clutched at her throat, her breathing short, laboured. *All these cards, all this time, had held the missing puzzle piece to her life, to her entire upbringing, her relationship with herself and her mother.*

A hurried knock at the door was followed by footsteps. She ignored the knocking until she heard Lee's anxious voice calling her, Alma's pleading whine, a painful echo now almost hysterical.

With a wild anger running through her, she flung the porch door open and stomped back into the living room, back in control.

'Please, Judith. Let me explain,' said Alma, reaching for one of the cards. 'I sent all these...'

'But I didn't know. I never knew. I didn't know any of it,' sobbed Judith.

'They promised. Promised to pass these on.' Alma visibly trembled, her hands unsteady, her voice shaking.

'I can't take all this in. Do you know how I struggled to build a relationship with my mum? I thought she hated me. But I now realise she hated the situation, the impossible circumstance we were both locked into. You took my childhood away.'

'But your mother agreed to take you on as her own. She was a good woman,' Alma said.

'Good? She never loved me. Everything I did grated on her nerves. If it wasn't for my father, I wouldn't even have the few precious happy memories I do have.'

'I'm so sorry. If I'd known…'

'I've wondered all my life why my mum, the woman I thought should have loved me unconditionally, just couldn't. And now you're here, thinking it will be okay?'

'And you've lied to me too,' said Judith, turning to Lee.

'I wanted to tell you. I thought getting to know me first would make it easier for you,' said Lee.

'Easier how? A man of God too. How could you? After everything I've done to help you, to bring your family here.'

'What's going on?' asked Matt, walking in on them. 'Judith?'

But Judith shook her head. 'Not now, Matt, please.'

About to insist, Judith recognised how Matt realised he'd walked in on something big. He nodded his agreement and took a step closer to her, as if to offer her his protection.

'I'm so sorry, Judith. Please,' continued Lee. I want us to be family. Want you to be a part of mine.'

'This is all my fault, don't blame Lee. I'm the one who persuaded him to get involved.'

'It's a shock for me too. I only found out about you recently. Mum also kept you from my life. I'm so sorry, Judith. I never wanted to reveal who I was to you like this,' said Lee.

'Please, let's talk about this properly, tomorrow. Not now. Not like this,' begged Alma.

'I don't know. Maybe,' mumbled Judith, wiping her tears, conscious of everything closing in on her, only

Matt's arm around her reminded her she was not alone.

'Come on let's get back to the fete. We can't miss out on Kerry and Maja's grand finale,' said Matt and Lee was already making his way towards the front door.

'I'm so sorry,' said Alma and she reached out to squeeze Judith's arm. Judith shook her off with force, more than a tetchy irritability and astonishment flooding her senses.

'Let's get back to the fete. I don't want to let Kerry down,' said Judith, shaking away her tears and tilting her chin in defiance as she followed them out with Matt close behind her.

Chapter 60

It was finally seven o'clock, the time for the grand finale to begin, the biggest surprise of all, the part of the fete Kelly and Maja had worked so hard on. The fete goers collectively moved to the area in front of the big screen and their excitement carried Judith along, though part of her felt detached, lost. Her mind raced blindly over the past sixty years of her life; fast forwarding then fast rewinding, images flashing at her, disconnected, another life.

'I'm not going to ask what that was all about, but please don't shut me out,' said Matt, pulling her out of her semi-present state.

'I promise, I won't. Let's get through the next hour and I will then explain it as best as I can.'

Matt squeezed her hand in agreement. 'No pressure,' he said. 'But I'm here for you.'

Judith focused on the present. The atmosphere around

her was undeniably electric; like fireflies dancing in the summer air, she could feel the electricity. She saw Kerry and Maja leaning into each other, whispering. She knew how nervous they were, could see it in the way Kerry bit down on her lip and Maja, a turquoise hoodie pulled over her soft-feathered pixie cut, bounced from one foot to the other on pink-striped trainers, looking tentatively towards the crowd.

'Good evening, everyone!' Kerry stopped, the high-pitched screech and then static preventing her from speaking. Maja looked on helplessly until Tom jumped on stage and fiddled with the microphone. 'Sorry about that,' continued Kerry. 'Thanks Tom.' She looked at Maja and continued, 'Thank you for being here and we hope you've had a great day so far.' The crowd cheered and Judith fought hard against the welling of tears behind her eyes, bit down on her lip. 'We hope you enjoy the next part of what has already been an incredible day.'

The music blasted out, the sound system speakers thrumming with the bass, and an image formed on the screen in front of the audience. The four-legged friends in the crowd barked with excitement. The pixilation converged to create a sweeping panoramic photo of the village, taken with a wide-angle lens, highlighting all the shopfronts, the village green with its old pump, and St Barnabas with its tumble-down cemetery, its arcaded narthex standing proud at its entrance.

'This is our village. It is our village for as long as we love it and appreciate those who live here, support and help us. Kerry's voice, clear and unwavering, sent goosebumps prickling up Judith's arm and Judith felt a burst of pride for the part she had played in bringing Kerry to this point, though at the same time it seemed to exacerbate her own lonely journey.

Next a number of pictures rolled in from the right to the left of the screen… Ian standing behind the counter at the shop, 'Always counting his takings,' shouted someone. Then a photograph which captured Paul pulling a pint at the pub, Zuzanna, at her sewing machine, showing off a glittering party dress she had made. Someone called out, 'That's my dress.'

The vicar welcoming his flock on a Sunday morning flew across the screen and little gasps of ooh and ahh were heard as members of the audience recognised themselves on the big screen, enjoying their two seconds of fame. Lou, standing behind the vicar, was pulling a face in the next image and everyone laughed as they noticed her, pointing, and smiling.

Lou complained about the angle of the next shot which showed her smiling as she watered her garden followed by a grainy photograph of Judith glowing under the tree lights at Lou's birthday party. Judith regarded Lou and Geoff, standing close together a few feet away from her. He beamed down at Lou, and she playfully slapped his arm, smiling as he whispered something in her ear. Judith smiled too, happy knowing her friend had found the beginning of a new happiness with Geoff.

The final two images showed Harry and Charlie riding their bikes through the village and Bill, with grass in his eyebrows and hair, proudly holding a basket of wild garlic stems and a handful of foraged mushrooms. He smiled broadly next to the huge compost area he had instigated for the villagers' use. *Such a great idea.* Judith had used more than a barrow or two of the fertiliser for her garden. She knew how grateful many in the community were and they appreciated, and supported, the initiative: BWNC – Bill's Waste Not Compost.

The cheers from the audience filled the sky with sparks of joyful electricity as if a constellation of stars had lit up their hearts.

'Truly amazing, wouldn't you say? But we must nurture it. We must, as a community and wider community, move forward, embrace change and welcome change. We must not be afraid to shake things up, accept something outside of our norms and we must push the boundaries of our comfort zones… it is about progress and sustainability.' Judith wound her arms across her waist and hugged herself.

The screen went blank, and another song burst forth from the speakers. A picture of Maja in the school's netball team kit alongside the rest of the team filled the screen and everyone cheered as Maja's voice crackled through the microphone. 'I am the person I have always been, and playing netball with my new friends is a dream.'

'Do we love the sea less because it is green and not blue? No, it tastes the same, welcomes us to swim and bathe in it, beckons us to enjoy summer days we have always loved so much,' said Kerry.

'This is one of the biggest hurdles I have had to face. I have had to work hard to persuade people to accept me,' continued Maja, 'and playing netball with such amazing people who don't say *no* has made it easier for me to get healthier and happier.' Maja stopped, her voice cracking as tears threatening to fall brightened her watery eyes. Her mother, pushed through the crowd, and taking her place next to her daughter, took Maja's hand in hers, nodding for her to go on. 'My mum is the strongest person I know and without her courage I wouldn't have the life I have in England, here with you... so thank you for making this easier, for making it possible for me to find my place at school and in the village and to Judith for being totally *zdumiewający*, amazing.'

The cheering and whistling was deafening. One or two dog-owners hushed their dogs' whines and barking, stroked them to calm the pets' jumping and wagging tails. The genuine love and support from the audience was evident and, this time, both mother and daughter broke down and hugged in front of everyone. Judith leaned into Matt, their bodies pressing closer, drawing strength from his strong arm wrapped around her.

Next a picture of the vicar burst through. He wasn't looking directly at the camera and his white cassock was awkwardly skewed across his shoulders. Behind him stood Megan and behind her Tom smiled, two fingers resting above Megan's head creating rabbit's ears. The crowd laughed and then fell silent.

The vicar got up from his seat, Lou's camping chair, and took a couple of steps towards the front of the stage, as if wanting to be closer to his audience, as if one with them. He coughed, and coughed a second time, clearing his throat.

'I stand here before you not only as your vicar, but as your friend, your neighbour.' Lee took a deep breath and added, 'your brother.' He scanned the crowd before he looked straight towards Judith. 'I'm not going to preach to you about forgiveness... because you have shown forgiveness. A Mark Twain quote, *Forgiveness is the fragrance that the violet sheds on the heel that has crushed it,* springs to my mind and I want to say thank you for seeing that I too am human, make mistakes and... and thank you for taking my family into the bosom of your community.' He motioned to Megan and Tom who sheepishly joined him on stage. 'Thank you for making us welcome.'

Ian raised his hands above his head and clapped, Paul and Kerry joined in and within seconds the entire crowd cheered, a crescendo building around them. Judith forced back the tears threatening to fall. Emotions were high, some evidently alcohol-induced, but people cried all the same, wiping their tears. Some approached the stage and shook the vicar and his family by the hand. They hugged and kissed. Tom looked uncomfortable but Megan beamed and squeezed Lee's hand tightly three times as he looked straight at Judith.

It was all okay. Not quite as Judith had predicted but it was and would be and something made her turn around. She looked past the heads of the crowd towards Alma, her mother, standing on her own, tears streamed down her face; her mother crying too. Lee's words rang in her ears, forgiveness.

'I just have to see someone,' whispered Judith to Matt and she slipped from his embrace. 'I'll be two minutes.'

Kerry asked everyone to quieten down. 'I don't want to bring down the mood of the day because it's been brilliant. But I wanted to show you all what I've been doing while I've been finding myself again.' Kerry clicked the remote control and her "Wall of Hope and Love" filled the screen. 'It's hard when you lose a baby. You lose a part of yourself that you've never really had the chance to get used to or know, yet you know you can never have what you've lost again.' She shuffled from one foot to the other and carried on. 'But in times of trouble and despair, there is always someone who jumps in, like a beacon to help you navigate your way out of that darkness again. I've got a lot of thank yous to make.' She pulled Paul up close to her. 'Firstly, to Paul who is the kindest, most patient man in the whole world. I love you Paul with all my heart. And our beautiful angel baby in heaven loves you too.'

Paul wiped his tears, but they still trickled down his cheeks and fell unchecked onto the front of his shirt.

'And then, just as suddenly, Maja came to me with an open mind despite having troubles and worries of her own. Together we created a video diary, and I hope you'll share and read and follow the blog. It's intended to be uplifting, informative and full of hope. Miscarriage is nothing to be ashamed of. It is no one's fault. It happens. And life has to go on after death. So, join me in celebration of love, hope and new life.'

Her voice cracked as she turned back towards Paul and went on. 'And I know this one will love you too,' she said, patting her tummy; a tiny bump visible under the fitted denim dress she wore.

Paul looked at her, confused.

The screen flickered into life again and a scan picture

burst across it.

'I'm pregnant, almost seventeen weeks. A boy. I'm sorry I didn't tell you sooner.'

Judith, caught up in the emotion of Kerry's news, whispered with a thrill, 'That's my "Four for a Boy". Wonderful news.' She searched the stage for Lou, hoping she would have heard Kerry's announcement. Paul picked up Kerry and twirled her around once, twice, three times.

'And finally, if I don't fall over dizzy,' said Kerry laughing, 'we've left the biggest thank you till last… Judith, our neighbour, our confidant, our mentor, our friend.'

The screen filled quickly with images of Judith around the village, talking to her neighbours, pruning her climbing roses, posting a letter, licking one of her sticky jam fingers, eating a sandwich on the green, tickling Jasper under the chin, smiling at Lou. Judith turned towards the stage, stopping mid-track for a few seconds, before pushing her way again through the crowds.

'Without this kind, thoughtful, compassionate, and giving woman many of us would have flowed adrift… and who knows what we might be doing now, how we might be feeling. Instead, we can stand here tonight, knowing we are where we are because we have a friend who cares enough to help us, to stop and ask how we are and to give her time, her love, and her energy to her community.'

Judith, finally by her mother's side, stood, listening with wide eyes, her hand over her mouth, stifling her exclamation. She put her arm through Alma's and drew her close, all the while with a tiny, tentative, tender smile on her face.

'Come with me,' Judith said to her, and they plunged into the melee together, back towards Matt.

'Wait a minute. I know this isn't the time, but I want you to know that I have failed in my life, but when I look at you, I know I've done one thing right. You're a beautiful, kind, intelligent woman. I'm proud of you.'

'Thank you. We'll talk. Properly. Tomorrow. The day after. And the day after that.'

'I'd like that,' said Alma.

Back in the warmth of Matt's arms, with her mother by her side, something in Judith shifted, her heart filled with love. She had found a new place in her community, or maybe this had always been her place, an old place from her life to bring her back home; it had been here all along, in the village, amongst friends and with Matt, and now, with her mother.

Kerry's words washed over her, consumed with happiness, Judith buried herself into Matt's arms and sniffed back tears of joy, of regret, but most of all of hope and the magic of new beginnings.

The last image burst across the screen: Kerry, Maja, Lee, Lou, Daniel, and Judith. Those faces, including her own, were her "Six for Gold". She pictured the postcard on the kitchen table: six magpies threaded together with a gold ribbon. She had finally found peace and love in a world which looked a little different now, newer, shinier. The seventh magpie, her mother, would always remain her biggest secret… at least for now. She had a lot to process, so many questions, yet she was comforted by the thought of the future.

Tina Turner's Simply The Best blasted out. Everyone joined in, singing the chorus, and above the church spire an impressive burst of fireworks shot up and filled the sky whirling with a spiral of colour. Spinning for some time, the vivid greens, oranges, purples, reds, and yellows filled the night sky until they disappeared into a thousand dazzling, falling stars and all that was left was their long, white tails. The children cheered and waved their sparklers, the smell of sulphur heavy in the air, tinged with a lighter sweet charcoal-like smoke. The celebratory bang of the final rocket marked the end of a truly marvellous village fete.

The night was one to remember and the village was never as closely knit or as emotional as they were that evening, and the Summer Fete remained the topic of conversation as the summer transitioned into autumn. The leaves turned golden and fell to the ground in a carpet of yellows and oranges. Roses faded and spiny stems and boughs revealed themselves, unabashed in their skeletal beauty against shorter days and darker mornings but still the village held onto love and hope. Hope for the future and hope for their village and finally Judith was happy to be older, to be wiser and to be in love. Secrets had unfolded yet she knew they had brought her back full circle to where she wanted to spend all of her tomorrows, with friends, with her new-found family and with Matt.

*** THE END ***

Acknowledgements

I am forever grateful to the team at Kingsley Publishers for their support in bringing this story into the world.

With huge thanks to my wonderful team of beta readers: Lia Seaward, Maria Amoss, Daisy Wood, and Elaine Graham-Leigh; your constructive critique, and unwavering support has been a Godsend at times of doubt and at times of procrastination.

Thank you to Kari Gibson and Michelle Swinea who acted as my sensitivity readers and for casting their eyes over the story for accuracy, better representation, and sensitivity. I have learnt a lot through your expertise. I am indebted to you both.

Finally, but by no means least, thank you to my partner, Alan Reynolds and my amazing sons, Christian, Alexei, and Angelo, for your love, support, and patience while I holed up in my Writing Room to write the very first draft of this story during the lockdown months of Covid and the ongoing pandemic.

About the Author

Born in London to Greek Cypriot parents, Soulla Christodoulou was the first in her family to go to university and later retrained to become a teacher.

Alexander and Maria was nominated for the RSL Ondaatje Prize 2021.

The Summer Will Come, a book club read in the Year of Learning Festival 2019, is currently under contract for translation into Greek and earmarked as a book to movie project.

Soulla is happiest writing in her pretty garden Writing Room and drinking tea infused with cinnamon sticks and cloves.

Connect with Soulla on her website
https://www.soulla-author.com/
Instagram: @soullasays
Twitter: @schristodoulou2
She loves to hear from her readers.

The Village House

"Romantic, descriptive, and evocative… The Village House captures the authentic spirit of a Cypriot village."
- *Nadia Marks, best-selling author of Among the Lemon Trees.*

Katianna receives a solicitor's letter summoning her to Omodos, a mountain village in Cyprus.

What is at first an inconvenient trip quickly becomes more attractive as she spends more time there. Flooded with many childhood memories, she falls in love with her roots and relishes in the relaxed pace and warmth of her cousin and the Cypriot people she meets. And then there's the simmering attention of the builder tasked with renovating the village house Katianna has inherited from her maternal grandmother.

Grappling with yo-yoing emotions, she returns home. But in London all is not well for her award-winning dating agency; her world is threatened, turned upside down, forcing her to question everything she believes in and has worked so hard for.

She travels back and forth and has to face the fact she has to sell the only connection left to her family.

But can Katianna have everything? Will she find a way to hold onto her business? Or will the pull of her heartstrings and the village house entice her to start over in a place closer to home than she ever imagined.

The Village House

SOULLA CHRISTODOULOU

Chapter 1

The building, in the heart of London, screamed success. Katianna relished it. Her patent heels clipped across the marble flooring, the echo bouncing across the bright, open space. She took the green coded escalator to the double-decker lifts, leather laptop case in one hand and designer handbag in the other.

The glass doors pinged opened, closed immediately after her. She pressed the button for the twelfth floor, the location of her dating agency, *Under the Setting Sun*. She looked straight ahead at the control panel; the buttons lighting up the company names as the elevator whooshed past each floor: Investment Management PLC, Kew and Press Lawyers, ARC Project Management, Cyprus Property Portfolio… her eyes stayed locked with the word Cyprus… the letter she had recently received on her mind, still sitting on her desk, but she shook the niggling, invasive thought away, refocused.

In her office, she tucked her handbag under her desk and smoothed out her black pencil skirt. She plugged in and switched on her laptop. She sat facing the glass-walled partition which afforded her with a view of her team and the open-plan workspace beyond. At eight promptly she went through the day's key activities with her PA.

'That's great, thank you Angie.'

'I'll get your coffee,' Angie said, her tight ponytail and wide-legged culottes swinging in time with each long step. Her yellow flat pumps coordinated nicely with the mustard of her trousers and echoed the colours of an uncharacteristically warm July. At almost six-foot Angie didn't need any more height. She towered over Katianna, who at only five foot four considered her own heels necessary, especially at work.

Angie was in her early thirties, a few years younger than Katianna, but her mature attitude and commitment shone through from the moment she said "anything it takes" in her interview five years before. Katianna recognised a kindred spirit in her and despite Angie's patchy work history hired her instantly never regretting it.

A real asset to the company, Angie was efficient, productive, proactive and loyal. She had become a good friend over the years and with life very much tipped towards work, genuine friends were hard to come by for Katianna. The glitz and glamour of award nights and ceremonies were just that and Katianna snubbed her friends' comments.

'Slow down,' they urged. 'Not everything which

shines is made of gold.'

But her circle shrunk as she rebuffed their comments telling them everything did in her world.

Katianna's sole purpose to be successful was all-consuming, her single-minded ambition her steed. Eight years before, she had won the court case against her business partner, also her ex-fiancé, to keep the business name. She had since spent every waking hour and every ounce of energy making the business a leader and had vowed never to be indebted to anyone ever again, especially in business. But in love too.

Judged by the UK and European Dating Awards' independent panel on reputation, success rate, approachability, and customer service, *Under the Setting Sun*, had been favoured many times over.

Framed awards hung in a perfect line across one wall and gave no room for doubt: UK Matchmaking Agency of the Year 2015 and 2018, International Matchmaker of the Year 2015, European Matchmaking Agency of the Year 2016 and 2018.

But achievement had come at a price; the ensuing months of working long hours and at weekends had pushed away the university friends Katianna had in her inner circle. The odd text or phone call was all she had time for now. She recognised a shift once they had husbands, wives, families of their own. She pushed aside the split-second prickle. She had her empire, didn't she?

She swiveled round in her seat to face the London vista laid out before her, the leather squeaking against the fabric of her skirt. This, all of it, she breathed, was worth every minute of working past midnight, waking at dawn, and missed lunches with friends. This is what made life worth living.

Every day she breathed in the success of the dating agency and her innovative approach had kept her ahead of the ever-growing competition and away from negative press increasingly associated with dating agencies and relationship apps.

Hers was different; clients plugged into a network of high-calibre, aspirational, professional singles. Supported by an assigned matchmaker, they worked towards the ultimate goal of a long-term relationship. Their sign-up package included professional photography, Myers Briggs-type indicator assessment which provided information on who each client really was and ID-checks on all members which ensured safety and security. Her matchmakers had backgrounds in psychology, counselling, and life coaching. Her newest recruit was a chartered psychologist and Associate Fellow of the British Psychological Society.

She took a call from John, her full-time accountant and finance manager. Running any business effectively relied on the owner's understanding of costs, money in and money out, and John handled that side of the agency for her; she preferred the company of people to figures and spreadsheets and she was instinctively yielding around him, trusting his knowledge and expertise implicitly.

John had been working with Katianna for almost seven years and he had been one of the first people she consulted with in terms of growing the business. It took off in its second year, more than tripling her forecasted income.

They rescheduled their monthly meeting around another appointment that had moved for John and said goodbye.

Katianna checked her emails and looked over the schedule of client photo shoots and website update meetings planned with her team; she kept a keen eye on the competition and read the main broadsheet newspapers and magazines every day. She followed trending hashtags, Instagram stories and LinkedIn news, including trends in the USA, Canada, and Europe.

She turned around, a knock-knock at her door.

'Come in,' she said, already gesturing to Warren, one of her advertising sales team.

'Have you got a minute?'

'Of course,' she said, nodding towards one of the black leather club chairs.

'I've got good news and bad news,' he said. 'The Mayfair Inn, Sherlock Mews and Devi Ahilya India have confirmed their online advertising for another year. I've increased the ad fee by 10%.'

'And the bad news?'

'One of the new restaurant accounts has paid for the key spot on our home page for twelve months.'

'Bad news because?'

'The Broadgate Hotel & Spa has already confirmed that spot for three months and paid-up front.'

'Use your negotiation skills to keep them holding on until then... offer them something else for the first three months and then the nine months, or even the year, on the home page.'

'I did that already. They're not biting.'

'Leave it with me. When did you last speak to them?'

'Day before yesterday.'

'Email across the details, your conversation notes, files.'

'I'll do it right now,' he said, making for the door. 'Thanks Katianna.'

She smiled at his retreating back. Warren was good at getting the advertising in but not so good with what she called "being cute"−keeping all sides happy when a pickle arose which thankfully wasn't often.

Her laptop pinged, Warren's email. She read the attachments, nothing to worry about. She was sure she could keep both accounts happy.

She pushed the laptop away and the letter caught her attention; the letter that had been mailed three times to her previous address. It was quite by chance she had bumped into her old neighbour who mentioned she had been holding onto post for her.

Katianna had hated sharing a letter box with Nosy Rosy, as she not-so-affectionately nicknamed her, who never missed an opportunity to ask why Vodafone were sending so many letters or why she received discount offer cards when everyone did their shopping online; her own daughter and three nieces did. Katianna had forced a smile and tightened her lips holding back on what she had really thought of her nosiness even though it was cloaked as neighbourly concern and kindness.

She took the envelope in her hand, felt the weight of it, in more ways than one, ran her fingers over the perforated edges of the Cyprus stamp and slipped out the thick cream sheet. She read the three short paragraphs again. She needed to book a flight to Cyprus when all she wanted was to stay in London, enjoy the rare hot summer and get on with running her business. She didn't have the time to take the four-and-a-half-hour trip to a country she hadn't been back to for years and recalled a client, two years ago, who the agency had successfully paired with a French lawyer. She believed they now lived happily in Paphos.

'Look at it as a well-deserved break,' Angie had said, 'on the island of l-o-o-o-v-e.' Katianna smiled, remembering how Angie had drawled the word.

Katianna had tried dismissing the unexpected wave of wistful affection. Her *yiayia* Anna had been the only grandmother she had known in her life and memories filled her; *yiayia* hugging Katianna tight, pinching her cheeks each summer in exaggerated awe of how much she had grown, plucking juicy purple figs, and picking grapes together.

Was going back to claim her *yiayia's* house a good idea? Her grandmother's passing had been painful, a shock, yet Katianna had not returned for the funeral still reeling from the deaths of her own parents; a stab of guilt poked at her, even more so now that the village house had been bequeathed to her and her parents were no longer here to know it. For a moment, tears threatened to fall but she pushed them away. There was no time for silly sentimentality and regrets. Living in the moment was all she had, and this is what she had right now; a house in the village waiting for her to what? Breathe new life into it? Connect with a life and a culture she had negligible ties with?

Her cousin Savva, who had linked up with her, after more than twenty years, put on the pressure, begging her to fly out.

'You can stay with me,' he said. 'I'm all grown up now.'

She had to go. She could not get out of this. Savva wouldn't take no for an answer and, of course she had to sign the legal documents for the house. Cyprus, it appeared, didn't recognise technological advancements and the solicitor insisted she visit to sign the paperwork in person with her identification: 'We have to have the original documents in front of us,' he repeated, though she wondered whether Savva had anything to do with their lack of enthusiasm to do things online.

Saying goodbye to her team was bittersweet; part of her looked forward to a break, a change of routine, and she had solved Warren's issue, with charm, so she was leaving on a high. Her team was the closest she had to family, yet she held them at a distance, preferring not to blur the lines between her work and their private lives. But she was admittedly going to miss them all as well as the buzz of the day to day in the office. As she left shortly after seven, she quietly relished the idea of disappearing for a few days, remembering her mother's words: *Rest is not an indulgence, it is essential Katianna. How can you be your best self if you don't treat yourself well?* Cyprus was going to bring her the rest she needed, she reassured herself.

Chapter 2

Katianna arrived at Larnaca International Airport exhausted and crampy; the pains in her tummy twisting her intestines with anticipation but her exterior façade portrayed nothing of her inner anxiety. It was nearly midnight by the time she exited the airport even though passport control had been efficient, and the queues had moved quickly. She hoped Savva was still waiting for her.

The flight from Heathrow Terminal 5 had been delayed by two hours because of "mechanical issues". The announcement had left her uneasy and anxiety consumed her entire flight despite the luxury of flying first class. All the while the whiney antagonistic voice in her head said: "You should have stayed at home. Leaving your business and gallivanting to God knows where…"

Katianna marvelled at the modern, bright airport remembering how she used to arrive with her parents and have to queue on the tarmac; the airport building too small to accommodate a full plane of arrivals. She walked out of the air-conditioned building with a renewed bounce.

The muggy heat of the night enveloped her and conscious of a sheen of sweat she brushed her hand across her forehead and upper lip. August, the hottest month of the year. Her clammy hand slipped against the suitcase handle as she dragged the oversized luggage behind her. Trying to keep it upright, she crossed the tarmac, no longer riddled with potholes and cracks as it had been years before, though the intense summer heat was the same. Her ankle doubled over as she caught her red stilettos on the edge of the raised walkway and her designer jacket slipped off her arm. Looking down at the heel, the leather had been shredded. Damn, she thought and gathering the jacket draped it over her shoulders despite the heat.

'Katianna,' Savva called from where he leaned against the shuttered kiosk, the streetlamp casting a harsh light.

She carefully navigated her way between the rows of parked hire cars and minibuses. As Katianna neared him, she took in his dishevelled appearance, yet his stance oozed a quiet, sexy confidence which took her by surprise. He was unkempt yet surprisingly attractive. He seemed bolder, more mature, in real life, not the soft, baby-faced man she saw on their video calls.

He threw his unfinished cigarette to the ground, grinding the stub into the tarmac and leaned in to kiss Katianna's cheeks, exhaling smoke over her shoulder. Katianna, taken by surprise, felt a blush of colour fill her cheeks. She had forgotten how kisses and hugs were nothing to shy away from in Cyprus, especially when greeting friends and relatives.

'I thought you said you were quitting?' she grimaced and then smiled as she waved the tendrils of Savva's cigarette smoke away.

'I was, until a week ago when the thought of my English cousin visiting stressed me out.'

'Very funny. You can't blame me. What's the real reason?'

'Lack of will power.'

'That's it?'

'That's it. Now come here and give me a proper hug.' He pulled her close.

'You stink like an ashtray,' she said, pulling away and giggling, surprised and delighted with the familiarity between them.

She liked the way she was able to connect with him even though her Greek was inferior to his fluency in English. But the closeness between them, there since childhood, was evident and flooded back like a ribbon-like flow of water, comfortable moving with the force of gravity, unperturbed by any babbles or ripples. They were almost twins; their birthdays only three days apart and it didn't take long for Savva to tease her about being older and therefore demanded respect.

'You haven't really changed at all,' she said.

As children they had been thrown together every summer holiday; they danced together, swam out to the floating raft at Santa Barbara beach despite words of warning from their parents, and as a teenager Savva had escorted her to clubs, keeping a close eye on anyone who dared approach her, ready to pounce with the protectiveness of a lion over his pride.

*****

The drive to the village from the airport took just shy of an hour and a half; Katianna took in the silhouetted view of tall buildings and huge lit billboards, almost unrecognisable to the landscape she remembered as a child.

The peaks of the Troodos mountains loomed darker still behind the buildings, with the stars twinkling like Van Gogh's *The Starry Night. S*he recalled a specific camping trip to the Kykko Monastery, a royal, Patriarchal Stavropygian Monastery located in the western part of the mountain range, twelve miles from the highest peak of Cyprus' Mount Olympus.

All those years ago, lying side by side with Savva, sharing the same sleeping bag, the same splintered stars had dotted the inkiest blue expanse which felt so close it was as if she could pluck one from its blanket. Savva had tried to grab one for her, huffing and puffing, exaggerating his efforts. The other campers had been woken by her laughter followed by the smack of the thrashing slaps from their parents; both had hidden inside the lumpy sleeping bag till they almost couldn't breathe, holding hands, their bodies squashed against each other's in innocence, as any brother or sister.

'Almost there already,' she said, disappointed when the car indicated at the final E-road exit for Omodos.

Omodos, she thought, coming from the Cypriot word "modos," meaning "taking your time," with tact, carefully. She had found the snippet of information on the in-flight magazine. She hadn't realised how popular a destination her ancestral village had become and felt a sense of pride shadowed by a sting of guilt at not having known it.

As a child, the drive from the airport seemed to take forever, the journey made almost in complete darkness with no lighting along the poorly tarmacked roads, pot-holed and rutted—dirt tracks—unlike the roads now, the majority brightly lit and well-maintained.

They arrived in the village, built at the slope of the mountains, the winding roads narrower than she remembered and the pretty stone village houses, with their tiled roofs and terraces and picturesque upper floors, glowing in the amber light of the streetlamps; those replaced at intervals with brighter bulbs shone at a sharp downward angle and she scrunched her tired eyes against their harshness. The sweet smell of grapes carried on the mid-night breeze as it swept over the vineyards towards the village. A stray cat, not straggly or emaciated like the strays used to be, ran out in front of the car, her shiny coat glinting in the headlights. Savva slowed down and the cat's eyes seemed to stare at Katianna.

Katianna shivered against a little tremor running through her, but she looked upon the cat crossing their path as a good omen and her black fur even more so. She slinked away and disappeared under a parked pick-up truck; battered and missing a back bumper.

*****

So where do you want to start today? I've taken three days off work to be your translator, chauffeur, whatever you need.'

'You're a real good sort. How comes you haven't been snapped up?' Katianna wiped her brow, already sweaty from the rising temperature.

'Who says I haven't?'

'Because your house is still a house, not a home,' said Katianna, pointing to the stark walls and clutter-free surfaces of the open-plan kitchen and sitting room.

'How is that observation going to help you sort out your *yiayia's* house?'

'Sorry. It isn't. It's a habit of mine… comes with the job.' She smiled, hoping to take the sting out of her comment. 'Let's start with breakfast and then you can accompany me to the house.'

'Sounds good. I want to know everything that's been happening. There's something different about you I didn't catch on our video calls. I can't put my finger on it.'

Chapter 3

'Black tea with cinnamon sticks and cloves, and a halloumi and mortadella toastie for me, thank you.' Katianna placed her order after Savva introduced her to Sofia.

Katianna had spotted the little café *stafilia kai meli* which translated as "grapes and honey" as they walked arm in arm across the village square and though Savva had tried to persuade her to walk further, Katianna's puppy-dog eyes had won him over.

'How delightful. I haven't been asked for a cinnamon and clove tea in years.'

'It's how my *yiayia* Anna made it. It seems right I should drink it now I'm back,' said Katianna.

'She was a wonderful old lady, so kind,' said Sofia.

'You knew her?'

'She was a grandmother to all of us growing up in the village,' said Sofia.

'I guess she would have been, yes. I wish I'd known her better, especially these last few years.'

'Well, there are many around here who can tell you about her,' said Sofia.

'Just a coffee for me, Sofia,' said Savva, interrupting them.

Katianna gave him a look; one she had perfected in the days of child minding to pay her university fees. Memories flooded her: piles of ironing, scrubbing shower doors until they gleamed, tidying endless toys, sleeping on her side on the edge of a single bed until her arm went numb while Jessica and James fell asleep, working with her laptop balanced on crossed legs on the sofa until after midnight, reading Eric Carle's *The Very Hungry Caterpillar* and Michael Bond's *Paddington Bear* Books over and over until she almost knew the stories word for word. She sighed, and then recalled the heavy hardbacks of J.K. Rowling which the family gifted her when she finished working with them two years later together with a generous bank transfer which put her in the black for the first time in four years.

'What?' he asked, cutting across her thoughts.

'You've taken me back to my nannying days… and not the good ones.'

'What d'you mean?'

'No smile. No please. No thank you.' She paused. 'You could at least acknowledge her. She's lovely and no wedding ring.'

'That's because she's not married,' he said, folding his arms across his chest.

'How come?' teased Katianna. Her lighter tone eased

the tension she picked up on and Savva gave her a half smile.

'I don't know. She's always lived in the village, never left. Opened the coffee shop when her parents died,' he said, avoiding eye contact.

'She looks happy.'

'They say happiness can come from the deepest sorrows, don't they?' said Savva.

'You're right. Kahil Gibran said something like, *when you feel joy, look to your heart and you'll find it's only that which has given you sorrow that is now giving you joy.*'

'I guess that's kind of true.'

'And she owns this place?'

'She spent all her inheritance breathing new life into the once derelict building abandoned by the previous owners. She's always here. Working.'

'Working but happy,' said Katianna, Sofia's situation closely mirroring her own.

Katianna sat a while, didn't say anything but her mind was already ticking with anticipation, an idea forming. Back in London and across the industry she was inevitably known as *The Matchmaker* and even though she was single herself she had this knack of pairing single hearts together and matching them fruitfully. With a first in psychology, she knew what made people tick and *Under the Setting Sun* had become more than a simple dating agency. It attracted clients serious about partnering and with a view to getting married, finding a life-long partner and it worked.

Sofia returned with their order served in a mishmash

of crockery.

'So pretty,' said Katianna, fingering the pretty floral teacup and saucer.

'Thank you, it meant a lot to my mother who received it as part of her dowry when she married. My intention was to use it temporarily and replace it once the business began making a profit but I'm glad I didn't,' she said, with a faraway look in her eye.

'I'm here refurbishing my grandmother's house and when it's done, I'm hoping to have a little celebration in memory of her life. I wonder…' she said, turning an idea around in her head. 'Would you cater for it and, of course, join me as a guest.'

'I'd be happy to arrange anything you need food-wise, but this place takes up all my time. But thank you for the invitation, that's sweet of you.'

'Don't say no to joining us just yet. Let me get sorted and once I have a date you can decide then.'

'She said, no, Katianna. Leave it,' said Savva.

Sofia's cheeks turned a fiery red. She grabbed the empty plates from the next table and scuttled off towards the serving hatch where Petros, her part-time chef, was already lining up the next round of breakfast orders.

'You embarrassed her,' said Katianna and slurping her tea she focused on its sweet, spicy fragrance to take away the sourness in the air.

'Me? You're the one going on about the catering and the invite,' he said and pulling his mouth with both fingers, stretched it wide, and waggled his tongue at her.

'You're not ten anymore,' she tutted, 'but I guess that's what so loveable about you.'

'Enough of me and how immature I am. Let's talk about you. What are your plans with the house?'

'Spruce it up and sell it. It's not convenient to keep it. I'm like Sofia with work leaching my time. And my life's in London.'

'The house is in pretty bad shape so sprucing may realistically need to be translated as refurbishing and even rebuilding in places.'

'It's been old and run down for as long as I remember,' she said, taking a bite of her toasted sandwich. The nutty aroma of the toasted, sesame-seed bread filled her nostrils. 'This is so good. The bread I buy from the bakery back home is good, Polish bread, but this is just heaven.'

'I'll tell George when I next see him. He's very proud of his baking skills.'

'And so he should be,' Katianna said.

'Eat and then let's get the solicitor out of the way.' Savva took the last swig of his Greek coffee as Katianna picked at the errant crumbs on her plate.

She wondered what the story was between Savva and Sofia, and she knew there was one; she felt it.

Printed in Great Britain
by Amazon

33798661R00182